Please return/renew this item by the last date
shown. Books may also be renewed by
telephoning, writing to or calling in at any of
our libraries or on the internet.

Northamptonshire Libraries and Information Service

Northamptonshire
County Council

www.library.northamptonshire.gov.uk/catalogue

SAY HER NAME

JAMES DAWSON

HOT
KEY
BOOKS

First published in Great Britain in 2014 by Hot Key Books
Northburgh House, 10 Northburgh Street, London EC1V 0AT

A CIP catalogue record for this book is available from the British Library.

ISBN: 978-1-4714-0244-9

Northamptonshire Libraries & Information Service WW	
Askews & Holts	

Hot Key Books supports the Forest Stewardship Council (FSC),
the leading international forest certification organisation, and is
committed to printing only on Greenpeace approved FSC-certified paper.

www.hotkeybooks.com

Hot Key Books is part of the Bonnier Publishing Group
www.bonnierpublishing.com

For Erin and Faye

'Twas in the middle of the night,
To sleep young William tried,
When Mary's ghost came stealing in,
And stood at his bedside.
O William dear! O William dear!
My rest eternal ceases;
Alas! my everlasting peace
Is broken into pieces.
I thought the last of all my cares
Would end with my last minute;
But though I went to my long home,
I didn't stay long in it.

From 'Mary's Ghost: A Pathetic Ballad' by
Thomas Hood

THIRTEEN YEARS AGO

Drip, drip, drip.

Drip, drip, drip.

Drip, drip, drip.

This was *really* starting to get on her nerves. Taylor Keane tightened the kitchen tap with all her might, even using a tea towel to gain a better grip, but the relentless dripping continued. Where was it coming from? Leaning over the sink, she twisted the handle and threw the window open, snaking her arm through the opening and into the balmy night air. She held out her open palm. It wasn't even spitting.

The strangest thing was, wherever she went in the house the volume of the drip remained consistent, like it was following her around. She may well have snoozed through Physics, but she was pretty certain that wasn't possible.

She opened the cupboard under the sink and, pushing past

about a trillion bottles of bleach, disinfectant and furniture polish, found the U-bend. A quick swipe of her finger confirmed it was bone dry. No leaks there.

Drip, drip, drip.

This was so typical. Her parents only went out one night a week to their ridiculous salsa class and she was left alone with a plumbing emergency. She'd called and called but they weren't answering their phones.

Worst. Night. Ever. Bad enough that Jonny hadn't come over like he'd promised. They were supposed to be watching a DVD/making out, but he'd cancelled, saying he felt 'fluey'. The scummy liar was probably down the arcade with his mates. Taylor cursed her fatal weakness for big arms and blue eyes.

Drip, drip, drip.

'God, that is so annoying.' She clutched handfuls of her tousled caramel-blonde hair and stomped out of the kitchen and into the lounge. Locating the remote control, she muted the TV.

Drip, drip, drip.

It seemed to be coming from above, perhaps the dead space between floors. She scanned the ceiling for bulges. Maybe she should just call a plumber . . . she was sure that's what you were meant to do in a leak situation. Surely her mum and dad would only thank her for preventing the collapse of the ceiling. It was almost 9 p.m. though, and she shuddered at what an emergency out-of-hours plumber might charge. She didn't even have ten quid in her purse.

She padded barefoot across the plush beige carpet into the hall and peered up the sweeping staircase to the first floor.

Maybe it was coming from upstairs – in fact the bathroom was the most likely source. It was worth a look.

Drip, drip, drip.

Louder, clearer than ever: thick, viscous drops landing on a solid surface. But where? She'd lived here her whole life (well, when she wasn't away at school) but suddenly the house seemed alien and strange. It was super-lame, but she really wished someone else was in the house right now.

Taylor put a brave toe on the first step. She arched her neck back, angling to get a look at the upstairs landing. The coast was clear. High above her head, the light fixture cast a claw-like shadow over the ceiling. She hesitated. A voice in her head whispered, *Don't go upstairs.* 'Get a grip, Tay,' she muttered to herself. With that, she took the steps two at a time, showing the house just how unscared she was. This wasn't some stupid horror film that Jonny had brought over to try to freak her out, it was real life and they simply had a leaky pipe.

Emerging onto the landing, she peeked around the banister. *Nothing to see here.* The water tank was in the attic, but horror film or not, there was no chance she was going up there by herself, not with spiders the size of kittens. Yet the dripping persisted. If anything, the liquid splattered with greater frequency – tapping out an increasingly hectic rhythm.

There were two possible sources on this floor: the main bathroom and the en suite in her parents' room. Clenching her fists, she arrived at her parents' room first. With dim streetlight filtering through the blinds, she found the room immaculate as always and with no evidence of flooding. She crossed to the tiny bathroom. Snapping on the light, she saw at once through the glass shower door that the dry cubicle was not responsible for the dripping. The toilet also appeared fine; there was no water on the tiles at all.

One option remained. As she returned to the landing, she cursed. The leak was worse still. The drips were now almost a current, as if liquid were pouring onto the floor.

She hurried into the main bathroom, pulling on the light cord. The bulb seemed to falter, wheezing and shuddering as it came on, only filling the room with a thin, stuttering, greenish glow. Taylor wondered if the leak was affecting the electrics. Everything else seemed normal, but the water was at its loudest. The shower curtain was drawn along the length of the bath. She suddenly felt exceptionally blonde. All that fuss and it was just the shower trickling into the bath.

The lights flickered again. Even dimmer. The prickly feeling in her stomach wasn't going away. *It's just the shower*, she told herself. Taylor inched over the tiles, steadying herself on the sink pedestal, catching sight of her ashen face in the ornate mirror that hung above it. She reached for the shower curtain, teasing the edge of the plastic veil. *Do it like ripping off a plaster . . .*

She yanked the curtain aside, only to knock bottles of shampoo into an empty, white bathtub. The showerhead hung expectantly over her, no water running from its face.

'What the . . . ?' Taylor groaned, stepping away from the tub. 'This is insane!' *Drip, drip, drip*. It was *so* loud. Where was it coming from?

And then she saw. In the very corner of her eye, she saw *something* move in the mirror. Something that wasn't her. Mouth dry, she turned to face the glass. It was *impossible*, but her reflection wasn't alone; something else waited within the frame. Taylor screamed.

The glass was no longer solid, more like a rippling silver pool on the wall. A slender hand, as white as marble but slick with blood, reached *through* the glass and clutched the basin, pulling itself from the reflection into the bathroom. Glistening red rivers ran from the dead fingertips, coursing through splayed fingers. It pooled around the taps and in the sink. As the hand reached for Taylor, thick red beads splashed onto the mosaic tiles.

Drip, drip, drip.

PRESENT DAY

Chapter 1

Hallowe'en

Piper's Hall School for Young Ladies aged 11–18 sat on the top of a rugged, exposed cliff-face, a cove much battered by high winds and higher waves. The school perched, gargoyle-like, high above the shore. Nothing about the architecture said 'school'; towers and turrets were topped with vicious metal spikes, while even the sprawling green playing fields were the colour of slate in the midst of a storm. By day it was a nightmarish vision, by night it was worse.

Locals referred to it by many names, some ruder than others, but all the townies in neighbouring Oxsley stayed clear. With good reason . . . it was every haunted castle from their childhood nightmares. Even from miles out at sea, you could see forked tongues of lightning reach down to lick the casements.

Worse than the sinister appearance, it was full of posho, toffee-nosed, boarding-school brats. Well, that was certainly

Bobbie Rowe's verdict on why anyone with an ounce of common sense would avoid her school.

The cold sawed through Bobbie's bones, the pathetic rubbish-bin fire doing nothing to keep their party of seven warm. They were gathered in a squat PE shed at the outer limits of the hockey pitch, the shutters over the windows rattling in the howling gale. Clamping her jaw shut was the only way Bobbie could stop her teeth from chattering like a cartoon woodpecker.

This whole evening was so lame. So lame she could cry. Bobbie didn't even *like* most of these people, and she certainly wasn't bothered about Hallowe'en.

'And the noise grew louder . . . drip, drip, drip . . .' The fun-size bonfire cast a demonic red glow across Sadie Walsh's ruddy face. 'The babysitter oh-so-slowly reached for the shower curtain and, taking a deep breath, she flung it open!'

'Oh God! What did she see?' squealed Lottie Wiseman, nervously chewing her hair.

Sadie narrowed her eyes in glee, building the anticipation until her audience was salivating for the grand reveal. 'The poodle was hanging from the shower rail, its throat cut, and blood drip, drip, dripping into the tub!'

The two guys on the opposite bench, who had no business being at an all-girls school at *any* time, let alone in the middle of the night, chuckled to one another.

'And on the mirror . . .' Sadie continued, a twisted, manic look in her eye, 'written in blood, were the words "Humans can lick hands too!"'

Lottie and Grace managed a coy faux scream for the

delectation of the smuggled-in boys. Bobbie did not scream, only shifting slightly to kick-start life in her gym-bench-numb buttocks. While boarding school turned some girls into ticking hormone bombs, it had only succeeded in making her excruciatingly shy around boys.

'Whatever, Sadie.' Sitting next to her, Bobbie's best friend Naya spoke out. 'I've heard that story a million times before, and FYI, it's an *old lady* and a dog, not a babysitter . . . why would a babysitter be going to bed at someone else's house?'

Bobbie giggled and pushed her geek-chic-but-actually-necessary glasses back up her button nose. Thank God for Naya – she just about made Piper's Hall tolerable. She noted that one of the local boys (the cuter of the two – the mixed-race one with closely buzzed hair) was also grinning but Sadie did not look thrilled at the negative review.

'Oh, I'm sorry, Naya. I forgot you were the expert on everything Hallowe'en related – my mistake.'

Naya pursed her full lips. 'I'm not saying I am, but you promised a *true* ghost story. Oh hi . . . is that Trade Descriptions?'

Once more Bobbie laughed. Sadie was full of crap at the best of times, and in an institution where laxatives were traded like cigarettes in jail, that was really saying something. 'Okay. You want a true story?'

The circle chanted agreement. Except Bobbie. At Naya's insistence she'd abandoned *Pride and Prejudice and Zombies* for this demented charade . . . *'It's Hallowe'en!'* she'd begged, *'one night a year . . . live a little!'* Naya would pay for this. Bobbie didn't know how, but she'd pay.

'Don't say I didn't warn you . . .'

15

'Sweet Jesus, Sadie!' Grace Brewer-Fay, the final member of their illicit party and reigning monarch, finally spoke. She could not have looked more bored if she'd tried. 'Can you just get on with it please? I don't want to be here all night.' The Head Girl delivered the last two words in precise, soap-opera seduction mode as she stroked the boy she was nestled against – the same cute Hollister model one. As Grace ran her fingers over the smooth, taut, brown skin of his forearm, Bobbie couldn't help but wonder what it felt like. He was *gorgeous*, and even keeping the admission in her head made her cheeks flush raspberry red. It was so silly, he didn't even know she was here; Bobbie was ever the chameleon, happy to fade into the wallpaper.

Sadie puffed herself up like a particularly proud peacock. 'Well this one *really* happened, right here at Piper's Hall.' Grace and Naya voiced instant disbelief. 'It's true! This all went down when my eldest sister was here! If you don't believe me, I'll ring her for you right now!'

Bobbie rolled her head on Naya's shoulder. 'Can we go?' she whispered, so only her friend would hear. 'I have like two chapters left to read and I was just getting to the big finish.'

'Are you kidding? We're getting to the good stuff!' Naya's New York accent, somewhat watered down after three years in England, always strengthened when she was excited.

'Who knows the story of Bloody Mary?' Sadie once more leaned into the fire. Any closer and her face was sure to melt. Bobbie reluctantly raised a limp arm and so did a couple of the others. 'You may *think* you know the story . . . but it's been diluted and changed as it got passed around. The true story,

16

the original, so to speak, started right here at Piper's Hall . . .'

'As if!' barked the second boy, whom she'd overheard the hot one call Mark. Bobbie always felt sorry for boys called Mark. Like who names a kid after something you wipe off a kitchen counter? It was just mean. He too was an Oxsley townie, muscular-stocky, and wore a gold stud in his left earlobe. Bobbie liked to imagine he was a farmhand or chimney sweep, but knew that was more her Oxsley snobbery than any truth. 'I've heard that story loads of times!' he went on. 'There was a film about it!'

'Yes, Mark, that's because so many Piper's Ladies have gone out into the world and spread it . . . the *real* story all started two hundred years ago when a Piper's Hall pupil called Mary Worthington killed herself. It was a night just like this one . . . lightning lit the sky and thunder crashed!'

Right on cue, the dingy storage shed shook under a mighty peal of thunder. Despite herself, Bobbie grasped Naya's arm.

Sadie revelled in the chance drama. 'One Hallowe'en, she went to her lover – a local boy in the village – to ask him to elope. In those days, it would have caused a huge scandal – a young Piper's Hall girl having an affair out of wedlock. When he refused, she begged, but he laughed in her face. He'd got what *he* wanted. So Mary ran back to the school in the pouring rain, found a length of rope, took herself to the bathroom and hung herself. The last thing she saw was her own reflection in the mirror as she dangled . . .'

'We've all heard that story!' Grace scowled, flicking her shampoo-ad blonde hair.

'Doesn't Bloody Mary refer to Queen Mary because she

17

killed hundreds of Protestants?' Bobbie breathed in Naya's ear as the dim recollection of a Year 6 History lesson swam through her memory.

Naya grinned broadly. 'I don't think Sadie got that memo!'

At the other side of the circle, Grace stood, hauling her beautiful boy bounty to his feet. 'Caine and I are off. We have better things to be doing . . .' Ah, so his name was Caine. *Caine.* Cool name. 'Bobbie and Caine' had a nice ring to it. *Yeah, that's gonna happen.*

'Just wait!' Sadie smiled sweetly, licking her lips. 'That was just the background . . .'

'I wanna hear the end of the story.' Caine plonked himself back onto the bench, much to Grace's obvious dismay. Poor Caine mustn't receive the Piper's Hall newsletter . . . no one defied Grace Brewer-Fay and lived to tell the tale.

Banshee winds threatened to lift the roof clean off the shed and Bobbie hugged herself tight. Sadie continued her yarn. 'There are so many different versions of what happened next, but everyone agrees Bloody Mary can be *summoned* . . . it happened right here in the school. A girl did it, a few years ago when my sister was here. There are rules. It has to be during the witching hour – midnight. You have to light a candle to help Mary find her way from the Other Side. You need a mirror too; you see, Mary's dying soul became trapped in the mirrors, unable to cross into the afterlife. And then, all you have to do is say her name five times . . .'

'What happens then?' Caine asked, eyes wide.

'No one has lived to say . . . they don't even find the bodies. They just vanish . . . or so they say.'

The room fell silent, hanging on the consequences of Sadie's last words until Naya started a slow handclap. Caine, white teeth twinkling in the dim light, joined in. His smile lit up his face further; Bobbie couldn't take her eyes off it. There were dimples. He was straight off a bedroom wall poster.

It was weird. Bobbie wasn't usually interested in guys her own age: teenage guys looked like little boys to her. The 'teenagers' she fancied on TV were all fake because the actors were really in their twenties. Caine was different though: no acne, no braces, no ill-fitting sportswear – he looked like the guys on TV. *He mustn't be able to move for girls hurling themselves at him at Radley High*, she thought, which made it even weirder that he'd go for Grace. She was certainly pretty, Bobbie mused, but then so were lots of poisonous flowers.

'They never find the bodies? Well isn't that convenient?' Naya whooped. '*And there was never a shred of evidence!*'

Equally unimpressed, Grace scowled. 'Well, I'm *so* glad we stuck around for the ending. When's the film version coming out?'

Sadie folded her arms and pursed her lips. Somehow, Bobbie foretold the next sentence before it had even escaped her mouth. 'Fine. You won't mind doing it then, will you?' *That* was the true crescendo to her tale, the other ending a false finish, drawing them to this inevitable conclusion. You could have heard a pin drop at the far side of the hockey pitch.

'What? Are you serious?' Naya replied. Lottie watched the scene with bushbaby eyes.

'I'll do it!' Caine offered at once, rubbing his hands together.

'No! Don't!' Poor Lottie was on the verge of mental collapse, judging by the look on her face.

Sadie stood, throwing down an invisible gauntlet. 'Well if the story is total rubbish, you won't have a problem summoning her.'

'Go summon a clue!' Naya snapped. Oh God. Bobbie had seen this happen numerous times . . . Naya Sanchez just didn't know when to back down. She braced herself for the oncoming storm. 'Why don't you do it if you're so tough?'

'Sigh. Rewind – I already did!' Sadie posed, hand on hip, every inch as stubborn as her frenemy.

'Then why aren't you dead?' Bobbie finally spoke up, hoping to douse Naya's fire. She pulled the sleeves of her heavy cable-knit jumper over her hands to keep them warm.

Sadie stalled at the centre of the circle, her parade rained on. 'I don't know! It didn't work. But Lottie will back me up, she saw me do it!'

Every head in the smoky outhouse turned to waif-like Lottie, who, frankly, would go along with anything her best friend said. 'It's true. She did it three nights ago . . . and she did it right, but nothing happened. It was really scary though!'

'You're kidding? The fake ghost didn't appear? Big shocker.' Grace's lips curled into an all-too-familiar smirk.

Sadie stood her ground. 'Okay. So do it. Or are you scared?'

Grace shrieked with laughter. 'Sadie, babe, do you really think that's going to work on me? I *invented* peer pressure.'

Sadie crumbled under the immense power of Piper's Hall's own Bloody Mary. That was the thing with Grace. She was like a cobra; she'd dance all night, but one bite and it was all over. Bobbie had no idea why Grace was as mean as she was – she must be pretty insecure to spend so much time picking on other people. Whatever the cause, Bobbie didn't care enough to try to reach out to the human cactus, quite sure she'd only get pricked for her efforts.

'Well I'm gonna do it!' Caine rolled up the sleeves of his hoodie and did a merry warm-up jig, like a boxer psyching himself up for a bout.

'What?' Grace sprayed venom.

'I'm gonna do it!' he repeated. 'It's Hallowe'en. I ain't afraid of no ghost.'

'I'll do it too.' Naya rose to her feet and approached Caine. 'What is it they say – "Everyone deserves one good scare on Hallowe'en"?'

'Get in!' Caine delivered a high five to Naya.

This could not be happening. This night was turning into a repeat of the Spring Ball fiasco (identical-dress-faux-pas flashback) and Bobbie knew just what was coming next. Grace vs Naya.

'You must be kidding!' Grace said, nostrils flaring. 'If you think you're creeping off into the night with my boyfriend, those last few brain cells must have finally lost the will to live.'

Caine's mate, Mark, sniggered and parroted the word 'boyfriend' under his breath. Caine didn't look thrilled either, but let it slide with a curl of his beautiful lips. New dimple action.

'Well, Grace, you'd better come too then!' Naya smiled like a flight attendant on speed.

Bobbie heaved herself off the bench, feeling her knees crack as she dragged her tired limbs towards Naya. 'Nay, let's just

21

go to bed. It's late.'

'Yeah, listen to Blobbie, Naya . . .'

Bobbie opened her mouth, poised with a witty retort, but as always, Naya leaped in first, wheels on fire. 'Don't call her that! I'll do what I want. Come on then, Sadie, which bathroom? Let's go. Bloody Mary, on the rocks.'

Chapter 2

The Summoning

The shrill, unanimously ignored pleas of Mrs Craddock, the housemistress, haunted the long corridors and high ceilings of the dormitory blocks. As it was Hallowe'en, the strung-out housemistress had allowed the young ladies of Piper's Hall some free cord to run riot with but, as midnight neared, her patience had finally run out.

'Ladies! Into your rooms now please!' She was a woman on the edge, but who wouldn't be after shepherding adolescent girls for twenty-five years?

Bobbie, Naya, Grace, Sadie, Lottie, Mark and Caine listened from downstairs, next to the fire escape they'd just crept in through. Their faces and hands were red and raw, even from the short dash across the rain-lashed hockey pitch. Naya was in a tug of war with the door, struggling to pull it shut in the fierce winds.

Checking the coast was clear, Sadie pushed on an oak panel located between the kitchen and dining room. 'I can't believe you have legit secret passages!' Caine said with boyish glee.

'Keep your voice down,' Grace snapped. 'Do you have any idea how much trouble we'll be in if we get caught?'

'Sorry.'

The so-called 'secret passages' had been Bobbie's only reason for agreeing to come to the school – the promise of *Scooby Doo* revolving bookcases and *Temple of Doom* caverns filled with bugs had appealed to her eleven-year-old self.

Turned out, the 'secret passages' were, in fact, little more than servants' passageways from when the main block of the school was a stately home. Allegedly there were priests' holes too, dating back even further, although Bobbie had never seen one. The corridors and stairwells weren't even 'secret' as such, but Lowers – the younger girls – tended not to use them once Uppers had over-egged how much trouble they'd be in if found trespassing in them. Oh, and naturally they were 'haunted'.

'Come on,' Sadie instructed. 'Follow me.' They slipped through the panel and into a narrow, carpet-less corridor, only marginally wider than Mark's blocky shoulders.

At the end of the passage, a rickety, creaking wooden staircase zigzagged all the way up the back of the old block, with exits on each floor. In a conga line they followed Sadie until they reached its exit point on the second floor, outside the dorms. Bobbie was wedged at the very back of the queue. She very much doubted anyone but Naya even knew she was there.

Behind the exit panel – a concealed door in the bay window on the landing between Austen and Brontë House – Bobbie could hear girls giggling and Mrs Craddock becoming more exasperated. Hopefully, the scurrying mass of girls would mask the fact that five pupils were missing from their dorms, not that Mrs Craddock checked anyway, at least not when *CSI: Miami* was due to start in five minutes.

'Wait until it goes quiet . . . it's way past Craddock's bedtime, she'll be asleep in a few minutes,' Sadie breathed, ear pressed to the panel.

'Whatever,' Grace moaned. Ironically, as Head Girl it was her responsibility to ensure all girls were in their dorms after 9 p.m. and to report any visitors trespassing on the school site. Bobbie couldn't suppress a curious smugness that Grace wouldn't get her wicked way with Caine, at least not tonight. Assuming they survived Bloody Mary, of course. She wasn't sure whether to laugh or cry. That said, if she was really honest, she was half curious to see if they'd go through with it, and if nothing else, Caine was particularly moreish eye candy.

The dorms, part of the original school building, were divided into four houses, each named after noted female writers – Austen, Brontë, Christie and Dickinson. The fact they weren't just labelled A, B, C and D was further proof, as if any were needed, that Bobbie's school was massively pretentious. Austen and Brontë were on opposing wings of the second floor, while Christie and Dickinson were the floor above that.

Sure enough, within fifteen minutes, footsteps and voices had faded to silence. Only the electric hum of strip lights and the pained moans of the storm filled the school.

'Right, let's get it on!' Sadie led the brigade out from their shelter.

Lottie left them to it, tiptoeing back to Christie House on the next floor. Bobbie hung back, tugging on Naya's arm. 'Why

25

are we doing this?'

'Oh come on, Bob!' Naya took her hand. 'I've done this at a hundred slumber parties. I'm just messing with Grace and Sadie! It'll be hilarious!'

'Really? Do explain.' She shrugged, incredulous.

'Duh! I go through with it and then spend the next week creeping around writing stuff on mirrors and hanging nooses everywhere! It'll spectacularly freak them out – I want to see Grace Brewer-Fay wet her bed!'

Bobbie watched as Grace hung off Caine's arm like a B-movie heroine. It was such an act; Grace had more testosterone than both boys put together. Would it be funny to take her down a peg or two? Hell, yes.

In the lead, Sadie and Mark reached Brontë House. Only a skittering night light illuminated the long line of peaceful dormitories – a dim silver light to guide girls to the fire exit. The coast was clear and the bathroom door stood ajar, awaiting them. Bobbie couldn't help but feel it looked a little ominous in the dark, on Hallowe'en night, in a raging storm . . .

She mentally threw a bucket of reality over herself. She should know better. Idiot kids all across the globe were chanting 'Bloody Mary' at mirrors; if it were true she was pretty sure the press would have covered it by now.

'Come on!' Sadie tiptoed into the shower room. Taking a deep breath, Bobbie allowed Naya to pull her across the threshold.

As always, the damp, tiled room carried the eggy scent of hair-clogged drains combined with an infusion of soap and shampoo. Behind the torn plastic curtains, the rusty showerheads leaked continually, dripping against the ceramic floor. Bobbie doubted even the most desperate spirit would be summoned to this hole.

'Shut the door,' Sadie commanded and Bobbie obliged. Sadie pulled open her shower bag, which she'd already filled with candles and matches from her dorm, and started to set them up around the long, communal sinks that stood before the mirror. This whole thing had been orchestrated to the finest detail – Bobbie wondered how long Sadie had been planning it. There was some sort of unresolved tension between Grace and Sadie: both were in 'The Elites', a long-standing Piper's Hall institution-in-an-institution. Every year, one or two girls from rich, powerful or famous families were initiated into a 'special club' to have secret get-togethers and generally be vile – sort of like the Masons but with lip gloss. From what Bobbie could ascertain as an outsider, Grace and Sadie constantly jostled for Top Bee/Queen Dog.

It was total bull. Because her mum was kind of famous, Bobbie had been invited to join in her first year. She'd declined because it looked like some sort of sugar-fuelled, miniskirted anorexia cult, and as a consequence had suffered ever since. She was social roadkill, not that she gave a rat's ass. Naya *had* badly wanted in, however. Grace, who had taken an instant dislike to the sultry American newcomer when she'd arrived in second year, had seen to it that it'd never happen.

Bobbie gave her reflection only the briefest glance in the long mirror, pausing to fluff her rod-straight mousy hair before switching her gaze to the infinitely more interesting Caine – the bronze tone of his skin and the velvet texture of his hair. When the Caine-reflection caught the eye of her own, she whipped

27

her head down, praying he hadn't noticed her staring. Or worse, what if Grace caught her in the act? She needed to get it together.

'Okay. Almost midnight . . . who's going first?'

Grace drew herself up to full height and admired herself in the mirror, smoothing flawless blonde strands of hair. 'I'm not doing it, full stop. It's for kids.'

'Then why are you here?' Naya repeated.

'Because I know what *you're* like.' Her voice was ripe with accusation.

Caine, apparently sensing the brewing catfight, stepped forward to the looking glass, pulling stocky Mark alongside him. 'We'll go first!'

The shorter boy whipped his arm back. 'I'm not doing it. What if it's real? I'm just gonna film it so I can mock you till the end of time!'

'What is wrong with everyone?' Caine's irresistible smile broke again. 'You are all so soft!'

Naya, hands on hips, joined him in front of the mirror. 'They don't make soft New Yorkers, honey.'

Bobbie raised an eyebrow, unsure whether Naya was trying to be alluring or not. If she was, it wasn't working. And then she felt her feet doing something almost alien . . . they started to move towards the others. It was as if Caine were a computer virus completely infecting her personal hard drive . . . all her usual heuristics were blocked, all the sensible self-defence invisibility mechanisms overwhelmed in her desire to impress a boy she'd met only hours earlier and hadn't even spoken to.

Naya looked to her, a mixture of shock and pride. 'Bobbie?'

'What?' she replied. 'I'm not scared. It's stupid.' She was annoyed that Naya thought she was a weakling when she knew the real her. Grace shot her a look of pity normally reserved for three-legged dogs.

'Go, Bobbie! Love a girl with balls!' Caine stopped. 'Well not like that . . . you know what I mean.'

Bobbie lost herself in his eyes for a second, the first time he'd given her more than a fleeting moment's attention. *He knows my name.* She pulled herself tall. Boys are like dangerous dogs – if you show fear they might eat your face. 'Well, let's get this over and done with before we all get expelled.'

'Yes please,' Grace agreed. 'Bloody Mary is one thing, state schooling is another.'

Sadie backed away to where Grace sulked and Mark flicked his mobile open and started to record their personal, low-budget horror film.

'Whenever you're ready. It's past midnight. If you dare.' Sadie whispered the last word like a somewhat camp crypt keeper.

The three of them looked into the mirror. Predictably, three reflections stared back. Bobbie: petite and delicate, hiding behind her thick glasses; Caine: tall, broad, swimmer's build; and Amazonian Naya: thick black locks tumbling about her shoulders. As unlikely a trio as you could find in a girls' toilet at midnight.

Noisily inhaling through his nostrils, Caine looked at each of them in turn. 'Ready?'

'Yeah.' Naya seemed less certain at this stage in the game. Bobbie responded with a slight nod.

'Okay. After three . . .' he continued. 'One, two . . . three . . .'

They stalled, no one wanting to go first.

'Come on!' he laughed. 'This time . . .'

'B . . . Bloody Mary,' Naya started and the others dutifully joined in, their voices low and monotone. Bobbie felt the air rush out of the room. The night itself had heard them start and held its breath accordingly.

'Bloody Mary . . .' The tension became too much. Caine and Naya dissolved into giggles and Bobbie joined in, not wanting to be left out of the mirth.

'Keep going,' encouraged Sadie from the outskirts. 'That's only two.'

They suppressed their laughter. 'Bloody Mary . . .' and again, 'Bloody Mary.'

The candles flickered and sputtered as a thin, icy breeze infiltrated the bathroom; voodoo shadows danced across the walls and all about the three faces framed within the mirror. The uplighting made their faces gaunt and hollow-cheeked, skull-like.

'One left.' Bobbie looked deep into Naya's eyes and saw that only an iota of bravado remained.

'All together,' Caine rallied them. Between the girls, he took Naya's right hand and her left. Bobbie's heart rattled against her ribs; she couldn't even breathe, let alone say the two remaining words. She looked to the furthest point at the back of the mirror. Crazy, but it seemed to stretch as if she were looking down a long, black tunnel. There wasn't even a reflection any more, but a dark passage. Miles away, at its furthest point, something stirred.

Caine's lips parted. Naya gave her a discreet nod. Bobbie

inhaled and closed her eyes.

'Bloody Mary.' They all said it together.

The light in the room dipped as if the candles were going to go out altogether. And then nothing. The bathroom was silent aside from the monotonous drips within the shower stalls. Bobbie looked to her companions. Naya was clenched so tight she could see the sinew in her neck. Caine chewed his bottom lip nervously.

Nothing.

Bobbie actually caved first. She cracked up and the others followed suit. Wild hoots of laughter tore from their lungs, a bizarre mixture of relief, hysteria and sheer embarrassment. For a fraction of a second, each of them had been well and truly suckered in. 'As if any further proof was needed . . . I'm such a massive loser!' Bobbie giggled.

'The look on your face was something else!' Caine pointed at Naya, doubled up.

'Me? Dude, you didn't look so hot yourself!'

Sadie was in a similar state, supporting herself against the wall next to Grace, who maintained her uncanny impression of a cold, wet fish. Sadie cackled, 'That was priceless! You looked like you were going to actively soil your pants!'

'Thanks for that, Sadie!' Bobbie offered her an outstretched hand, which Sadie shook. 'Okay, I'll admit that was diverting fun for a Hallowe'en night. Well done on a first-rate frightfest. Now, I don't know about you but I'm going to bed.'

'Thank God for that,' Grace sneered. 'Caine?'

'Babe, we gotta head back. I'm staying at Mark's tonight.'

Grace's lip curled with disappointment before she

remembered who she was: nobody's fool, and above all else, a Piper's Hall Lady. 'Fine. I'll catch you later then.' She swept out of the bathroom, closely followed by Sadie.

Caine cringed at Mark. 'Dude, never mind Bloody Mary, I'm in deep trouble now!'

'She'll get over it,' Naya smiled sweetly. 'No offence, hon, but she drags a different village boy up here every weekend. Can you find your way out?'

'The way we got in?' Mark replied.

'Yeah, you're a quick study.'

'Good times tonight, girls.' Caine said 'girls' like 'gewls' and Bobbie kind of loved it. She wondered where he was from – it wasn't a local accent. Caine embraced Naya in a friendly hug. 'See you soon, yeah?' He approached Bobbie with an identical gesture, which she awkwardly returned. Her heart stopped beating and she forgot to exhale, taking in a giant mouthful of his boyish scent – washing powder and macho deodorant. It was a nothing, throwaway gesture to him – he'd never think about it again and she'd remember it forever. Typical. 'Good to meet you, Bobbie – cool name by the way.'

'Yeah. Thanks.' Her tongue was tied in a fat knot.

Checking the coast was clear, the boys made for the exit and Bobbie turned back to the dark rectangle of the mirror, blowing out the candles. They may not have summoned a spirit, but something had sure been awoken deep inside Bobbie. She shook her head and sent her inner simpering girl to the naughty corner; she was meant to be above the Judy Blume stuff.

Bobbie followed Naya out of the shower room, not even noticing the monotonous *drip, drip, drip* that echoed off the tiles.

DAY ONE

Chapter 3

The Message

Bobbie was woken up the same way she was every morning, by Naya singing at the very top of her voice. In Spanish.

'Dear God,' Bobbie pleaded, rolling over in bed. 'Won't you please give it a rest? It's a Sunday – a whole day specifically designed for rest!'

She shoved her head under the pillow, but Naya kindly removed it and sang a few words in her ear. 'Wakey-wakey. Places to go, people to see!'

'Are you tripping? It's Piper's Hall. There are no places to go, literally.'

'Come on, it's Sunday. Church!'

Bobbie sat bolt upright in bed, pushing her hair out of her face. 'What?'

'Got ya!' Naya giggled. 'But at least you're up now. Come on or we'll miss breakfast.'

Now that they were Uppers, Bobbie and Naya were lucky enough to have a twin room – the Lowers sometimes had to squish four girls in a room the size of a sardine tin. Comparatively, this was luxury.

'Do you think I look fat?' Naya stood in front of the mirror, prodding at an almost non-existent belly.

Bobbie pulled her duvet back. 'You're insane, you know that?'

'I swear I'm giving up carbs . . .'

There was a tap at the door and Mrs Craddock stuck her head into the room. 'Roberta, dear, phone call for you.'

That meant only one thing: time for the weekly update from her mother. Bobbie wrapped her dressing gown around her body. 'Naya, will you save me some breakfast, yeah?'

'Sure thing, hon.'

She walked with Naya as far as the office next door to Mrs Craddock's quarters, which the girls called the Lodge for some unknown reason. Bobbie had earned her reputation as one of the 'good girls' (last night notwithstanding) so was left unattended in the poky room.

'Hi, Mum.' Bobbie surprised herself with how solemn the greeting was.

'Bobbie? Are you okay, sweetheart?' her mother yelled. Her mum never spoke in anything less than a bellow.

'Hi, yeah, sorry, I'm fine. I just woke up.'

'Okay, I was worried for a second! You shouldn't freak Mummy out like that, darling!'

'Sorry. How's New York?'

'Sweetie, I've hardly been outside since I stepped off the plane – I haven't so much as set foot in Barney's. Rehearsals have been absolutely non-stop. I've barely had a chance to scratch my arse, darling!'

Bobbie wasn't sure what she was meant to say to that. In New York it was still pretty early in the morning. Bobbie guessed her mum had just staggered in from a cocktail party or something and was calling her before she collapsed. This was the part where her mum would endlessly complain about the director, the script, the theatre, all the time loving every minute of her madcap existence. 'But you will fly over for opening night, won't you, darling?' her mum finished.

'Perhaps,' Bobbie replied. 'My exams are coming up after Christmas – I need to work.'

'Oh, don't be such a drama queen, darling.' That was rich, coming from her. 'You can fly over from Heathrow in less than eight hours and you can revise or do whatever it is you do on the plane! I'll even get a driver to collect you from the school.'

'Okay, Mum, whatever. I'd love to see the play.'

'Of course you would, it's absolutely the best play I've ever been in!' She said that about *all* the plays. 'How is school, darling?'

Bobbie shrugged before remembering you can't hear shrugs down the telephone. 'Yeah, fine.'

'Bobbie, I don't pay the astronomical fees for *fine*!'

'Oh, it's *marvellous*, Mum, I can't get enough. They'll have to surgically remove me from the place when I turn eighteen!'

'Don't be sarcastic, Roberta, you'll get wrinkles.'

'I thought that was frowning?'

'Don't get smart either! You know Mummy loves you, right?'

'I love you too, Mum.' And she did. Not everyone would like a semi-famous, semi-faded actress for a mother, but Bobbie hadn't ever had any other mums and she loved the one she had. She was insane, but always at the end of a telephone. Some of the girls at Piper's Hall were lucky to get an annual visit from a nanny.

'Extra-big transatlantic kisses please!' her mum ordered.

Bobbie made an enormous smacking noise down the phone, confident that no one was around to hear. She was wrong. An immaculate head snaked around the door. It was the Principal, Dr Price. 'Mum, I have to go. Love you.'

'Love you too, sweetie.'

Bobbie replaced the receiver. Dr Price entered the room, dressed in a slick, tailored skirt suit, even on a Sunday. The Head was a beautiful woman in her late forties, if slightly angular, reminding Bobbie of the laconic, ice-cool women in the de Lempicka paintings they'd studied in Art. She had a neat strawberry-blonde bob and looked down at Bobbie through heavily hooded eyes. 'Sorry to interrupt your phone call . . . er . . .'

'Roberta, Miss.'

'Roberta, that's it. But you'll miss breakfast if you're not careful.'

'Sorry, Dr Price. I'll go now – I'll have a super-quick shower.' Bobbie was always so shy around the teachers for some reason, even though she'd known many of them for almost five years. Her grades were FINE, her behaviour was GOOD, her attendance was PERFECT – as such, Bobbie had been able to glide under the radar all the way through her time at Piper's Hall. She clammed up especially badly around Dr Price; not only was she in charge but she was always so poised and glamorous, whereas Bobbie was well aware that even when she was in her uniform she looked like an urchin.

She didn't need to ask why the Head was in school on a Sunday. Bobbie knew a workaholic when she saw one, and rumour had it she was going through a 'bitter divorce' too. Head down, she slipped past the Principal and awkwardly tottered back to the dorm to grab her wash-bag.

The thought of what charred offal horrors might be left in the canteen at 9 a.m. on a Sunday spurred Bobbie into action. She'd twisted the shower to life before even remembering last night's escapades. In the light of the day, the bathroom was a whole other room. She faced the smeared mirror, splattered in the toothpaste, zit pus and lip gloss of at least a dozen girls, and grinned at herself. What had they been thinking? *So* lame.

Then she recalled Caine and her insides were suddenly candyfloss. Bobbie placed her glasses on the side of the sink and studied her face in the mirror, which was no longer a black tunnel of doom. She wasn't *ugly* by anyone's definition, but she was no Grace or Naya. Certainly not what boys like Caine were looking for anyway. Bobbie figured there were two types of girls in the world: ones who wore tights even in thirty-degree heat and ones who got their legs out. She was in the former category, the Graces and Nayas of the world were in the latter. Thank God she hadn't told anyone about her crush; The Elites would crucify her.

The mirror started to steam up and she pulled off her robe. Roll on the Christmas holidays when she'd be able to shower in a room without the collective DNA samples of twenty other girls. At least the water was hot. The pressure wasn't bad either and she let the jet pummel her back for a few minutes before washing her hair. She had the shower room to herself for once – a rare luxury – and she'd have stayed longer if her stomach hadn't been rumbling.

She twisted the shower nozzle off and, not wanting to get soap in her eyes, blindly reached for her towel on the rail. She curved an arm around the curtain, waving it left and right, unable to locate the towel rail just outside the cubicle.

Her hand brushed against someone – specifically someone's hair.

She recoiled. Bobbie was sure she'd been alone. 'Sorry! I didn't know there was anyone . . .' She wiped the water out of her eyes and gingerly pulled back the mildewed shower curtain. The washroom *was* empty.

Bobbie wrapped the towel around her soaking body and listened carefully. The room was thick with steam and there was a constant *drip, drip, drip* from the shower, but the room was deserted. 'Hmmm,' Bobbie said, stepping out of the shower stall and onto the cool tiles. 'That's weird.' Perhaps she'd grazed her hand on the towel, but it really had felt like hair.

As the extractor fan creaked and groaned, removing the excess steam, Bobbie saw the mirror clearly. Someone had written in the condensation on the glass, little streams of water running like veins from the words.

It didn't make any sense to Bobbie. The two words simply read:

FIVE DAYS

Chapter 4

Sunday

Bobbie didn't dwell on the watery words, her growling stomach taking precedence. If she thought about them at all, she dismissed them as the name of a new boy band that some horny fan-girl had dedicated the mirror to. By the time the steam on the mirror had faded, she'd already forgotten about it.

The canteen was a high-ceilinged hall in the old building, with grand wooden beams arching up to a point – Bobbie always liked to imagine she was inside Noah's ark. Leaded slit windows only allowed in meagre light on even sunny days so today the room was especially bleak and oppressive. It was the end of the sitting so the room was about half full – the competitive bulimics compensating for the absence of the competitive anorexics. Whatever the competition, boarding school sure had a way of bringing out the killer instinct in high-achieving teenage girls.

As Bobbie shuffled past Grace and the rest of The Elites, who always sat at the informal 'head' table, she could hear

41

them whispering about what she was wearing or something equally trivial; they always did. Bobbie rolled her eyes. She didn't know what disgusted her more: the existence of a blatant hierarchy that the teachers chose to ignore, or that everyone seemed oblivious to the fact that the plural of elite is *elite*. Bobbie couldn't even be bothered to get involved – she was *never* going to be the cleverest, prettiest or fastest. That said, she was one of the best writers. That was *her* thing.

Naya waved her over. 'Hey, I grabbed you a bit of everything.'

'You're the best.' The pre-mixed scrambled eggs didn't look edible, but Bobbie took a stab at a rasher of bacon.

'What's the plan for today?' Naya asked.

'Dunno,' Bobbie admitted through a forkful of congealed beans. 'I was going to work on that new story I was telling you about.'

'No, that's boring! Let's head into Oxsley! Oh come on, not like there's anything else to do, is there?' she said, picking up on Bobbie's lack of enthusiasm. 'Sit around here and watch paint dry?'

Piper's Hall is what paint watches when drying gets too exciting, Bobbie thought. On a weekend, Piper's Hall Ladies are supposed to better themselves in some way that would enrich their applications to Cambridge or Oxford. Bobbie took a creative writing class on Saturday mornings, but Sunday was all sports stuff – *so* not her thing. 'Yeah, okay. We could hit the library.' Not as dull as it sounded; the librarian was keeping some Susan Hill books to one side for her *and* they had free DVD loans.

'Child, you know how to party!'

'Ooh, or maybe we could go hover outside the off-licence

42

and see if we can lure men into buying us drinks with the promise of sexual favours like slutty booze sirens?' Bobbie's voice was rich with sarcasm.

'Very funny. But I wouldn't mind hanging with those guys from last night. They seemed fun, right?'

As the image of Caine's face ran through Bobbie's mind, her cheeks became so hot, she knew they must have blushed a deep crimson shade. 'Yeah, they seemed nice.'

Naya seized on her red face. 'Roberta Rowe! Do you have a little crush? You wanton tramp! Which one?'

Bobbie couldn't look her in the eye and lie. 'No! You know what I'm like.'

'Babydoll, we gotta do something about your boy issues or people will start to think you're same-sex oriented, which, by the way, is fine. I totally support your life choices. Speaking of which . . .'

At that moment, Sadie Walsh entered the dining hall, a pale imitation of her usual outdoorsy self. 'Sadie isn't a lesbian.' Bobbie had no idea why she was defending her.

'She is! I'm not judging, but everyone says she has an internet girlfriend in New Zealand!'

Bobbie rolled her eyes. 'Well then, it *must* be true!'

Sadie, dark shadows circling her eyes, shuffled to the servery and took a meagre breakfast before walking towards them, zombie-like.

'Girlfriend is looking busted,' Naya whispered. 'You think she's sick?'

'Ssh! She's coming!'

Sadie flopped her tray onto their table. 'Can I sit here? I

43

don't have the energy for The Elites today,' she said listlessly.

'Sure,' Naya said.

'Are you okay, Sadie? You look a bit peaky.'

Sadie looked for a moment like she was going to bite her head off, but clearly lacked the energy. 'I'm not sleeping very well.'

'What's up?'

'Weird dreams.'

'Can you remember them? My mom says all dreams have a meaning,' Naya offered.

'Yeah, but isn't your mum a Scientologist?' Bobbie couldn't resist.

'Thanks, Bob.'

'No, I can't remember, but the last two nights I've woken up in like a fever, covered in sweat. Maybe I'm getting flu or something.'

'Must have been quite a nightmare . . . or maybe it's one of *those* dreams. About anyone in particular, Sadie?' Naya grinned salaciously.

'Ha ha, very funny. I don't know. And there's a leaky pipe somewhere near our dorm – it's been dripping for days now. It's completely doing my head in.' She pushed her soggy cereal away. 'I'm not even hungry, and I'm always hungry.'

'Look.' Bobbie cleared the bowl onto her tray. 'Why don't you go back to bed? It's Sunday.'

'I can't. I coach under-16s hockey, duh.'

'Don't take it out on her,' Naya snarled.

Bobbie lifted the tray, ready to clear it. It was way too early for a Naya bitch-off. 'I'm going to get ready. Come and get me when you want to head into town.'

Naya backed down at once. 'I'll come with you now.'

Excellent, catfight avoided. As they walked towards the exit, Bobbie chanced a look over her shoulder. Sadie really did look gaunt and grey, and the writer in Bobbie couldn't help but think of the word 'haunted'.

A single-decker bus rolled through the windswept, lonely moorland that backed Piper's Hall. The sky and road were matching shades of melancholy grey and the air was ripe with the petrolic whiff that follows a thunderstorm. Today a mist lingered over the moors, part fog, part drizzle.

The bus itself was roasting hot from those foot-level heaters that feel like ankle hairdryers. Bobbie wondered if there was steam coming off her soggy duffel coat as every window fogged up. She and Naya shared one iPod, the headphones hanging between their heads like a telephone cable. They skipped duds and repeated favourites all the way into town in companionable quiet.

On arrival at Oxsley, they headed straight for the library and Naya hoodwinked the librarian into thinking they were eighteen so they could borrow *Psycho Killer*, *Rage* and *Hatchling 3: The Spawn*. There was a tea shop in Oxsley, but it was a proper tea shop with scones and Earl Grey rather than venti mocha fraps so there was little else for them to do other than enjoy the freedom.

Naya checked her phone as they plodded down the damp library stairs. 'Caitlin says that they're all at the graveyard. You wanna go?'

'I've made my feelings about the graveyard clear, have I not?'

Bobbie thought hanging out in the graveyard was disrespectful on about a hundred different levels of wrong.

'Yeah, I know, but Mark's there. He was kinda cute. I liked his arms. They were some . . . masculine arms he had right there.' Here was the real reason the Piper's Hall Ladies came into Oxsley – the fleeting possibility of an XY chromosome.

Bobbie's attention pricked up. If Mark was there . . . 'Is Grace with Caitlin?'

'You mean is Caine with Mark?' They trundled past the war memorial and started towards the church.

'That's not what I said.'

Naya grinned. 'You know my *abuelita* used to say I was psychic . . .'

'Caine is cute.' Bobbie rearranged the scarf around her neck. 'But Caine is also with Grace. The end. I'm so not little Susie Homebreaker.'

'Girl, there's no home to break. The gossip as I heard it was that Caine was going out with some girl in his year at Radley High and it totally mashed his head so he dumped her. He's a free agent. Just because Grace likes him doesn't mean anything.'

Bobbie's heart did a curious flippy thing at that information. She snorted. 'It means she would rip out my eyes and wear them as earrings.'

'Don't be scared of Grace Brewer-Fay. She's all talk.'

'The heads on pikes outside Christie House say otherwise.'

Naya cackled – she had such a filthy laugh, it was fabulous. 'Come on, Bob. Let's go stare at boys for an hour. It's biological destiny, why fight it?'

'God, as if Caine even knows I'm alive. He'd never go for

someone like me in a million years.'

Naya looked at her like she'd sucked on a lemon. 'Don't make me go all Tyra on your ass, Rowe. You are a rare and beautiful pearl.'

'Oh you are so full of crap! But okay, let's go.' Bobbie caved in in return for Naya buying her an iced bun from the tea shop. It's the little things.

St Paul's was a decaying, much-weathered village church on the road leading out of Oxsley. It was a squat structure with a moss-covered loping roof and square steeple – no spire – but four vicious-looking spikes on each corner. The unkempt church grounds rippled with wild grasses and weeds, the headstones standing at drunken angles where the ground had subsided with time. The place had that abandoned, end-of-days feel that put Bobbie on edge. The sprawling graveyard tumbled over the land between Piper's Hall and Oxsley – literally dead space. Bobbie could see the nearest gravestones from her bedroom.

The gaggle of noisy 'youths', as the churchwarden called them, was in stark contrast: a rainbow of American Apparel hoodies and fluoro trainers. Grace and Caitlin (her second-in-command) were perched on a stone sarcophagus, swinging their legs. With them there were four guys in total, two strangers joining Mark and Caine. As they entered the churchyard through the lychgate, Bobbie saw Caine was separated from the rest of the group, practising stunts on one of those tiny little bikes with bars on the back wheel.

'Hey, hey, hey!' Naya announced their arrival.

'Hi!' Caitlin waved them over. Caitlin was a lovely girl somewhere under all the make-up, but her parents paid full-fee

47

– a polite way of saying she hadn't exactly passed the entrance exam with flying colours. It was a good thing, then, that she was as pretty as any Disney princess. Her looks and minted parents had ensured she'd been initiated into The Elites. 'Hey, everyone. This is Charlie and Tom . . . you already know Caine and Mark, right? This is Naya and Bobbie. They go to our school too,' she said in her bubblegum voice.

'Bobbie,' said the ginger one, Tom. 'Is that short for something?'

'Yeah.' Bobbie was bored already. Clearly they'd been invited for pairing purposes. Gross. 'It's short for Bobbilene.'

Behind her, Caine laughed, hopping off his bike.

'Wow.' Tom didn't get it. 'Your parents are way harsh.'

'Tom, you div, she's messing with you.' Caine joined them. 'Is it Roberta?'

Bobbie nodded with a shy smile. Suddenly the 'ironic' mittens-on-a-string hanging out of her coat sleeves weren't so ironic and she feared she looked dangerously like someone on a day out with their carer.

Grace took a swig of the cheap white wine they'd illicitly bought at the corner shop in Oxsley. 'Anyway,' she said, 'Bobbie doesn't have parents. She's a test-tube baby.'

Oh God. Bobbie prayed for the earth to swallow her up. Better yet, she wished she could invent a time machine to go back in time to stop herself telling Naya about her parentage, therefore removing from history the fateful night when Naya had got drunk on Malibu and blabbed to Grace.

'What?' Mark said, attempting to keep a football off the ground.

'Grace, don't be a bitch,' Naya snarled.

'It's fine.' Bobbie drew herself tall (which was still only shoulder height to Naya or Caine). She'd learned early that people could only exploit a chink in your armour if you let them find it. 'I was conceived by artificial insemination.'

'What?' Tom said, clearly not the sharpest tack.

Bobbie took another deep breath. 'My dad is basically an anonymous sperm cell.' She went on. 'I like to call him Spermy. I also like to imagine a giant sperm cell coming home at the end of the working day with a bowler hat and briefcase.'

By this point Naya and Caine were in hysterics. It was possible Caitlin got the joke or that she laughed because everyone was laughing. Even Grace seemed quietly impressed.

'You're weird. But funny. I like it,' said Charlie – who, with his floppy hair and pudding face, looked like the chubby joker type himself.

'It's not weird.' Caine sat back against a headstone, opening a family-sized bag of Haribo and getting stuck in. 'It's just families, ain't it? They're all messed up. My mum left my dad for my uncle and then my dad tried to stab 'em both.'

Bobbie laughed despite herself. It was the way he delivered the news, like most people would deliver 'I have two sisters and a pet cat'. 'Seriously?' she asked.

'Yep. That's how we ended up down here in the middle of nowhere. I'm from Croydon.'

'Wow,' said Naya. 'We're like the screwed-up parent gang.'

'My parents are so dull it's not even funny,' Grace put in.

'No way.' Caine bit a jelly ring in half. 'The ones that look normal are secretly the weirdest.'

Naya turned to her blonde nemesis. 'So, Grace, I wonder what kinky little secrets your –' She stopped because that was when the blood started to gush out of her nose.

Chapter 5

Coincidence

Lots of things happened at once. Caitlin responded with an 'ew', pulling her legs onto the stone coffin. Conversely, Grace shot forward, unbothered by the blood and ready to help. Caine sprang to his feet. It took Bobbie a second to snap into action and reach for her friend.

'Oh God,' Naya gurgled.

'Pipe down. Tip your head back and pinch your nose.' Grace was surprisingly good in a crisis, it transpired.

'Are you sure you're meant to do that?' Bobbie rummaged in her satchel for tissues.

Grace looked at her as if she'd only just realised she was present. 'Of course I'm sure.'

'It's fine.' Naya accidentally smeared lumpy red-purple blood across her cheek. 'I used to get nosebleeds all the time when I was a kid.'

Charlie quietly disengaged from the group, looking pale and peaky at the sight of so much blood. Blood was now gushing from Naya's nose, thick droplets splattering onto the path, the dots rapidly joining. Naya took a handful of tissues from Bobbie and held it to her face, tilting her head towards the sky.

Bobbie saw spots of blood on her scarf where Naya must have splashed her. A third spot landed on the grey wool. That was when she realised it was coming from her own nose.

'What the . . . ?' She turned to see Caine dabbing at his nose too. A channel of blood ran from his left nostril to his full top lip. Bobbie held her fingers to her nose, but warm, viscous liquid trickled through the gaps.

'Oh my God.' Grace's face contorted. 'Have you been sniffing something? What did you take?'

'Nothing!' Bobbie cried, raising her already ruined scarf to her nose. The blood seeped into the wool, a fast-growing crimson cloud.

'Oh give over,' Caine snapped, wiping the blood away with the back of his hand. His didn't seem quite so bad.

'This is a thing,' Tom explained. 'It's to do with high pressure. A lot of people get nosebleeds when a storm's on its way.'

Naya pulled her tissues away and examined the damage. Her face was covered in gore. 'I think it's stopping.'

Bobbie felt her nose and gave an experimental sniff. Hers too seemed to have run dry.

'Do you get nosebleeds too?' Naya asked.

'Never,' Bobbie said. 'I never had one before.'

'Me neither,' added Caine. 'Except one time I got hit with a basketball.'

'Are you okay?' Caitlin looked horrified, holding her knees to her chin and grimacing through mascara-laden lashes.

'I think so,' Naya replied. 'Man. Pretty intense.'

Grace eyed them suspiciously. 'That's the freakiest thing I've ever seen. I've never heard of synchronised bleeding before.'

'I'm telling you, man, it's the weather.'

Mark laughed and gave a slow hand clap. 'Oh I get it. Very funny.'

'What?' Caine looked to his friend.

'It's a wind-up, innit? Cos of last night. Mate . . . you properly had me. How did you do it? Did you squirt the blood up there, or have you got like pellets, like on TV?'

The penny dropped for Bobbie. The dare. 'Bloody Mary.' As she said it, blood ran into her mouth. Nothing else tastes like blood: coppery, oddly expensive-tasting.

'Oh I see.' Grace pouted. 'Very funny. Psych.' She didn't sound impressed.

A frown furrowed Caine's handsome face. 'Mate, it's not a joke, I promise.'

That half knocked the smile off Mark's face, but his eyes said he was still expecting a raucous 'GOT YA!' any second now.

Bobbie had to admit, it was a pretty big coincidence. If it had been just her and Naya, she wouldn't have been too concerned, but *three* of them? The same three who'd said that name in front of the mirror. Her eyes suddenly stung.

She chastised herself; that was what made coincidence a thing – you recognised them because they happened all the time. One time she'd run into her cousin outside Topshop on Oxford Street even though they'd had no idea that each were going to be in London that day. That had been pure coincidence and no one had blamed a ghostly curse.

Nonetheless, the same mixture of fear, disbelief and smeared blood read on each of their faces – even Grace looked a little spooked. 'It must have been a sympathy nosebleed.' Bobbie tried to laugh it off, adopting her chirpiest tone.

'Aw, you're such a good friend,' Naya said, trying in vain to clean her face – she looked like one of the flesh-hungry zombies from the books she liked reading. 'You couldn't let me have the spotlight, even for a minute, could ya?' Naya winked, acknowledging the irony.

'Come on.' Bobbie took her friend's hand. 'Let's go to the tea shop to clean up.' As they walked away, Bobbie saw the look in Caine's eyes. His expression was grim – the local boy unable to laugh it off. Saying nothing, he watched them go and Bobbie felt his eyes on her all the way down the path.

On a Sunday evening, the girls of Piper's Hall were expected to dress smartly for Sunday roast in the great dining hall, which was also attended by the school priest. Each week he led prayers, which everybody lip-synched or ignored altogether. He sat with Dr Price, Mrs Craddock and Grace on the head table. Dr Price politely smiled and nodded as he moaned about the lack of faith in today's society.

Bobbie, as usual, sat with Naya and a few of the more pleasant girls from Brontë House. She wore a dotty vintage dress with her favourite cardigan – a huge woolly beast that had once belonged to her dead grandfather. 'I'm telling you,' Naya recounted her graveyard ordeal, 'it was really scary. I totally thought I was gonna croak it.'

'Did you see a bright white tunnel?' Bobbie grinned. 'You

are such a drama llama. It was only a nosebleed.' Bobbie refilled her water glass from a battered metal jug. By the time they'd convinced the old lady who ran the tea shop that they hadn't been in a gang fight (or wanted to eat her brains) and cleaned off the blood, they'd had to head back to Piper's Hall to spruce themselves up for the roast dinner.

'Still. It really freaked me out. I like actually feel nauseous.' Naya turned directly to Bobbie, abandoning her sticky toffee pudding and custard. She looked at her with big chocolate-button eyes. 'Bobbie, if I die, will you make sure loads of people come to my funeral?'

Bobbie chuckled. 'Of course I will. What are friends for?'

'That's like my greatest fear. That no one would care if I died.'

There was a glimmer of genuine sadness in Naya's eyes. Every once in a while the bluster cleared and Bobbie got glimpses of how skeletal Naya's esteem really was. 'Whatever happens, I'll be there, okay? And I'll make sure they play all your favourite songs, even the embarrassing ones.'

'You're the best.'

Bobbie was distracted by Kellie Huang, who wore the shortest, most buttock-skimming skirt ever, approaching the top table. That was a bit of a no-no while people were still eating. The skirt was a no-no at any time.

'What's up with Kellie?' Naya asked.

'Shh, I'm earwigging. I imagine she has a cold bottom.'

While Naya giggled, Bobbie tuned in to what they were saying. Kellie spoke to Mrs Craddock and Dr Price at the same time. '. . . I think she might really be ill.'

'What's wrong with her?' Mrs Craddock asked. Bobbie

guessed they were talking about Sadie, who roomed with Kellie.

'I don't know. She was kinda freaking out though.'

'Kind of *freaking out?*' Dr Price half smiled. 'Could you be more specific?'

Bobbie *knew* Sadie hadn't been well when they'd seen her at breakfast. Kellie went on. 'I dunno. She wouldn't leave the dorm though.'

Dr Price looked to the housemistress. 'I'll check on her after dinner,' said Mrs Craddock.

The problem with having a writer's brain, Bobbie thought, is that you start seeing patterns and relationships where there are only boring facts. Sadie was ill, they'd had nosebleeds. They'd *all* been in that bathroom at midnight last night. Suddenly her stomach shrivelled up like a raisin and she couldn't face her pudding.

Coincidences. More coincidences. When it's icy, people slip over. This doesn't make ice evil. The fact they'd all been sneaking around in the middle of the night probably explained why they were all feeling off colour today. Bobbie cursed her overactive imagination for arriving at 'haunted mirror' before 'logical explanation'. There was *always* a logical explanation.

After dinner, Bobbie changed into her pyjamas and fished her writing pad out from under her bed. It was a camel-colour suede notebook that her mum had brought back after filming an episode of some BBC drama in Norway, and even the touch of the thing made her want to write in it.

Naya was trying to gain access to Sadie, so Bobbie had the dorm room to herself. She wrote best to Danny Elfman's melancholy choral scores, which now played in the background. The suites were brooding and dramatic, a lot like her prose.

Where I once felt warm, spongy contentment inside, there was now only a hollow absence. An abyss of sorts. Yes, that was it – a void like a black hole in the coldest corner of space, she wrote. *It was as if one night, as I slept, some unseen hand had pulled a plug within and all the joy seeped away, leaving me empty. Eternally drained.*

Bobbie chewed her pen. She always wrote by hand first, only typing up the sections she was happy with. She'd once uploaded a short story to an online writing colony and it'd had like six thousand views. As soon as she got out of Piper's Hall and didn't have so much needless school writing to do, she'd start working on a novel – the only problem being she had more ideas in her notebook than she could ever hope to feasibly turn into novels.

Naya entered the room – her pyjama shorts revealing miles of gorgeous olive leg. Her endless black hair was twisted into a knot on top of her head where she'd washed her face. 'What ya doin?'

'Writing . . .'

'Is it the one you were talking about?'

'The suicide one? Yeah.'

'Get your Plath on, girl.'

Bobbie laughed. 'Oh I intend to. How's Sadie?' She rested her pen inside the notebook and closed it up – she'd rather die than show someone her writing at draft stage. What's more, she couldn't deny a ping of nosiness about their classmate.

'Between you and me it looks like worst case of PMS I've

seen in a while – she's howling and sobbing and saying she wants to go home. Girlfriend needs a hot-water bottle and a Nurofen, stat.'

Bobbie rolled off her bed. 'The sympathy spring has truly run dry for you, hasn't it? I'm gonna go brush my teeth.' She dragged her wash-bag off the dresser and sloped out of the dorm, the floor tiles freezing cold on her bare feet.

The hallway was deserted. Mrs Craddock had already turned the hall lights out so only a pale glow filtered through from the dorms. On Sundays it was standard for girls to retire to their rooms after supper. Last scraps of homework were hurriedly completed ready for the next day and the dreaded Sunday night/Monday morning malaise fell over the dorms. As Bobbie padded down the hall, her warm feet stuck to the floor, making a tiny suction noise as she went.

The bathroom was empty but smelled of fresh mint toothpaste and perfumy floral shower gel. As ever, the room was humid, never entirely drying out. Someone must have just finished. The shower head made a steady, echoing drip into the cubicle. Hating to see water wasted, Bobbie reached into the stall and squeezed the lever tighter. She frowned. The drip continued. It must be inside the pipes somewhere, out of her control.

Drip, drip, drip.

Bobbie brushed her teeth for the recommended three minutes, before filling the sink to wash her face.

Drip, drip, drip. God, that was annoying.

She took off her glasses and rested them next to her wash-bag. Earlier, at the chemist in Oxsley, she'd bought some

58

new foaming-cleanser-miracle-spot-defence and was keen to give it a try. After all, it promised 'results' after 'just one wash'. Who knew; it might just transform her into a supermodel. Her eyes tightly shut, she scrubbed her T-zone as directed before rinsing her skin. With a blind hand she felt around for her towel. She patted her face dry, making sure she'd cleared all the soap from her eyes.

When she reached for her glasses, they'd gone. 'Where are –'

The bathroom door slammed shut. Bobbie jumped, knocking her toiletry bag onto the tiles. Her conditioner rolled under the sink. 'What the . . . ?' They'd been right there a second ago. She checked the floor, but they weren't amongst her toiletries.

Stepping over her spilled things, she tugged the door open and looked out into the corridor. Without her glasses, her vision was pitifully weak, like someone had rubbed grease over her field of sight. Squinting through the gloom, she saw a figure at the furthest end of the corridor, heading towards the staircase. 'Hey! Did you pick up my glasses?' she called after what she assumed was another student.

The girl didn't stop. She headed further into the shadows. Her head was down, her stance hunched. She moved almost like she was sleepwalking.

'Excuse me! Those were my glasses!'

If this was some lame joke, Bobbie really didn't have the patience. She was an Upper now; she was meant to torment the Lowers, not the other way around. 'Can you come back please? It's not funny.' Bobbie took off down the corridor after the girl. Her feet slapped against the freezing floor.

The girl seemed to be heading into Austen House at the

far end of the corridor. Bobbie stopped and frowned. Instead of heading right across the landing, the other girl pivoted and headed down the stairs. Perhaps this wasn't just Austen versus Brontë rivalry. Nonetheless, Bobbie wanted her glasses back. Without them, everything was a disorienting blur, as if a dense fog had crept into the school halls. She followed the girl.

Bobbie reached the top of the stairs just in time to see a head of dark hair, almost ebony in this light, slip around the bend at the foot of the staircase. 'Oh, come off it!' Bobbie hurried after her, taking the steps two at a time. This was the 'Accy Area': a break-out space with some sofas, a TV and a table tennis set. The girl was nowhere to be seen. It was way too late for hide and seek. What's more, with no other pupils milling about like ants and all the lights off, it didn't look like her familiar old school any more. With long, strange shadows stretching across the floor, it almost felt like the walls were leaning in towards her. Bobbie dug her nails into her palms. When she swallowed, her throat was tight.

There was another stairwell leading down to the reception and main exit and further black corridors to the left and right. The space smelled heavily of the cabbage they'd had earlier. Above her she heard faint laughter – some girls in Brontë getting ready for bed. 'Hello?'

Bobbie crossed the Accy Area to the top of the next staircase. Sure enough, the girl was already silhouetted in the milky moonlight flooding the main entrance. The intricate leading in the glass panels cast shadows over the floor: curling, twisting vines and leaves. She just stood in the centre of them, facing the door, back to Bobbie. That was weird. Bobbie paused on the first step down. The other girl was wet . . . in fact she was dripping onto the tiles, a black puddle glistening like an oil slick about her feet. She was fully clothed, but soaking wet. 'Hey,' Bobbie asked. 'Are you okay?'

There was a crash and a squeal from the floor above and Bobbie whipped her head around, almost tumbling down the stairs in shock. With sweaty palms she gripped the banister. 'Give it back, you bitch!' some girl screeched, followed by shrill laughter. When Bobbie turned back to the stairs, the curious girl was no longer by the front doors. Bobbie frowned. How could she have moved so fast? Bobbie warily descended the remaining stairs to the hallway. Okay, weirder still. The floor wasn't even wet. Bobbie stooped down and ran a finger over the floor: dusty and bone dry. She'd *seen* that girl dripping all over the tiles. Or had she? Her eyesight really was dreadful without her glasses.

There was a sinking sensation in Bobbie's gut – the kind you get when a lift drops too quickly. The hallway was freezing cold, much colder than the stairs. Her skin prickled and she had a powerful urge to get far, far away from this place. Perhaps she should look for her glasses tomorrow morning . . .

Bobbie flinched, startled. The girl was silently waiting at the end of the corridor beyond the reception desk – towards the nurse's station and the Head's office. Just waiting. Bobbie tried to focus, but it was futile – she could hardly see beyond her hands. 'Look, ha ha, very funny, but can I have my glasses back please?'

The girl was framed by the tall, arched window at the end of the hall. She stood as still as any statue, almost unnaturally still. Bobbie could just about make out long, lank hair hanging rod straight from a skinny frame. Well, at least she was cornered now. 'Listen, I won't grass you up – I just want my glasses back.'

The girl's pale face was almost in focus. Bobbie realised that something about the girl wasn't right. There was something wrong about the way she was standing. Was she hurt? Maybe she needed help.

'Stay there, okay?' Arms held out in front of her body, clutching at the dark, Bobbie approached the shadowy girl.

Chapter 6

The Olden Days

The Head's office door swung open in Bobbie's face. Light flooded the corridor and Bobbie screamed – she wouldn't have had herself down as a screamer, but she'd been holding her breath and then the door burst open and then and then ...

Her head teacher's hand flew to her chest before she composed herself. 'Oh my goodness me! You'll give an old lady a heart attack! Roberta, isn't it?' Dr Price stepped out of her office, laptop bag on her shoulder like she was leaving for the night. 'What are you doing down here? Is there something wrong, dear?'

'I ... Someone ran off with my glasses.' Bobbie stepped back and pointed to the end of the corridor, to the arched window.

There was nothing there. Well, there was a comfy armchair for visitors to use, and a spiky pot plant, but no *person* stood in the window, certainly no creepy, weird, silent girl. 'Oh, Roberta, you're going to kick yourself.'

'What?'

'They're on your head, dear – your glasses. I do that all the time too. Don't worry,' she added with a faint smile, 'it only means you're cracking up.'

Bobbie checked her hair. Sure enough her glasses were tucked behind her ears and resting on the crown of her head. No way . . . she'd put them by the sink. She was *not* some flaky ditz. 'But I . . .'

Dr Price smiled. Even when she smiled, the Head was a little glacial. 'Don't worry, I won't tell anyone if you don't. Now off to bed, young lady, it's a school night.'

'Okay,' Bobbie said. She was frustrated but wasn't about to enter into an argument with the headmistress. What was she going to do? Stamp her foot and swear there was some stupid Lower running off with her glasses who'd then somehow put them on her head? 'Sorry.'

'Not a problem. Now scoot.'

Bobbie ran all the way back to her dorm, not wanting to spend a second longer than necessary in the draughty corridor. The whole way she couldn't shake the sensation of eyes on the back of her head. She shut the bedroom door behind her and dived onto Naya's bed. 'Naya, something really super-weird is going on.'

Naya's copy of *Heat* had flopped to the floor and she was half asleep with her bedside light still on. 'What?'

'This is going to sound mental, but I think I just saw Bloody Mary.'

'Girl . . .' Naya rolled onto her front, burying her head in the pillow.

64

'It's true. Someone took my glasses out of the bathroom.'

Naya lifted her head. 'Oh well then, it's definitely Bloody Mary. Call the hotline now.'

'Don't,' Bobbie moaned. 'I followed her because I thought it was just a Lower, but there was something *wrong* with her. It was really scary.'

'Of course it was. Everything in this school is scary at night. Go to sleep. In the morning you'll feel like a total moron, I promise.'

Another thought occurred to Bobbie. 'Naya, is this you?'

'What?'

'You said before we did the mirror thing that you wanted to freak Grace out . . . Is this all some sort of prank?'

Her friend propped herself up onto her elbows. 'Girl, I swear on my mom's Louis Vuitton handbags that I someday hope to inherit that this is nothing to do with me. It's nothing to do with anything – you're freaking yourself out. Go. To. Sleep.' She flopped back down onto her pillow.

Bobbie realised she wasn't going to get any sense out of Naya now, and her friend did have a point. Everything *would* feel different in the morning. She looked around their dorm, at the embellishments they'd made – their furry throws, their framed photos, their Hello Kitty, John Green and *Satanville* posters. It felt safe. 'Can we keep a light on?'

'I don't care. Just stop talking.'

Bobbie couldn't remember falling asleep. She read through her story for a bit while Naya lightly snored, but she must have nodded off eventually. She didn't even remember closing her eyes – for the longest time she stared at the centimetre gap under the door to check that no feet were coming past their room.

'MARY!'

Bobbie was in class. It was the music room – the same floor-to-ceiling bay windows and the view overlooking the hockey pitch. Only, for some reason, everything was different. For one thing, although it was November, it was mild and sunny and the classroom smelled of freshly mown grass. The furniture was arranged differently for a second; all the music stands and instruments had been cleared away. Now there were rows upon rows of vintage-looking individual desks – the sort Bobbie had only seen wheeled out for exam time. They were the really old-fashioned ones with the surface that lifted up to reveal a compartment within.

This all felt very odd. There was a summery haze over the room, as if she were seeing the world through a Vaseline-smeared lens. A couple of girls milled around her, distributing exercise books, but they moved in half-time as if they were walking on the moon.

'Mary!' the same voice trilled.

Bobbie looked behind her, only to realise she was in the last row. She wore her hair in a neat plait, something she hadn't done since she was very young.

'Mary Worthington, are you listening to a word I'm saying?' Bobbie didn't recognise the teacher. She wore the scratchiest-looking cardigan and skirt combo Bobbie had ever seen, with thick wool tights sagging around conservative court shoes. It took her a moment to realise that the severe woman was glaring at her.

'Me?'

'Well, is there another Mary Worthington whom I don't know about?' The girls tittered, all looking at her. They were all strangers. Prim, white girls, all wearing the Piper's Hall uniform, but a slight variation of the one she was so familiar with. The kilts were longer and the white socks were higher. 'Could you please answer the question?'

Bobbie felt her cheeks blaze. 'I . . . I don't know, Miss.'

'Of course you don't – you were half asleep. Miss Worthington, do you have any idea how *lucky* you are? A girl like *you* in a school like *this*?' The word *lucky* stung like a slap.

The bell rang out, the same bell that still rang out to signal the change of lessons. The girls gathered their belongings. 'Don't all charge at once, please.'

The other girls glowered at Bobbie with barely concealed disdain, giving her a wide berth as they filed past her out of the classroom. Bewildered, Bobbie followed them. This was a dream, but it felt fragile somehow, like she was on the very verge of waking up. A dream made out of the finest spun sugar.

The hallway looked almost identical to how it did now, but Bobbie sensed this was some time ago – the way the teacher was dressed, the lack of display boards, the blackboard where there was now an interactive whiteboard. There were subtle differences everywhere.

Bobbie drifted, feeling lost in her own school. Sideways glances and whispers all aimed at her. She couldn't be sure, but the loudest whisper sounded something like 'Scary Mary'.

It was one of *those* dreams. She was half in it, half looking in on it. She wasn't herself. She didn't feel like Bobbie Rowe, she felt sadder, like there was nothing to look forward to, nothing to laugh about. She felt a kind of inky, hopeless black inside, the type of which she'd only ever written about. Wanting to be away from the other girls, Bobbie ducked into the nearest toilet. There was something she had to do.

The ground-floor bathroom was almost the same as it was now – the pipework all painted a sterile jade-green colour to match the aqua-green tiling. Bobbie crossed to the nearest mirror.

She woke up at once.

Dawn was breaking outside of the dorm windows, the curtains barely holding back the light. At some point in the night, Naya had crawled into bed alongside her. Either the conversation or a nightmare had spooked her – Naya often snuck in if she'd had bad dreams. Bobbie snuggled up next to her for heat and, if she was honest, security. Tonight the bad dreams were hers. With Naya there she felt safer.

Bobbie was almost too scared to close her eyes. She couldn't remember what she had seen in the mirror. It had been too awful.

DAY TWO

Chapter 7

The Vanishing

It took a superhuman effort for Bobbie to drag herself out of bed the next morning. Her sleep had been so shallow, so wafer-thin, that it barely counted as rest. In daylight though, it seemed safer to close her eyes and so she deployed the snooze button three times.

Naya was no longer beside her and the other bed was empty, so Bobbie guessed she must have crept out to beat the shower stampede. Breakfast was at seven and classes didn't start until nine, so it was her call as to whether she showered and got into her uniform before or after eating. Bobbie eventually flopped out of bed at ten to eight, the last possible minute she could join the breakfast queue. Grabbing a pair of leggings, Naya's Yankees hoodie and some flip-flops, Bobbie trudged towards the bathroom.

She hadn't got far when she realised something was wrong. Instead of eating breakfast, girls were scurrying up and down the hallways and in and out of each other's rooms like agitated

71

bees. The air was loaded – a buzz of activity and nervous chatter. Caitlin emerged from one of the rooms in Brontë and hurried towards the stairs. 'Caitlin, what's going on?'

'Oh my God, didn't you hear? Something's wrong with Sadie. No one's even allowed in Christie. Some people are saying she's . . . she's dead.'

The floor started to spin until Bobbie forced it to be still – the rumour mill was clearly working overtime. She gripped the banister at the top of the stairs for support. 'What? No way.'

'Swear down. I'm gonna find Grace. She'll know what's going on.'

Bobbie took off down the stairs at once. She knew how fast gossip could travel around this place. Last year Maisie Spence-Guillame had told *one person* she'd slept with Mr Granger, the vaguely handsome Maths teacher, and within *two hours* the police were in school. It hadn't even been true, but it showed you had to watch your mouth in a school that had ears.

Naya was stationed in the Accy Area, acting as another node of information with Lower girls crowding around her. They parted to let Bobbie through. 'Naya, what's going on?'

'Oh there you are. We have no idea – nobody's saying anything. Just that something's wrong with Sadie.'

Bobbie let out a mighty sigh of relief. 'Oh thank God – Caitlin said she was dead.'

'She might be,' said ferret-like Rose Clarkson. 'No one's been in or out of her room. Dr Price and Mrs Craddock are up there now.'

'Be real.' Naya gave her a stinky glare. 'If there was a dead girl upstairs don't you think we'd have seen some police or an ambulance by now?'

'Not necessarily,' whined Rose.

Mrs Craddock leaned over the landing balcony that overlooked the Accy Area, looking harassed. 'Girls! Dr Price says she wants you in uniform and in the main hall in fifteen minutes. No arguing, no exceptions.' The gaggle of girls around the table tennis set started firing questions at the housemistress. 'Oh, just get on with it, girls! Go!'

Naya pouted. 'They can't possibly be making us go to lessons. If Sadie *has* died, we'll at least get a couple of days off, right?'

Bobbie raised an eyebrow. 'You're all heart.' Her appetite for breakfast was now non-existent. 'Come on, let's get front-row seats in assembly.'

Unfortunately, everyone wanted front-row seats. Once they were in the grey with claret trim of the Piper's Hall uniform, Bobbie and Naya had to settle for a position in the third row. Bobbie's heart was an unswallowed lump at the back of her throat, refusing to go down. It was more than just nosiness or curiosity – Bobbie *needed* to know what had happened to Sadie. There were only so many coincidences she was willing to write off.

Rumours and speculation bounced off the oak-panelled walls of the main hall. Thick-framed portraits of former headmasters looked on with stern disapproval. 'Meningitis', 'pregnancy' and 'suicide' were popular suggestions, although Bobbie was particularly impressed with 'she injected heroin she bought from a tramp in Oxsley'. Still, she didn't crack a smile. Her jaw was clenched tight and she chewed on the inside of her cheek until Dr Price blew into the room, as collected as ever, but with a steely glint in her eye.

'Settle down NOW.' She wasn't taking prisoners. Every girl fell silent. The Head took her place at the podium and looked out across a sea of gossip-hungry faces. 'This is very, very serious. Sadie Walsh is missing from Christie. No one has seen her since lights-out last night.'

There was a ripple amongst the crowd. Naya whispered something in Bobbie's ear but she shushed her.

'Quiet!' Dr Price went on, smoothing her strawberry-blonde bob. 'I don't care what's going on, what's been said, what anyone has done – legal or otherwise. *All* that matters is finding Sadie and making sure she's safe. If anyone knows anything about her whereabouts I need to know right now.'

More mutters as each girl asked their neighbour what they knew. Bobbie found herself short of breath. She and Sadie weren't bosom buddies or anything, but the thought of something happening to her was awful. There was something else too, a niggling feeling that there was something she should be remembering.

'If you don't stop chatting I'm going to get really angry, ladies. I do not want to hear gossip, ideas or speculation. Obviously Sadie has gone somewhere and I don't believe for a second that she didn't tell someone where she was going.'

This time, at the point where someone *needed* to stand up and confidently say 'she eloped to New Zealand with her internet lesbian lover', the room was as quiet as a chapel.

'You don't need to say anything now, but if you do, genuinely, know something about Sadie please see me at once. Clearly

I am going to be very busy dealing with this all day and the police are on their way. That means the rest of you need to make sure you are in the right place at the right time. You will all go to first period at once, is that understood?'

There was a droned 'Yes, Miss' by way of response.

Bobbie made her way to class on autopilot. First period on a Monday, cruelly, was double English Lit and, unusually for her, she hadn't done the reading homework. As she filed into class, she overheard Grace talking to Caitlin, both of whom, even at times of crisis, were so effortlessly gorgeous they made the kilt and blazer look like a fashion statement rather than a uniform. Grace always proudly displayed the gold Head Girl badge on her blazer like she was the sheriff of the goddamn town. 'God, she's such an attention whore,' Grace bitched. 'She'll be in Oxsley with some dykey Radley High girl who looks like Justin Bieber. I bet you anything.'

Bobbie ignored them and slipped into her seat. The lesson was on Poe's *The Fall of the House of Usher*, which she should have been excited about, but she couldn't focus. A worry worm bored into her skull. She drummed her HB pencil on the side of her exercise book, her fingers overloaded with energy. Fragments of ideas, noises and images sloshed around her head – nothing making any sense. Nosebleeds, her dream, the girl in the corridor . . . how did that connect to Sadie . . .? Then another piece of memory flotsam drifted to the front of her brain, something she'd completely forgotten.

The pencil slid from her fingers and rolled to the floor with a sharp ping.

She stood, almost knocking her chair over. The metal legs made an ugly screech as they scraped along the floor. Grabbing her books, she turned and darted for the door, almost colliding with Miss Foster, her English teacher, as she entered the room. 'Bobbie, where are you . . . ?'

'I have to talk to Dr Price.' The lie felt lumpy on her tongue, but it would have to do. Bobbie knew Miss Foster would assume she had information about Sadie and let her go without hesitation. With her head down, she ducked past the teacher. This was so unlike her, but she knew there was no way she'd be able to work until she knew the answer to the noisy question that roared inside.

The first mission was finding Lottie Wiseman, Sadie's BFF and room-mate. She did a ton of languages – where would she be? Bobbie initially set off towards where she knew Naya had Spanish, banking on Lottie being in the lesson with her, only to have a last-minute change of heart.

Instead, Bobbie left the shiny Millar Wing, with its clean sandstone walls and glass partitions, and headed back to the old building, towards Dr Price's office. It made sense to Bobbie that those nearest to Sadie (including Lottie) were probably still being interrogated.

There was an open concrete courtyard in the middle of the school, and a fine drizzle had turned everything charcoal grey to match the heavy cloud that squatted above the school. Bobbie darted under the rain shelter and slipped in through the fire escape on the opposite side of the quad. Few lessons were taught in the old part of the school any more; only the music room, hall, dorms, canteen and offices were situated there.

As such it was eerily quiet at this time of day, with almost all the girls either in classrooms or shivering on the playing field.

Bobbie ducked past the dinner ladies setting up the dining room and straight into the entrance hall, which seemed so different in the light of day. Her pursuit of the mystery girl seemed so much longer ago than last night. Now, fuzzy amber light diffused through the stained glass in the grand front doors, shining down on the reception desk. Lorraine, the school's long-standing receptionist, looked up to greet her. 'Hello . . .'

'Bobbie.'

'That's it! Is everything okay, love?'

'Yeah.' She used the same lie again. 'I need to see Dr Price.'

'Well, she's in with the police at the moment, dear. Is it about Sadie?'

'Sort of. Yeah.' Bobbie leaned past the desk and glanced down the corridor towards Dr Price's office. Sure enough Lottie and Kellie, her other room-mate, were waiting on the sofa near to where last night she'd seen the awkward figure of the girl. The impossible ghost girl.

'Okay, love. Go wait with the others.'

Bobbie thanked her and shuffled down the corridor, trying to think of a way she could phrase this without sounding like a crazy person. Poor Lottie, who looked gaunt and frail at the best of times, looked awful, eyes red from crying and her face clammy and grey. If Sadie *had* been planning something, her best friend evidently hadn't been in on it.

Kellie looked up at her. There was a long black hair trapped in her lip gloss and for some reason it really bothered Bobbie. 'Hey hey hey, Bobbie. Do you know something about Sadie?

Did you see her last night?'

'No,' Bobbie admitted. 'I need to speak to Lottie.'

'Me?' she sniffed. 'Why?'

Bobbie took a deep breath, suddenly not sure what to do with her hands. She clasped them in front of her to keep her fingers still. 'Can you remember Hallowe'en night?'

'Yeah.'

'You know Sadie's dumb story about Bloody Mary?'

Lottie's eyes widened. 'Yeah.'

'Well, can you remember when Sadie said she'd already done it? You said you were with her.'

The skinny girl now looked thoroughly confused. 'Yeah, so what? She did it in front of the mirror inside her wardrobe.'

Bobbie's pulse felt much too fast. 'Did you do it too?'

'No.'

'When did she do it?'

Lottie thought about it, forehead creased. 'It was Tues— no, Wednesday night. Yeah, it was after choir.'

Bobbie had to reach out and steady herself against the wall. Her feet felt disconnected from the floor. Just as she'd feared. This couldn't be happening. 'That was five days ago.' The last word got caught in her throat and came out as a hoarse whisper.

The message on the mirror. *Five days*.

Chapter 8

Five Days

Bobbie burst into room E7, the door clattering against the back of a chair that had been left too close. 'Can I help you?' asked Mr Carlos with his trademark pout and an arch of his over-plucked brows.

Bobbie pushed her glasses back up her nose. 'Yes. I'm sorry . . . but Dr Price needs to see Naya at once.'

Naya caught her eye and knew immediately this was a lie. Mr Carlos dismissed her with a flourish of his arm. 'Okay. You'd better go and see what she wants.'

'Yes, sir.' Naya tucked her chair under and swung her bag onto her shoulder. Bobbie was steered back into the corridor – one of the sterile, plastic-smelling ones in the new annex. The Millar Wing had opened during her first year at Piper's – it was all exposed brick and inspirational posters: YOU ARE EXCEPTIONAL.

'What's going on? You look like you survived something,' Naya said with a swish of ebony hair.

'Naya, I know what happened to Sadie.'

'O and M and G. I knew you were hiding something!'

Bobbie dragged her away from the classroom, and any eavesdroppers, towards the stairwell. 'I think . . . I think it was Bloody Mary.'

Naya waited for the punchline. 'Say what? Is this what you were babbling about last night?'

Bobbie sighed, frustrated. 'I'm serious. Five days ago Sadie said "Bloody Mary" five times into her bedroom mirror and now she's gone. After we did it, I saw a message in the mirror that said "five days". I wish I were kidding. I'm not.' Naya's face fell before she shook it off. The taller girl giggled under her breath. 'What?' Bobbie prompted.

'No way. Just . . . no. This must be the final part of Sadie's little joke. Girl, when I see her, I'm gonna . . .'

Bobbie knew at once there was something more. Naya was many things, but an effective liar was not one of them. 'Naya, what is it?'

'It's nothing.'

'Naya . . .'

Naya reached into her cotton tote bag. She pulled out her lesson planner. 'Look. Some moron graffitied on it.'

Bobbie took the diary from her and turned to the current week. In small, scratchy ink letters were the words *five days*. It was written in the box for Sunday – the same day she'd got the mirror message. Bobbie inhaled as if winded. 'Oh God.'

'Oh come on – this could all be part of Sadie's . . .'

'No!' Bobbie snapped, louder than she meant to. Her cheeks flushed. 'Can Sadie mess with my eyes too? And my dreams? I am *seeing things*, Naya.'

Naya rolled her eyes before taking hold of Bobbie's tie and leading her down the first-floor corridor like a dog. When they reached the vending machine, Naya slotted in some coins before a can clattered into the dispenser. She handed Bobbie a Coke. 'Here. Have this. Your eyes are doing a weird bulging thing and it's wigging me out.'

Bobbie accepted the Coke and took a sip. She hadn't realised how badly she needed the sugar. There were some padded chairs outside the careers office and Bobbie fell onto one, her legs feeling hollow. 'Thanks.'

Naya sat alongside her. 'Let's regroup. You genuinely think a ghost killed Sadie? Bob—'

'I don't know. Maybe. People don't just vanish. Oh God, poor Sadie . . . she must have been so scared.'

'Bobs . . .'

'I know. It sounds all fifty shades of crazy. But you know that bit in the films where you just want everyone to hurry up and accept that the seemingly impossible thing is a possibility? Well . . . that.'

Naya managed a wry laugh. 'I hear that. But . . . it's a bit of a reach. I don't even believe in ghosts.'

'Neither did I until I saw one.' Bobbie sipped on the Coke. 'It's all too much. The day after we said her name we *both* got messages. We *all* got nosebleeds. I saw a girl downstairs . . . Mary. I dreamed about her . . . in the dream I *was* her. Talking about ghosts *is* pretty stupid, but so is denying what's right in front of you.'

Naya took a theatrically deep breath. 'Okay. Let's suppose for a second I buy all this. What do you wanna do about it?'

'I don't know. We only have until Thursday . . .'

'Until?'

'I don't know.' There was a spiky lump lodged in her throat. 'Until whatever happened to Sadie happens to us.'

The truth finally seemed to hit Naya. Her cheeks lost their glow, fading from the colour of coffee to the colour of very milky tea. 'Oh God.'

It was Bobbie's turn to be the supportive one now. She gripped Naya's arm. 'No, it's okay. That means we still have nearly four days to stop her. I hope. Last night, if she'd wanted to hurt me, she could have, but she didn't. For whatever reason, she's given us five days.'

'To say goodbye.'

'There's the spirit,' Bobbie chided. 'I think she *wants* something. Look, maybe if we can work out who she was . . . is . . . what happened to her. There *has* to be a way to stop her.'

'What? You reckon we can talk her out of ripping our skin off or whatever?'

Bobbie winced. 'She *might* be a friendly ghost . . . like Casper.'

'Honey, tell that to Sadie and anyone else fool enough to do what we did.'

Bobbie squeezed the Coke too hard and a fountain sprayed onto her tights and the chair between her legs. 'Naya, you're a genius.'

'I am?'

'Yes. This has happened before.'

With the school in utter chaos – fluorescent police jackets flashed in and out of classrooms and the houses like wasps – no

82

one noticed or cared that Bobbie and Naya hadn't returned to their classes. Girls were being pulled out of lessons at a steady rate for questioning about Sadie so they took full advantage of the madness.

They went to the library reading rooms, knowing that two Uppers wouldn't look too out of place – for all the librarian knew they were on free periods. Bobbie checked no one was watching before logging onto the system and accessing the internet. 'What are you looking for?' Naya asked. Bobbie ignored her and typed MARY WORTHINGTON PIPER'S HALL. The first few searches were about the 'oldest hall in Ohio' that had apparently been owned by a Mary Worthington. The next ten or so all referred to a character on the TV show *Supernatural*. The legend of this girl was worldwide. Most of the Google hits were Facebook pages for modern-day, real-life Mary Worthingtons. 'Anything?' Naya prompted.

'Nothing useful. Oh wait . . . look at this.' Bobbie clicked on a link. It was one of those awful 'ask anything' websites where people post questions before members log on and answer. Bobbie read the original post aloud. '"Watched the Bloody Mary episode of *Supernatural*. Is this like a real thing? Well scary LOL!" There's a load of answers and then someone said this: "I heard from a friend in the UK that it really happened at some fancy boarding school."'

'Holy crap.' Naya pulled her chair closer. 'That's us.'

'Yep.'

Naya leaned in. 'What about the alumni page on the school website? If she was a student here . . .'

Bobbie could have kissed her – why hadn't she thought of

that? 'See, that's why I love you. You're beautiful *and* clever.'

'Snap!' Naya grinned.

Bobbie found the Piper's Hall website and then clicked on the link to the alumni pages. It was divided up into sections – decade by decade. 'There must be thousands and thousands of girls on here.'

Naya chewed her lip. 'Was there anything in your dream? Like were they all in flares and stuff?'

'No.' Bobbie took her glasses off and rubbed her eyes. 'At a guess I'd say Thirties or Forties.'

'Worth a look.' Bobbie did so, also checking the 1920s and 1950s as a precaution, but there was no record of a Mary Worthington amongst the lists of former pupils. 'That's weird. In the dream, I – I mean she – was definitely a student. I was in uniform.'

'In the story, she committed suicide,' Naya said. Bobbie altered the search to PIPER'S HALL SUICIDE. This time there was a positive result, but it concerned a Piper's girl who'd killed herself in the Nineties while at home. Bobbie disregarded it and Naya shrugged, at a loss. Another idea occurred to Bobbie. 'Can you remember? On Saturday night, Sadie said something had happened while her sister was here.'

'Yeah.'

'Do you know *her* name?'

Naya shook her head. 'No – the middle sister was here at the same time as us, but the eldest one had left by the time we got here. Just look for Walsh – it can't have been too long ago.'

Bobbie looked through the last two decades. Sure enough there was a Claudia Walsh who'd graduated four years before and was now at Oxford, and then there was a Tabitha Walsh who'd left thirteen years earlier. That was quite a bit older than Sadie; Bobbie wondered if perhaps they were stepsisters. Bobbie brought up the alumni list for Tabitha's graduating year. She scanned the names until something caught her eye. 'Oh that's weird. Look.'

'What am I looking at?'

Bobbie pointed at the two names at the very end of the list.

Abigail Hanson and Taylor Keane – always in our thoughts.

'Well, what's that supposed to mean?'

'Let's find out.' Now in full-on detective mode, Bobbie googled ABIGAIL HANSON PIPER'S HALL and hit enter. 'Jackpot.'

This time they'd struck gold.

Police escalate hunt for missing schoolgirls . . .
Parents' plea to missing pair . . .
No evidence of foul play in double disappearance . . .

Each story came with an accompanying picture of the two girls. Abigail was a devastatingly pretty brunette with cheekbones to die for while Taylor looked like a cheerleader or something, all bronzed skin and tousled off-blonde hair. 'How have we not heard about this?' Bobbie wondered aloud.

'If there were no bodies, I guess there's no case.'

Bobbie opened one of the news reports. It *had* made the national news, but at the time she'd been only about four and

85

living in her limited, childish world. Both girls had vanished from their homes: Abigail in London and Taylor on the Welsh borders. That made no sense. Apparently it hadn't made a lot of sense to the police either. Two girls vanishing on the same date, miles apart. From what Bobbie could tell, the only lead was that the two girls had run away together, although neither took any belongings.

They'd vanished. Just like Sadie. A jagged, icy feeling chilled Bobbie from inside out, starting in her spine and spreading through her bones. 'I would literally bet anything in the world that five days before they vanished they were in front of some mirror . . .' She didn't need to finish.

'Try searching for more missing girls,' Naya suggested. Bobbie did so and there was only one positive result – another Piper's Hall girl some eight years before Abigail and Taylor. Same story – another girl who seemed to drop off the face of the earth. Naya puffed her cheeks out. 'I bet there are more – from before everything was online. Why don't we all know about this? My mom might have sent me to a different school . . .'

'Who'd believe it?' Bobbie's eyes were wide. 'Bloody Mary is a ghost story. Hundreds of kids must do it every day . . . only the ones who do it *here* vanish in a puff of smoke. And do you know what the really funny thing is? We can't say we weren't warned! Sadie told us exactly what was going to happen.'

'Bobbie. We're going to disappear aren't we? Something's going to come for us.'

Bobbie wanted to say, *Yes, it looks pretty likely*, but she couldn't – she couldn't say it to Naya and she couldn't admit it aloud. It felt like quitting. 'No. We still have three and a half days. We can . . . stop her somehow.'

'How?'

'I . . . I don't know. I'll think of something. I'm sure we've been given five days *for a reason*. In my dream . . . I . . . she didn't *feel* evil. She mainly felt *sad*.'

'Maybe if we spoke to Sadie's sister or something . . .'

The final search on the first Google page caught Bobbie's eye. 'We might not have to. Look.'

Haunted Piper's Hall. The TRUTH about Abi and Taylor.

Bobbie clicked on the link at once. It was a pretty basic online journal. In the pursuit of a single-minded obsession, no creativity or thought had been taken with the layout of the blog. Every post was about Bloody Mary. The most recent post, at the top of the page, was little more than stream of consciousness.

The more I say the less people believeme I don't know why I bother or howmany timesi can say it . . . what they don't undersatdn is that she is in my head. She is watching me too.

The blog's author was one Bridget Horne, according to the banner at the top of the page. Even the most recent post was almost ten years old. Bobbie scrolled down. The older the posts got, the more cohesive and sane they seemed. Naya stopped her. 'Look at that one.'

I told the police everything I knew. I told them about the dare. I told them about BM. I'm sure you can guess what their reaction was. I don't know what else I can do except warn people. Never, ever say her name.

'A bit late for that, isn't it?' Bobbie tugged her hair off her face. 'Wait! If this Bridget was a Piper's Hall girl . . .' Bobbie switched tabs back to the Piper's Hall alumni pages. Sure enough there was a Bridget Horne on the list. One click and it brought up her contact details. 'Ta-da!'

'You think the contacts are kept up to date?'

'They should be – they send out a newsletter and invites to the yearly luncheon and stuff. You know the motto . . .'

'*A lasting, lifelong sisterhood.*' Naya did a pretty good impression of Dr Price.

'It's worth a go.'

They went to lunch as normal, aware they'd missed the entire morning session. Bobbie couldn't bring herself to swallow even the smallest amount of food. The one mouthful of soggy pasta bolognese she attempted turned to cardboard on her tongue, requiring a gulp of water to force it down. She was like a dog with a rag. Her foot tapped impatiently under the long dining bench, waiting for the bell for the afternoon session to sound so she could continue with her mission.

This afternoon she had a proper free period, but Naya once more had to cut class. It was getting a little risky.

There were so many rules at Piper's Hall, and she had obeyed them without question for so long that Bobbie often forgot how ludicrous they were. Right now, the fact they were only allowed to use mobile phones from 7 to 10 p.m., and only then in their dorms, seemed especially insane. But this was the institution that had special paths and corridors for Uppers and a blanket ban on black socks. Another rule was that girls weren't allowed into the dorms between lessons or during study sessions, the (accurate) thinking being that girls would use their frees to sleep.

As the bell rang out and everyone else made their way to period four, Bobbie and Naya had to go to the Lodge to use the phone. 'Do you think anyone saw us?' Naya asked.

'I don't think so. But maybe you should go to Drama just to be on the safe side?'

'Are you crazy? I'm not missing this to listen to Ms Flemming bang on about the freaking Stanislavski System.'

Bobbie chuckled and checked the coast was clear. God only knew where Mrs Craddock was – she was off duty until five. Somewhere down the hall a hoover purred as the cleaners went through the bedrooms. Activity surrounding Sadie's room in Christie House seemed to have died down, although the police cars on the front drive suggested the officers hadn't left yet. With any luck, their presence would keep teachers out of their way.

Taking the crumpled piece of scrap paper out of her blazer pocket, Bobbie started to dial the number last listed for Bridget Horne.

'Do you want me to do it?'

'No, it's okay.' Bobbie listened to the phone ring.

'Maybe they're all out – it is the middle of the day.'

'Or maybe it's totally the wrong num—'

On the sixth ring, someone answered. 'Hello?'

'Oh, hi. Is that Bridget?'

'No. Who is this?'

Bobbie had a name ready off the alumni list. 'This is Clarissa True. I was in Bridget's year at school.'

The voice on the other end was tentative, nervy. 'Oh. Well, dear, this is her mother.'

'Is Bridget there?' Bobbie knew that over ten years after graduating from Piper's Hall, it was highly unlikely Bridget still lived at home, but she hoped they might get her new number.

'Did you say your name was Clarissa?'

It felt like there were bubbles in her heart. 'Yes.'

'Did we ever meet, dear?'

'I think we did.' Bobbie reached into the dark. 'At that show . . .'

'And you knew Bridget well?'

She didn't like the past tense one bit. 'We were close at school, but y'know, we sort of just lost touch . . . after what happened.' It seemed like a safe bet that an unexplained double disappearance had sent ripples through the year group.

There was a pause at the other end of the line. 'I see. Well, thank you so much for getting in touch. I shall be sure to tell Bridget that you rang.'

Bobbie scrabbled to keep her on the phone. 'Isn't there a way that I could speak to her myself?'

'At the hospital?'

'Yes.' Bobbie's blagging skills were being tested to the limits. 'Don't they have like a time when I could ring?'

There came another pause: a barely audible, sad sigh.

Although her tone was as full of forced cheer as yellow paint, Bridget's mother sounded tired. 'That's sweet of you, but Bridget doesn't really say much any more. Least of all on the phone.'

Bobbie looked to Naya, who just shrugged. 'Erm . . . what was the name of the hospital again? I'll send a letter.'

'Oh that would be nice – I think she'd really appreciate that. There haven't been too many letters or phone calls since she went into care full-time. It's the Psychiatric Care Unit at the Royal Seahaven Hospital.'

Bobbie took care to keep the victory out of her voice. 'Thank you, Mrs Horne, I shall send a card later today.'

'Thank you, Clarissa. You take care now.'

She ended the phone call and looked to Naya. 'This just keeps getting more and more messed up. Bridget is on a mental ward in Seahaven.'

'No way. That's just past Oxsley.'

Bobbie nodded. 'I know. I think we need to pay –'

She was halted in her tracks. A silhouette loomed tall in the frosted-glass door panel. The door creaked open, Dr Price's slender frame somehow filling the space. Bobbie's heart plummeted in her chest and shot into her throat simultaneously.

The Principal's eyes narrowed, glaring daggers at them. 'And just what do you think you two are doing?'

Chapter 9

Cracking Up

'Well?' Dr Price's cool tone was betrayed by the anger in her eyes.

Bobbie tried to speak, but her heart still blocked her windpipe and only a strangled gasp emerged. Naya wrapped her arm around Bobbie. 'Bobbie was really freaked out about Sadie. I thought it might make her feel better if she rang her mom.'

'Oh for crying out loud, Miss Sanchez. I would expect better from Lowers, never mind Uppers. Furthermore, Mr Carlos informs me that you left Spanish this morning, apparently at my say so?'

Bobbie decided to try something radical – the truth. 'I'm really sorry, Dr Price. I was freaking out about Sadie. It's my fault. I asked Naya to sit out Drama because I had a study session.' She made her eyes go as wide as they possibly would.

It worked a charm. 'I have to say, Roberta, this is *most* unlike you. In six years you've never been a moment's trouble, and this is the second time in two days I find you in the wrong place.'

More Rowe doe eyes. 'I'm sorry. I . . . I just . . . I'm really worried about Sadie.'

Dr Price pursed her lips. 'We all are, which is why I *need* the Uppers to set an example to the younger girls.'

Bobbie nodded solemnly, feeling a little guilty. Then Naya asked a question and Bobbie swore the floor tipped like the world had been punched off its axis. 'Was this what happened when those girls vanished thirteen years ago?'

Boom. Dr Price actually flinched. Even the robot-headmistress-with-no-soul reacted to that bombshell. Her jaw clenched and her eyes flickered with what could easily be panic before she regained control and replied. 'How do you know about that? That was a very long time ago.'

'Everyone knows,' Naya said casually, like it was no big deal.

'I very much doubt that's the case.' Her voice became ever so slightly shrill before she cooled herself. Bobbie could tell she was trying to downplay the past. But why? For the first time Bobbie questioned if the event had been somehow covered up. 'Do I really have to explain the effects a bit of gossip and hysteria could have on the school at this time, Naya?'

Bobbie felt her cheeks blaze, ashamed. Her primary-school need to please the teacher had never faded.

'Now you both listen to me, and listen carefully. Those girls both vanished miles and miles away from Piper's Hall. Clearly what happened, although most upsetting, had nothing to do with the school. Is that clear? I want no further mention of this or you'll both be in isolation.'

Neither girl argued. Bobbie dared not even look into her eyes for fear of turning to stone. In six years at Piper's, Bobbie had only ever known one girl be placed in the Isolation Room – a girl who tried to hurt another girl with a knife in a dining-room brawl. Dr Price was deadly serious if she was even threatening it.

'Bobbie. If you want to call your mother you have five minutes. I'll be waiting outside the door. Naya, I want you in class immediately with a written apology to your teacher for your poor punctuality. Go!'

Naya said nothing, slinking past the Principal, her head heavy with shame. Bobbie picked up the phone and dialled her mother's number – with Price lurking outside she'd *have* to call her now. Bobbie calculated it was about eight in the morning in New York; hopefully her mum wouldn't be at rehearsals yet. She answered on the second ring and Bobbie greeted her. 'Bobbie, darling!' Her mum sounded husky, like she'd just woken up.

'Hi, Mum.'

'Oh, darling, you sound dreadful – whatever's the matter?'

'Did I wake you up?'

'Yes, but that's all right. There was this ridiculous party last night, sweetie – you would have died. Rooftop swimming pool at Soho House. Private party for Jared's fortieth. Utter decadence like you wouldn't believe!'

Bobbie tasted tears at the back of her throat. She didn't even know why – something to do with the familiarity of her mum's voice. She could see her now – the bird's nest of expertly bleached hair on the pillow. Last night's lashes still attached to panda eyes.

The idea that time was running out caught up with her, a

fantasy hourglass hovered over her head, sand pouring through at an alarming rate. What if she never saw her mum again? 'Mum, can you fly home?' The words popped out before she could stop them.

'What?'

'There's something really weird going on. I can't explain it.'

'Don't scare Mummy, darling. What's going on? Are you in trouble? Is it drugs? It's drugs, isn't it? I shouldn't have been so liberal, should I?'

'No. No. God, no, it isn't drugs.' Bobbie took her glasses off and pinched the bridge of her nose, forcing back the threat of tears. She could feel herself regressing, becoming the little girl who just needed her mummy. 'Mum, I'm scared.'

There was a pause. 'Darling, is someone giving you a hard time? Tell me who it is and I'll have Dr Price expel them. It's very simple. That's your problem, sweetie, you're too nice. You trust people and they completely take advantage. What have I always taught you . . .'

'Please, Mum. I just really miss you. I wanna see you.'

'Bobbie, if you won't tell me what's wrong, there's nothing I can do, is there?'

Bobbie closed her eyes. Her head felt like it was full of noisy, jagged images and ideas rattling around like broken glass and nails. She felt powerless, useless. 'You wouldn't understand.'

'Of course I do, darling. We all get homesick. I miss home all the time – what I wouldn't give for a bit of proper bacon right now. The Christmas holidays will come around before you know it.'

The first tear found its way out. A fat, warm thing, it dribbled down the inside of her nose and dripped off her nostril onto the phone stand. She couldn't tell her mum that there was nothing beyond the next four days. There would be no Christmas – she wouldn't even make it to Bonfire Night. 'Mum, please . . .'

'Come on, Bobbie. You have less than two years left at school. I think you can cope. Mummy needs to be in New York at the moment. I thought you understood that.'

Wiping the tear away, Bobbie nodded. 'I know.' She pulled herself together, knowing she would never convince her to fly over and, from the fate of Taylor and Abigail, that her escaping to New York wasn't going to work either. Bloody Mary would find her however far she ran. Deep breaths. As tempting as 'little girl mode' was, she'd have to dig deep for 'strong like she-wolf'. This was just a wobble – she could do this, she had to. 'I'm sorry. It's been a hard couple of days.'

'This isn't like you, darling.'

'I know.' Bobbie closed her eyes and imagined borrowing strength from her resilient mother through the telephone cables. 'I'll be fine.'

'Are you sure? Do you need money?'

If only it were that simple. 'No. I'm okay. Just ignore me.'

'Okay, sweetheart. I need to dash. I have a shiatsu massage at ten with Chloë Sevigny. I'll leave my phone on though . . . If you need me, just give me a call.'

Bobbie pulled her knees under her chin, feeling flaccid. 'Sure. I'd better get to class.'

'Kisses, sweetie!'

'Bye, Mum.' She hung up the phone.

Bobbie attended Philosophy for the rest of the afternoon and then had to lip-synch through choir practice too. Her mind couldn't focus for a second; it was hard to concentrate with an enormous, noisy, ticking clock clicking out the seconds. For the first time in her life, every minute counted and she keenly felt she was wasting them.

She went to supper with Naya, but could only face a tragic bowl of vegetable soup. Solids were a no-no. Naya looked similarly unimpressed, poking some sort of gelatinous stew around her plate. 'Do you think there's carbs in this?'

'It seems likely,' Bobbie replied listlessly.

She stuck her tongue out. 'Man, I feel gross. Even the smell of it makes me wanna hurl.'

Bobbie knew how she felt. The mood around Piper's Hall was even more sober than normal. The clocks had gone back the week before so night had fallen just before five and the evening mist seemed to curl in off the sea even sooner. The outdoor areas were dank, cold and cloaked in an impenetrable fog.

The atmosphere inside the dining hall was no better. With Sadie still missing, and all the scandalous gossip fried off, all that was left was worry and genuine concern – both for the missing girl and at the lingering notion that all was not well with their school. Piper's Hall was always depressing, but now it also felt *unsafe*.

The girls ate in a respectful quiet, with solemn whispers into friends' ears rather than shrieks and whoops at the end of a day of lessons. Dr Price watched over them from the head table, which was within Bobbie's earshot. After the main sitting,

Grace and Caitlin approached the Head.

'Dr Price?' Grace said, her voice newsreader serious. 'Me and a few of the Ladies –' by that she meant The Elites –'would like to organise a search party for Sadie. Or perhaps record a YouTube appeal?'

Uh, you two-faced harpy, thought Bobbie. Anything to win favour. 'That's so thoughtful, Grace,' Price replied. 'But I rather think the police have everything in hand.'

'Okay, let us know if you need any helpers.' Grace and Caitlin almost bowed away from the table. Bobbie surreptitiously rolled her eyes.

Another brilliant Piper's rule – no Wi-Fi in dorms – meant that at the first opportunity, Bobbie had to rely on faltering smartphone reception on her mobile once dinner was done and they were back upstairs. Eventually she successfully Googled the Royal Seahaven. Naya sat on her bed, nail-filing manically, even twitchier than usual.

'Got it,' Bobbie declared.

'What?'

'Visiting hours for Seahaven. Tomorrow, ten till twelve or two to four.'

'You're really gonna do it?'

'Yep. I'm not gonna sit around waiting to turn to dust or whatever. You know, it's really obvious now that Sadie knew there was something going on. You saw how crummy she looked yesterday.'

Naya didn't disagree but she did stop filing. 'How are you gonna get out? You need written permission to leave the grounds on a weekday.'

Bobbie shrugged. 'I don't care. The worst Price can do is expel me. If we don't figure out what this is all about . . . well, it'll be much worse.'

The right corner of Naya's mouth curled upwards. 'You know what, Bobbie Rowe? I kinda like this new empowered espionage thing. It's very sexy.'

Bobbie laughed. 'And I think you've been in an all-girls' school too long.' She took her wash-bag off the peg on the back of the door. 'I'm gonna use the bathroom while it's busy. That place is freaking me out.'

'Good call.'

At this time of the evening, it was normal for there to be a queue and today was no different. The sombre mood had even infected the halls of Brontë House. Although there were two shower cubicles in the bathroom, there were also two girls waiting outside the door, slouched against opposite sides of the corridor like bookends. Perfect. She wouldn't have to use the shower alone.

The girls in line, two Lowers, muttered about rumours that some escaped bearded lunatic had got into the building and abducted Sadie. Being older and wiser, Bobbie reassured them that wasn't the case, but neglected to mention the fact that she seriously thought a ghost might have something to do with the disappearance. After a ten-minute wait, a girl in a matching towel-dress/towel-turban combo declared the shower was free.

Once in the bathroom, Bobbie peeled off her dressing gown and stepped into the shower block. When her neighbour got shampoo in her eye and swore loudly, Bobbie couldn't help but be comforted. For the first time in six years, she was thrilled to be showering alongside her fellow classmates.

Bobbie relaxed. She remembered a time before Piper's Hall when she'd spent many evenings alone with the nanny while her mum was working. She'd only ever been able to sleep peacefully once she heard her mum get home. This was the same; with the girl in the next cubicle she could unwind. She washed her hair and even conditioned it for the suggested five minutes before rinsing. The tense, uptight nerves in her shoulders clicked as they loosened.

It was only when she turned the shower off she realised there was no longer any noise coming from the next stall. The other girl must have finished and slipped quietly out of the room while she was daydreaming under the jet. Bobbie braced herself and refused to be deterred. It was fine. She was in a brightly lit bathroom surrounded by dozens of other girls. Nothing could possibly happen.

Drip, drip, drip.

She'd heard that noise before. The thick, echoing drops that sounded like they were nowhere but everywhere at the same time. Bobbie towelled herself off as quickly as possible, avoiding the long mirror. It was steamed up and she didn't want to see what was in it. She remembered the way the reflection had stretched back like a black tunnel.

Drip, drip, drip.

The lights flickered, buzzing and dimming. They stuttered, almost going out. Bobbie slipped on the wet tiles, reaching for her dressing gown in haste. She wanted out of this room. Tying it at the waist, she reached for the door.

Drip, drip, drip.

She froze. The thin plastic curtain was pulled across the right-hand cubicle, but it *wasn't* empty. Although the shower was off, a silhouette stood behind the curtain. Arms hung at her side, her head tilted slightly to her left, lank hair hanging over her shoulders.

Drip, drip, drip.

'Hello? Penelope, is that you?' Bobbie's throat was tight. The silhouette didn't answer – didn't even move.

A voice raged in her head: *Get out! Run!* But her feet moved towards the shower stall. Bobbie had had enough of peekaboo with the mysterious figure. 'What do you want?' Bobbie's voice was the thinnest of whispers. 'Mary?' She reached a damp, trembling hand towards the shower curtain.

Behind her, the door slammed shut, sealing her in.

Chapter 10

The Intruder

Bobbie had spent her whole life sneering at girls who screamed, but it turned out she'd just never had a reason to do so. She screamed. Again. Although, at least this time she screamed a swear word rather than just whimpering – a fraction tougher. She twisted around just in time to see a familiar figure pull the door shut and slide the lock in place. 'What the . . . ?'

Caine leaned back against the door, out of breath. 'Man, that was intense.'

Bobbie turned back to the shower stall, ropes of wet hair swinging about her face. She pulled the curtain to one side. As she'd somehow known it would be, it was totally empty aside from stray hairs and residual soap suds. Her next thought was, *Are either or both of my nipples showing?* Thankfully they weren't, but she pulled the robe tighter across her chest. 'Are you insane? What on earth are you doing?'

The lights hummed and returned to their usual brightness. 'I had to see you.' He wore a black hoodie, hood up. He'd planned his break-in carefully, dressing like an urban ninja. *'I had to see you.'* What was that supposed to *mean?* This was a lot to take in. Surely not . . . a feeling somewhere between cartoon butterflies and nauseous panic fizzed in her stomach.

'Do you have any idea what would happen if you got caught in here with me?'

'You'd be expelled?' he shrugged.

'I didn't mean Dr Price, I meant Grace. She'd rip my arms off and use them to beat you to death.' Caine laughed, but stifled it. 'Caine, what do you want?'

He stiffened, more serious than she'd seen him. 'Come off it – you were in the graveyard. That was just the start of it. There's some serious *Paranormal Activity* crap going down.'

Bobbie's mouth fell open as a million sentences raced to get out at the same time: he'd seen things too; she'd totally forgotten he was there at all; what had he seen? The tornado in her head stopped because if he was here, saying this, that meant everything was really real. Just like that, the impossible came true. 'You've seen her too.'

He didn't say anything but he puckered his lips and drew a deep breath in through his nostrils. No words were necessary because his eyes alone said exactly how scared he was. 'What did we do?' he finally muttered.

Bloody Mary was real. It was overwhelming. The validation was at once both brilliant and terrifying. *There's no such thing as ghosts.* The refrain that had helped her sleep countless times in the past, on nights when the pipes creaked or branches scraped against her window, was now redundant. There *was* such a thing as ghosts, and they'd both seen her. In that moment, in that bathroom, Bobbie found herself living in a different world – one where fantasy was reality.

'What? Where?' She pulled herself together. 'I'm sorry, I should have been in touch. I . . . I could have asked Grace for your number.'

'Yeah.' Caine gave a wry smirk. 'That would've gone down well.'

Bobbie returned his smile and the mood in the bathroom lightened. 'God, how did you even get in here? You must have a death wish.'

'Same way we got in on Saturday. I saw you queuing in the corridor with those other girls and waited until you were alone.'

The secret passage. 'Well, I respect your kamikaze style, but we *cannot* be found in a bathroom. Needless to say, questions would be asked. You'll have to come to my dorm.'

Another semi-smile. 'Because that's less dodgy?'

Bobbie raised an eyebrow. 'Don't get any ideas.' As if he would. 'Naya's there.'

'Again . . . that's better?'

'Wash your mind out, young man.' Bobbie tutted as she opened the door no more than an inch. The corridor looked clear, but a couple of dorm doors stood open. Mrs Craddock's shrill voice echoed from somewhere in the distance. 'We're gonna have to make a run for it. You know I just spent five minutes convincing some Lowers that our school had impenetrable security and strange men couldn't get in.'

'I'm not a strange man.'

'You are if anyone catches us – got that?'

He chuckled. 'Got it.'

A girl emerged from her dorm to enter the one next door. Bobbie shut the door at once, giving her a minute to leave the corridor. 'Are you ready?'

'Yeah.'

'Okay.' Bobbie stuck her head into the corridor. 'Run.' She took off, her wash-bag swinging at her side and with Caine on her heels. There were six doors and a bend in the hall to contend with. Her pulse pounded in her skull. She kept her eyes fixed on their destination, not daring to slow for even a second. Almost throwing herself at the door, she pressed down on the handle, tumbling inside.

She hauled Caine across the threshold and, checking no one had seen them, slammed the door shut. It hadn't occurred to her that Naya could well be naked. As it was, she was clipping her toenails over the waste-paper bin.

At first her face registered shock before changing to one of pure smutface. 'Roberta Rowe, you little minx.'

Bobbie rolled her eyes. 'He's here about the ghost.'

Naya looked immediately less interested. 'Oh.'

'Yes. *Oh* is right. Caine . . . make yourself comfortable.' He pulled out the desk chair and Bobbie arranged herself as demurely as she could on her bed. In the terrycloth robe there were approximately two positions she could sit in without flashing him. This was far from ideal. She took her glasses from the bedside table and put them on. She really should also do something with her hair before it turned into dreadlocks.

Caine unzipped his hoodie and let it hang over the back of the chair. He wore a white cotton band T-shirt that seemed to know exactly where to cling. In other circumstances,

105

circumstances in which she didn't feel like her head was exploding, this would have all been pretty sexy. As it was, Caine's lips, biceps, chest and dimples (although very much in her bedroom) were the least of her worries. On the plus side she didn't feel awkward and tongue-tied any more. All that shyness seemed so inconsequential now, not to mention immature. 'So what's going on?' he asked.

'Your guess is as good as mine.' Bobbie dragged a reluctant brush through her knots. 'You go first. What did you see?'

'I only really noticed today. At first I thought I was imagining it – like my eyes were playing tricks on me or something, yeah?'

Naya suddenly looked more concerned now that *two* people had seen something weird. 'You're actually serious? What did you see?'

'Have you got a mirror? I'll show you.'

'Sure.' Naya climbed off her bed. 'In the wardrobe.' She opened the cupboard to reveal the mirror on the inside door. Each room had an identical wardrobe – a bulky wooden unit big enough for the clothing of two or three girls.

'Come and see.' Caine crossed the room and Bobbie followed. The three of them were reflected together, just as they had been on Saturday night.

'What am I looking at?' Naya appeared unimpressed. Caine angled the door, taking in different views of the room.

'Hmm,' he said. 'Can you open the door a bit?'

'No! What if someone sees you?' Bobbie remembered the last girl who'd smuggled a boy into Piper's Hall. Dr Price had only just stopped short of branding a scarlet letter on the poor girl's forehead.

'Just for a second.'

Naya exhaled noisily, but did as told. She held the door open. Now the mirror also held the reflection of the Brontë House corridor. It was gloomy, but their lights cast a sickly pool down the landing. In the mirror, Bobbie could see the last two rooms and the fire escape. 'There,' Caine whispered, not moving, the way you do when you don't want to scare a timid woodland animal. 'Can you see it?'

'See what?'

'Look at the very edge of the mirror. In the corner.'

Bobbie squinted. At first glance there was nothing to see, but then she looked harder. In the darkest recess of the corridor next to the fire escape, as far away as possible, stood the girl. Entirely still, she waited just outside their dorm. The thinnest sliver of light hit her skin. She held her pale hands together in front of her body, her hair once more hanging over her face. Bobbie gasped and whirled around, stumbling into Caine as she did so. The real corridor was deserted. She looked back at the reflection. As if startled, the girl with the black hair inched further into the shadows. 'Oh God.'

Caine held Bobbie tightly, his warm fingers wrapped around her upper arm. He squeezed her like he *needed* to be believed. 'She's in *every* mirror. If you look close enough, she's there.' His eyes widened. 'Serious. I can see her on the side of the road in my wing mirrors. She's in shop windows when you walk past them. She's e*verywhere*.'

'Oh God,' was apparently all Bobbie could say any more. She could taste tears at the back of her throat – not sad tears, *scared* tears. The girl in the mirror still waited.

'What do you mean?' Naya stomped back to the mirror. She angled it inwards, elongating the view down the corridor. Mary, if that's who she was, shied away from the light, edging into the darkness. Naya dropped the wardrobe door like it was hot. 'No way! No effing way!' Naya's fingers shot into her hair as if she wanted to scratch the image out of her head.

'Naya, keep it down,' Bobbie urged, closing the bedroom door.

'But it's impossible! How can she be in the mirror but not . . . ?' The taller girl tugged her hair off her face, stretching the skin into a mask of alarm. 'I mean, how? How can it be real?'

Bobbie took her hands and steered Naya towards her bed. If she didn't calm down Mrs Craddock would be at their door in seconds. Naya's eyes were wide, darting around, unable to focus.

'I don't know,' said Bobbie. 'We'll figure it out . . . we're getting closer, remember?'

Naya took a deep breath and held up a well-manicured finger for attention. She seemed to reel in the crazy a little. 'There is a ghost in the mirror.' Bobbie nodded. Naya went on, 'I guess I didn't really believe it until now. I really thought it was Sadie punking us.'

'It's not. It's all true. She's watching us.' Bobbie turned to Caine. Their eyes met and it finally felt like she wasn't on the life raft alone. 'It's like she's following us.'

Caine's breath shook. Relief. 'Least I'm not imagining it. I thought I was legit cracking up.'

Bobbie laughed a feeble, shaky laugh. 'I wish we were.'

'What the bloody hell is going on? This ain't right. Like impossible. I don't believe in ghosts.'

108

Bobbie filled Caine in on the limited amount she and Naya had learned that afternoon, which, when recounted, sounded like nothing at all. She finished on telling him about Bridget Horne's incarceration at the Royal Seahaven.

'Well, I'm coming with you,' Caine said after she told him about her plan to visit.

'You can't,' Bobbie said without any reason.

'Why not? I've only got Sports Science on a Tuesday morning. They won't even know I've gone. I can pick you up.'

'You have your own car?'

'Yeah – well, I drive my mum's. Don't you? I thought you lot was all minted.'

'Piper's Hall Ladies are not allowed cars on site,' Naya said in her crisp mockery of the English accent. She still sat rigidly on the edge of her bed, but the colour had returned to her cheeks.

A plan hatched in Bobbie's mind. 'Listen. Naya, if we both sneak out tomorrow we're more likely to be caught. If I go with Caine you can cover for me if anyone asks. Do you mind?'

'Do I mind not going to a mental asylum to ask about ghosts? Gee, let me think . . .' She fixed Bobbie in an unimpressed gaze.

'You're actually the best.'

'That doesn't fix anything though – you still have to break out of this place – and it's swarming with police.'

'I'll think of something. Caine, can you pick me up from the end of the cliff walk at like nine?'

'Sure.'

There was a rap on the door and all three froze, staring slack-jawed at the exit. 'Girls, it's Mrs Craddock. May I come in?'

Chapter 11

Girl Talk

'Hide,' Bobbie breathed. She threw herself at the door. 'Just a second!'

'Why?' The voice on the other side of the door was immediately suspicious. The door handle wavered. Bobbie pressed it shut. 'Let me in, please.'

'Get in the wardrobe!' Naya hissed.

'No effing way! There's a *mirror* in there!'

'Girls! What's going on? I'm not in the mood for any shenanigans tonight, I can feel a migraine coming on.'

'Bobbie's naked!' Naya hollered.

'Oh thanks, Nay.'

'I've seen it all before! Now please let me in.'

'Caine, you'll have to – there's nowhere else,' Bobbie pleaded in a whisper. Their mattresses were on those blocky bed things, with no room underneath for storage, so the other obvious hiding place wasn't an option.

He gritted his teeth and a frown furrowed his brow. Muttering an array of expletives he opened the wardrobe and stepped amongst the clutter of shoes. 'Sorry . . .' Naya sealed him in. Caine screwed his eyes tight shut as darkness engulfed him. Bobbie's heart went out to him – there was no way she could be in there alone, face-to-face, with *her*.

Bobbie gave a nod and opened the door. 'What a lot of nonsense.' Mrs Craddock blustered into the dorm. 'Lights out early tonight, ladies. Dr Price's orders.' Naya groaned, but she went on. 'Use the bathroom now, and then you may read, but you *must* stay in your dorm. Obviously I don't need to explain why.'

The wardrobe shook slightly. Naya pretended to trip over thin air to bump into it – and it wasn't nearly as casual as Bobbie would have liked. Craddock didn't look convinced. Poor Caine – what was going on inside that cupboard? What could he see, his face centimetres from the mirror?

There was one last thing she had to do before they could get him out, however. Bobbie reclined back on her bed with a sigh. 'Is everything all right, Roberta?'

'I feel awful . . . I've had really bad diarrhoea.' Bobbie had learned at a very young age that *no one* questions diarrhoea – like who's gonna check the toilet after you've been? It was the ultimate skiving sickness. 'It must be something I ate.'

Mrs Craddock had dealt with more than her share of vomit and diarrhoea and didn't seem fazed. 'Oh dear. Have you been more than once?'

Bobbie knew how to play it. 'Yeah. I went and then had to go again like right away.'

'And have you been sick?'

'No. But I *feel* sick.' She was careful not to be too hammy.

'Poor dear, must be a tummy bug. Drink plenty of water. Naya – keep an eye on her and come and fetch me if she gets worse.'

'Yes, Miss.' The housemistress turned to leave. 'Obviously if you need the toilet, go, but otherwise – stay inside from now on, please.'

'Yes, Miss.'

As soon as the bedroom door clicked shut, the wardrobe burst open and Caine tripped over his feet in his haste to get out. 'Shh!' Naya caught him.

'Are you okay?' Bobbie sprung off her bed.

'I could see her. Right behind me in the wardrobe.' His eyes were wild and beads of sweat gleamed on his dark skin.

'It's not real,' Bobbie said, although she was far from convinced. 'It's only a reflection.'

He looked to the floor, as if ashamed of his fear. 'It looked real.' Caine grabbed his hoodie, gripping it tighter than he should. His lips were pasty. 'She's coming for us.'

They waited ten minutes or so to ensure that Mrs Craddock had finished her rounds before smuggling Caine out of their room. Bobbie walked him back to the secret passage while Naya kept a lookout. Luckily, it seemed either the warning from Price or the threat of an escaped axe-wielding psychopath had kept all the Piper's Ladies securely in their rooms, and no one interrupted their stealthy prowl back to the hatch on the staircase.

Caine pulled the passageway door open and turned back to her. 'If this weren't so messed up, it'd be pretty cool.'

112

'What? The passages?'

'Yeah. We ain't got these at Radley!'

Bobbie whispered. 'There's one in the theatre too – so the servants could carry drinks in and out when it used to be a ballroom. There's meant to be priests' holes too.'

Caine frowned. 'What's a priest's hole? Sounds kinky.'

'Don't they teach History at Radley?' Bobbie smiled.

'I'm a Geography kinda guy.'

'Back in the day it was illegal to be Catholic. The original owners of the house were sympathisers so built little hidey-holes for priests on the run. Or so they say. I've yet to see evidence of this.' She shrugged.

'Man, your school is so much cooler than mine.'

Creamy moonlight flooded the landing, catching Caine's cheekbone and lips. All of a sudden, Bloody Mary was purged from Bobbie's mind. 'Okay.' She pulled her dressing-gown belt tighter. 'You sure you'll find your way out?'

'I wedged the kitchen door open with a rock.'

'They teach you that in Croydon?' Bobbie couldn't resist and Caine beamed back.

'Oi! Don't be talking smack about the Croydon massiv'!' he grinned. 'Nah. It's a dump. Better off out here in the sticks.'

There was a long silence. It probably wasn't *that* long, but it felt like an eternity. Bobbie knew that moments like these, goodbyes, needed filling. She didn't know what to do. She didn't know what to say. If this were one of her stories, her main character – the off-kilter-hipster-girl-with-issues that guys wanted to rescue – would say something profound or deep or even just plain cute. Nope. She had nothing, which she guessed meant that the real Bobbie Rowe was neither pin-up sexy *nor* adorable-kooky-funny. Great. 'I guess I'll see you in the morning then,' was the best she could do.

'Yeah.' Caine exhaled like he'd been stuck in suspended animation too. Or was that just the optimism node in her brain working overtime? 'Sweet dreams, yeah?'

'Oh that's likely.' Bobbie grimaced.

Caine slipped into the hatch, using his phone to light the way. 'Think happy thoughts. Or, you have my number now, just call me.'

Although she couldn't be sure, Bobbie was pretty sure she experienced her first swoon. That is, if a swoon felt like a strawberry-milkshake tsunami starting at your feet and levelling everything in its path until it got to your head. She actually had to steady herself against the portal. 'I'll leave my phone on in case *you* get scared,' she replied. *Nice save*, she thought. Caine chuckled and vanished down the servants' stairs.

She did think nice thoughts. She thought of the goodbye all the way back to her room, replaying the scene over and over, squeezing every last drop out of the memory – with time on her side she was able to think of about fifty funny-cute-sexy-witty goodbyes. Dammit.

When she arrived back at their room, Bobbie found Naya nervously perching on her bed. As soon as she walked in, Naya sprang off the bed and grabbed her. 'Oh God, what took you so long – don't leave me alone!'

'Sorry, I had to make sure Caine got out okay.'

Naya pouted. 'Oh I bet you did! Held his hand the whole way?'

Bobbie suddenly found it hard to look her in the eye. 'No . . . it's not like . . . that.'

'Look, normally I'd be up for an all-night boy summit, but, hello – ghost-mirror-woman!'

Bobbie took a deep breath. 'I know.'

'Bob, can I come in with you tonight?'

The fear burned bright in her eyes; Naya was fraying at the seams, about to fall apart. 'Of course. And we'll keep the lamp on. All night if you want.'

A tear glistened in the corner of Naya's eye. 'Thank you.'

They distracted each other for a while, bitching about Grace mostly, until Naya fell asleep first, her heavy breaths falling on Bobbie's ear. Bobbie closed her eyes and imagined it was Caine lying beside her. The idea came out of nowhere, but she was surprised to find she liked it. A lot.

But then thoughts of Sadie leaked into her head and she felt guilty for feeling happy. Bobbie wondered what her poor parents and sisters were going through right now. They must be going out of their minds with worry. She used thoughts of Caine to block thoughts of Sadie and that made her feel guiltier still.

So lost in it was she that it took her a moment to realise that she was dreaming again. It felt so real, so vivid, that she could easily have been awake, and she hadn't even been aware of falling asleep.

The gag-inducing stench of disinfectant filled the ground-floor girls' toilets. Bobbie sat on the seat of a toilet in a locked stall, her knees tucked under her chin. Once more she was in the old, starchy uniform. Itchy woollen socks were pulled all the way up her shins, ugly hobnail shoes finishing off her legs.

Bobbie didn't know why, but she was scared. She was hiding. She was hiding in a toilet cubicle.

Then she knew why. There was an unmistakeable laugh: the 'Mean Girl Laugh'. It was then as it was now. Cruel, harsh, mocking laughter – girls trying to outdo each other with cattiness. She wasn't alone in the bathroom. 'Have you ever heard her speak?'

'I don't think she knows how to! Perhaps she's deaf and dumb.'

'Don't be so mean, she's new,' said a third, kinder voice.

'Oh don't be such a goody two-shoes, Judy. I mean, she's positively backward.'

Bobbie sat as still as she could on the toilet. She knew two things: they were talking about her, and she would rather die than be discovered.

'You know, she has *quite* the reputation in Oxsley.'

'How do you know?' the third girl, Judy, asked.

'It's a small, inbred town! Everyone knows everyone!' Bobbie pictured them preening and pouting in front of the mirror the way Grace and Caitlin did today. 'You do know she's a *bastard*, don't you?' The offending word was whispered in awe and scandal.

'You never!' said the second girl, who sounded as airheaded as Caitlin.

'It's true. I'd be surprised if her whore of a mother even knew who her father was.'

'Susan, that's an appalling thing to say!' Judy scolded.

A soggy puddle spread across the hem of her skirt, Bobbie's

tears soaking into the charcoal-grey fabric. The words cut through her, dragging across her bones.

'Don't be so naive!' Susan went on. 'Everyone knows she's here for free – her mother doesn't pay a penny.'

'Because she passed the entrance exam . . .' Judy argued in vain.

'I heard it's because they didn't know what to do with her at Radley Grammar,' said the airhead girl.

'I think you two are absolutely beastly.'

'Heavens, Judy. If you like her so much why don't you be her best friend?' Susan chided.

There was a pause. 'No thank you,' Judy said finally. 'She's so queer. She scares me.'

All three girls laughed. The Mean Girl Laugh.

Bobbie awoke, back in her bed. The heating hadn't come on yet so the bedroom was bitter, her breath clouding. Dawn was still hours away. Her pillow was damp with tears.

DAY THREE

Chapter 12

Asylum

The sadness of the dream lingered long after she'd woken. It was like a heavy, leaden shawl around her shoulders. She burrowed further under her duvet, blocking out daylight. God, she hated Tuesdays. Mondays held so much promise for the week ahead, Bobbie always thought, but by Tuesday the novelty had worn off and you were still miles away from the weekend. She had a feeling this Tuesday would be even more of an uphill struggle than most.

Bobbie closed her eyes, her heart still feeling a little broken. If that sort of bullying was what Mary experienced at Piper's, perhaps it went some way towards explaining why her spirit hadn't moved on. As Bobbie understood it, a lot of people thought that ghosts were spirits of the dead with unfinished business: ethereal fingers desperately digging nails into the fabric of this world without passing on to the next.

Of course, that opened a whole RE can of worms that Bobbie *definitely* didn't have time for.

Bobbie remembered Sadie's original tale about how Mary had committed suicide in the bathroom. The cruel laughter of the girls made her skin crawl. If that had chip-chip-chipped away at Mary over the years, it was no wonder she hadn't wanted to live. Bobbie felt wretched and hopeless, and they weren't even her memories. Assuming Mary had killed herself, what unfinished business could she have left? Were they meant to complete the business on her behalf? Bobbie sighed. If someone kills themself, the burst bubble of potential leaves nothing *but* unfinished business.

The glimpses of Mary's past she saw were telling, but went no way to explaining Sadie's fate, or what was going to happen to them on Thursday. Time was galloping away.

It was almost time to meet Caine. Eight thirty-five. Bobbie kicked the duvet off. Mrs Craddock had already been in and given her permission to stay in bed. Bobbie had gone through the necessary martyr act: *'No, I'll be fine, I just need a shower and maybe a bite to eat,'* before Craddock announced she was much too weak to attend lessons.

Depending on whether Craddock came back to check on her, she was off the hook. That said, there was still the hardest task to accomplish: getting out of Piper's Hall without being seen.

She dressed quickly. The disguise, she had to admit, was genius. She'd swept her hair into a messy topknot, found some riding boots and borrowed Naya's Barbour jacket. The massive insectile sunglasses and McQueen scarf were the cherry on the cake. She looked every inch the horsey mummy dropping off a Lower at the school gates. The Piper's Hall student body was made up of about twenty per cent day pupils. In the hierarchy they were the lowest of the low and mostly stuck together for company. The theory was that only those hard core enough to give up their parents and home cooking were truly worthy of calling themselves Piper's Ladies.

The bell for registration would sound at eight fifty-five. This was the only time of day where people came and went with any regularity. It was now or never.

A few girls were milling about Brontë, getting the last bits they needed for class or changing into uniform after breakfast. Walking through the school in disguise was too big a risk. Bobbie weighed it up, and the fire escape was a better option than the secret passage, as that would bring her out by the kitchen just as the staff were clearing up from breakfast. Only one problem: it was alarmed. Idiot girls were *always* crashing into the 'push to open' bars, however, with such regularity that teachers and Craddock hardly ever seemed to investigate. The alarms turned off as soon as the door was shut again. At least, that's what Bobbie hoped.

Without her real glasses her vision was a fuzzy mess, but the corridor looked deserted, so she tiptoed to the exit. She gritted her teeth. Timing was key; she'd have to clear three flights of noisy, rickety metal stairs before someone attended to the alarm and caught her in the act. *Come on, Bobbie. Quick and clean.* Taking a deep breath, she pushed through the fire escape.

The alarm, a nasty, low buzz like an angry bee, sounded throughout Brontë House, but Bobbie didn't look back. Taking the stairs two at a time, she almost glided down the damp iron railings, letting gravity pull her along. She didn't stop to think about how many eyes might be seeing her through the windows she darted past. With any luck, she'd be nothing more than a blur.

The ringing stopped. Bobbie pressed her back against the wall. If she looked up she could see through the holes in the corrugated metal. No one stepped onto the fire escape. Perfect. Just as she'd hoped, someone else on her corridor (probably the poor soul who had the room next to the fire escape) must have come out and simply closed the door. Bobbie breathed a shaky sigh of relief. She continued down the steps. When she reached solid ground, she got her bearings: she was on a functionless patch of grass just to the front of the staff car park. Hopefully all the teachers would be in by now. Sticking close to the walls, but avoiding the windows, Bobbie prowled the school perimeter to the front entrance.

Perhaps those 'boarding school for spies' novels weren't such a waste of time after all.

At the front of the school, there was a doughnut-shaped driveway with a fountain in the middle designed for the purpose of dropping off pupils at the main entrance. Pupils entered through a nondescript door at the end of the old wing, while only visitors were allowed to use the grand double doors flanked by grumpy, weather-worn stone lions.

Most parents or nannies acted as chauffeurs, slowing the BMW or Mercedes for only the briefest of moments to offload their offspring, but some walked their kids to school too. Bobbie knew this would look a lot more convincing if she had a dog of some sort, as many parents chose to combine the journey to school with walking the family pet.

As casually as she could, she fell into step alongside a trio of mums emerging through the visitors' entrance. They'd probably been in to pay a library fine or to get tickets for a piano recital or something equally lame. Either way, it was perfect timing; they were even dressed similarly. As they approached the end of the drive, Bobbie pulled ahead of them – the foreboding building behind her getting smaller and smaller with every step. By the time she stepped through the curling wrought-iron gates at the end of the drive, Bobbie realised she was light-headed from holding her breath.

She'd done it. She was actually free.

Far below, the waves crashed onto the rocks – a roar and then a shiver as the tide rolled back over the shingle. A battered-looking Fiat with one door a different shade of red to the chassis waited by the turnstile to the coastal pathway. That *had* to be Caine's car. She darted across the road and saw two people in the front seats – Caine and Mark. What was he doing here?

Bobbie tapped on the window, and Caine twisted around to open the back door for her. 'Nice outfit,' he said, eyeing her up and down. 'You know Hallowe'en was last week, right?'

'Very funny. It's a disguise, and one that apparently worked. Hi, Mark. No offence, but why are you here?'

The stockier boy rolled his eyes. Caine answered. 'Mum needed the car today. Mark said he'd drop us off cos he has a free.'

'Oh. Okay.'

'Yup, today I'm a taxi service. I must be mad – going to a freaking loony bin in my free. I should be in bed, man.' Checking over his shoulder, Mark pulled out into the road and started on the journey towards Oxsley. At this time of the day, the traffic was awful – this could take forever.

'Anyway.' Caine sat sideways on so he could talk to both of them. Today he was wearing a cute jumper that looked like vintage skate gear. The deep maroon totally worked against his dark skin. 'You gotta see this.'

'Gotta see what?'

'Dude, where's your phone?' he asked Mark.

'In my pocket. Just watch where you're putting your hand.'

'Dream on, mate.' Caine gingerly fished the iPhone out of his pocket with pincer fingers while Mark drove. 'It's the video Mark made while we were doing the dare.'

'You told him?' Bobbie's skin suddenly felt hot. She didn't like the idea of dragging more people into this, and if she was really honest, she sort of liked having Caine to herself.

'I didn't need to. Look.' He handed her the phone all ready to go – she just had to press play.

She really didn't want to see this, but knew she had to. Pressing play, she waited for the show to start. It was surreal seeing it all happen *to* them. In her head, it had all seemed more epic, but the video showed the three of them standing in a poky bathroom with terrible lighting. The flickering candlelight illuminated them, but that was all she could make out. There was only a suggestion that even *they* were reflected in the mirror. The noise was better though. She could hear their giggles – the first time they'd lost their bottle.

Then the real thing started. *'Bloody Mary,'* they all said, looking dead into the mirror. There was a pause and they repeated the refrain. How could they have been so stupid? Now, sat in the car, Bobbie wondered who or what in her life had led her to

126

believe she was invincible. She thought of the girls in her year: drinking, smoking, eating junk as if none of it mattered, simply because they were young. They all assumed that bad things only ever happen to other people – old people. She'd been just as dumb. They'd played Russian roulette and got the bullet.

In the video, as they finished the fifth 'Bloody Mary', Bobbie scrutinised the clip. The candles flickered, and for a second the video was almost pitch-black. The room settled before they'd burst into hysterics. Bobbie held the phone centimetres from her eyes, desperately looking for a hint of the girl in the mirror, but at the same time scared to see her face. 'I can't see anything.'

'It's not something to see. *Listen*,' Caine told her. He reached over and bumped the volume up to full. Their laughter and chatter became noisier. 'Can you hear that?'

'Us?'

'No. In the background.' Bobbie shook her head and Caine held the speaker to her ear. That was when she heard it. Behind all their giggling, a baby was crying. It was faint but unmistakeable. The baby *howled*, the cries rattling inside her skull. There was something unique about that noise – a crying baby – a noise you instinctively *have* to stop; hearing such distress was unbearable.

'Oh my God.' Bobbie stopped the video. 'That's impossible.'

'Is there any way there could have been a baby in school?' Caine asked.

'Well, we do have a mother and baby wing,' Bobbie deadpanned.

'Serious?'

'What do you think? I'm kidding!' Bobbie smiled and Caine

127

smiled back. He was gullible and it was kind of cute. 'There's no babies at Piper's Hall ... this ... baby ... it can't be real. It's *her*.'

Mark shook his head in disbelief. 'You know what – I think you are getting each other all fired up. I am not buying all this *Woman in Black* shiz.'

Bobbie looked to Caine, who looked back sympathetically. 'It's all real,' she said. 'I had another dream last night. About her. I think she's trying to show me why she killed herself.' Caine frowned, and turned to sit properly in the passenger seat. 'What?' she prompted.

'Nothing,' he said. 'Just ... just that I've been having weird dreams too.'

Bobbie sat forward, clinging to the back of his chair. 'About what?'

'I dunno. They were ... I don't wanna say.'

Mark rocked back in his seat, laughing. 'Oh my days! You had a proper filthy dream! You have to tell us, man!'

Even with his skin tone, Caine visibly blushed. He said nothing. 'Caine, it might be important ...' Bobbie said, although she suddenly felt the most irrational jealousy of her life towards the dream girl.

'You know what?' Caine finally admitted. 'I couldn't talk about it even if I wanted to. I was so out of it ... I mean, in the dream it was half like it *was* me and half like I was *watching* it.'

'That's how I felt too.'

Mark carried on cackling. 'Dude ... it was hot though, right?'

Caine said no more, but a coy smirk crossed his lips and Bobbie experienced her second ever swoon.

The Royal Seahaven Hospital didn't look unlike Piper's Hall, except the hospital was set amongst the outskirts of woodland, making the approach feel even more intimidating somehow. As Mark drove down the long, oak-lined drive, Bobbie recalled *The Shining* and *The Wolves of Willoughby Chase* and suddenly this didn't seem like such a great idea.

The trees cleared and the hospital came into view. It was an old building with modern features artificially grafted to its bones – gleaming handrails and sliding doors on an antique hospital. It did nothing to make the place any more inviting.

Mark drove past the ambulance bay, following signposts towards the psychiatric unit. The Charity Sawyer Ward was set behind the main hospital, a square structure with square windows neatly arranged in parallel lines – not a curved edge anywhere in sight so as not to upset the mad people within, Bobbie thought.

'I gotta get back to school for second period. I can come back period three if you need me to.'

'Nah, it's cool – we can get the bus into Oxsley,' Caine suggested, and Bobbie nodded agreement. At this stage, she was so nervous she could taste bitter bile at the back of her mouth. This didn't feel like playing or 'being mischievous' any more; this was serious – they were about to break into a hospital to interrogate a person with a mental illness.

That was the whole problem, though. What if Bridget Horne wasn't ill? Or what if she was and *they* were seeing things too? Bobbie wished she'd grabbed something to eat before she left school; her whole body felt hollowed out and empty, like the rotting jack-o'-lanterns left over from the weekend.

'You okay?' Caine sensed her unease.

'Not really. We could get in serious trouble for this. Like police trouble.'

He shook his head. 'We're just visitors. There's no law against that.'

Bobbie nodded, trying to absorb some of his calm by osmosis. Caine got out of the car and she followed, smoothing down her outfit. On the drive over, she'd let down her hair and swapped the sunglasses for her usual ones. 'We're just paying a visit,' Bobbie said to herself as much as Caine.

Mark pulled away, heading back to Radley High, leaving them in front of the mental hospital. It was surprisingly quiet. Bobbie had half expected there to be wailing, flailing mad people struggling inside straightjackets, even if she knew that was purely TV territory.

A first few marble-sized drops of rain spattered onto the tarmac. 'Come on, let's get inside.' Caine put an arm around her and steered her up the steps. Automatic doors slid open, and the reception area was pretty much like any doctor's surgery: a desk, a couple of padded chairs in eggshell blue, tatty posters about how one in four of us will experience mental-health problems. The only difference was that the room was secure. Access to the rest of the building was behind tightly shut security doors, guarded by a man in uniform.

Bobbie forced herself to smile for the receptionist. 'Hi, we're here to see Bridget Horne, please.'

The receptionist, an impossible-to-age, obese woman with a red face and salt-and-vinegar odour, tapped something into her computer. 'Okay, sweetheart. Take the lift to the third floor and there's a waiting room.'

Bobbie almost keeled over. Surely it couldn't be that simple. There was an obnoxious honking noise and the security light above the double doors changed from red to green. 'Go on through,' said the guard. 'Third floor.'

Not needing to be told twice, the pair hurried through. As soon as they were in the lift, Bobbie exhaled for what felt like the first time in five minutes. 'Why was I so nervous?'

'I know,' Caine agreed. 'I guess it's just a hospital.'

The lift arrived at the third floor and they stepped out into another NHS room, only this one had Radio 2 playing at a low volume. It had that awful hospital smell – alcohol hand gel mixed with vomit and disinfectant. The air was oddly sweet too, like someone had been spraying room freshener.

This time Caine approached the reception desk. 'Hi, we're here to see Bridget Horne.'

The nurse at the station – a handsome ginger-haired guy in his twenties – looked surprised. 'You're here to see Bridget?'

'Yeah,' Bobbie said. 'Friends of the family.'

The nurse – David, according to his name badge – looked her up and down sceptically. 'Bridget doesn't get visitors other than her mother.'

'I know. It was her mum who asked if we'd come. I think she wants Bridget to see more people . . .' Bobbie felt awful lying. Bridget was alone and her only visitors were here for selfish reasons.

'Can you wait here, please?' David swiped a security pass through a card reader and entered the ward. Craning her neck,

Bobbie looked through the glass in the door. He was talking to another nurse or a doctor – it was hard to tell when they all wore those pyjama scrubs. Eventually, he returned with a kind-faced Asian woman dressed in normal clothes.

'Hi, I'm Dr Kahn. David says you'd like to visit Bridget?'

'Yes please,' Caine said.

'I have to say, this is quite unusual. Bridget is a very anxious patient, and doesn't really enjoy visits – not even from her mother.'

Bobbie could see this failing, but it only made her more determined. They'd got this far. 'Please. I . . . we just want to help.' That much was true. Anything they could do to stop Mary might help Bridget too. Dr Kahn didn't seem convinced, so Bobbie jumped in again. 'Please. If you could just tell her that . . . that . . . we're on day three.' Instinctively she knew she shouldn't mention Mary's name.

Dr Kahn looked even more confused but, with a sigh, swiped her way back onto the ward, leaving them in reception. When she returned moments later, the bafflement on the doctor's face was next level. 'Okay. This is very strange, but she says she'll see you.' Behind the desk, David dropped his pen in shock. 'Do either of you have mirrors on you, or anything reflective at all? We can't have any mirrors on the ward – it triggers Bridget's psychosis.'

Bobbie rummaged through her satchel and found a pressed powder compact with a mirror inside the lid that actually belonged to Naya. She handed it to David who placed it behind the counter. Caine gave over his phone, which had a shiny chrome cover.

The nerves were back. As Dr Kahn led them onto the ward, Bobbie's tummy crunched painfully. Without thinking about it, almost like her hand was seeking its own comfort, her fingers found Caine's. He gave her hand a squeeze.

The patients were an eclectic bunch. From what Bobbie could tell, this must be a mixed ward – mixed nuts (why her brain thought *now* was the time to make lame and offensive puns was anyone's guess). The ward didn't look unlike a classroom: in the centre of a shared area there were two large tables set out for activities. There was a man in his forties, receding hair slicked down on his head, painstakingly cutting letters out of a magazine. The scissors precisely followed the edge of the R he was cutting. On the other side of his table a black woman with a shaved head was writing in a diary in the most minute handwriting Bobbie had ever seen, almost as if she had challenged herself to write in the smallest letters ever. The microscopic notes filled entire pages.

On the next table, a younger patient, a guy not much older than them, was having a tantrum, a nurse calmly trying to reason with him as he stamped his feet. 'Okay.' Dr Kahn stopped them outside the door to a side room. 'Bridget doesn't really leave her room, so you'll have to see her in there.'

'That's cool,' Caine said, although he now looked twitchy. Bobbie could feel the palm of his hand, red hot against her skin. Dr Kahn opened the bedroom door, but Bobbie saw only darkness inside – the curtains drawn. With a clenched jaw, and clutching Caine's hand like a security blanket, she entered the shadows.

Chapter 13

Bridget

It took Bobbie's eyes a moment to adjust to the gloom. Thick drapes hung over the single window, letting only pencil-grey light bleed in around the edges. Bobbie could make out rough shapes – a single bed, an empty desk under the window, a single plastic chair, a functional wardrobe. Like trying to find a specimen in the nocturnal house at the zoo, it was only on second glance that she even realised there was a figure in the room.

Bridget was pressed into the corner where her bed met the wall, sitting with her knees tucked under her chin – the exact same way Bobbie had crouched on that toilet in her dream. Only the whites of her eyes were immediately visible. She peered out through curtains of greasy brown hair, which hung over her shoulders. Bobbie wondered how long it had been since she'd seen the sun – her face was so pale it was ghostly, with raccoon circles around each sunken eye. 'Hello, Bridget, these are your vis—' Dr Kahn began.

'You called her, didn't you?' Bridget slurred. It was hard to age her; on the one hand she looked haggard, older than her thirty years, but at the same time she seemed like a frightened little girl, curled up in a ball on the bed.

Bobbie's eyes widened and she gripped Caine a little tighter. He gripped back.

Dr Kahn spoke again. 'Bridget is taking some quite powerful anti-psychotics, that's why she's so drowsy.'

It seemed to take Bridget a great deal of effort to hold her head up. It hung to one side – her posture not unlike the silhouette Bobbie had seen in the corridor two nights ago. 'Leave us alone.' Bridget peered at Dr Kahn.

'I'm not sure that's such a –'

'It's fine,' Bobbie assured the doctor.

'Are you sure?'

She nodded. 'Yes.'

'Okay. I'll be just outside if you need anything.' Reluctantly, Dr Kahn left, closing the door behind her.

'Do you want the light on?' Caine asked Bridget.

'No.'

Bobbie gestured at the plastic chair. 'May I?'

'Doesn't matter, does it?' Bridget picked at a corner of her pillow with fingernails she'd bitten down to the quick. 'You've only got a day and a half left, you can do what you want.'

On the chair there was a large wash bowl with a bedpan and jug inside. Bobbie realised that Bridget never left this room – certainly not to go to a bathroom. Bathrooms had mirrors in. Not making a fuss, Bobbie placed the apparatus under the chair and sat on it. Caine hovered at her side, unsure of what to do with his hand now that she'd returned it. 'We saw your blog,' Bobbie started. 'I'm Bobbie, by the way, and this is Caine.'

'She told me your names.'

Bobbie glanced up at Caine. 'What?'

'She knows you now. You let her in. She can see inside you. She *knows* you. Always looking in through windows.'

Swallowing hard, Bobbie said: 'We did the summoning. In Piper's Hall.'

Bridget giggled. 'Why else would you be here? I knew it'd happen when everyone forgot about us. While people remembered what happened to us, no one would be fool enough to say her name. I guess we're old news now – day-old bread. Time for the next generation.'

'Forgot about who?' Caine asked, clearing his throat.

'Me and Abi and Tay.' Maybe it was the darkness, or perhaps the medication, but Bridget's swollen pupils were gaping black holes in her face, drawing Bobbie in.

'W-what happened to them?' Bobbie tripped over her words. 'I'm sorry to ask, but if there's any way we can stop it from happening to us.'

'You can't.'

'Please . . .'

'Five days,' she snapped. 'You get five days and that's it. It's all wound up and then it just tick, tick, ticks away until time runs out. You wound it up and you can't stop the clock.'

'Please, Bridget. Tell us what happened. We'll believe you.'

She seemed to perk up at that, snapping out of her rut. When she spoke she was animated, bordering on manic. 'There was a house party in Oxsley. Some girl, she had a really pointy face, was telling us why she was so scared of Piper's Hall – a ghost story about a girl called Mary who threw herself off the cliffs into the sea. There was an urban legend – although I never understood why it's *urban* given that the school's in the middle of the countryside – that if you called her name five times she'd appear in the mirror.

'We all thought it was a load of crap of course, but when we got back to Piper's Hall – we were in Upper One – Abi thought it'd be hilarious to give it a whirl. That's Abi for you – nothing's too stupid to try . . . I remember once she snorted sherbet because she heard you got high off it. I swear she sneezed for an hour afterwards.' Bridget chuckled wildly at the memory. 'We did it in the Uppers' Common Room toilets. It was just the three of us – we even lit a candle, just like in the story. Taylor had the worst fit of giggles ever – it took us about a year to say her name . . .'

Caine chipped in: 'Bloo—'

'DON'T SAY IT!' For the first time, Bridget moved. She sprang across the bed, agile as a cat, and clamped a hand over Caine's mouth. His eyes widened with shock. 'Don't say it,' she whispered. 'Never say it. Haven't you learned? She's always listening in.' She let go and Caine backed away with shaking breath.

'What happened next?'

Bridget crawled back onto the bed, returning to her den like Gollum. 'We said it once, then twice, then three times, then four times . . . and then I stopped. I saw something in the corner of my eye. Right at the back of the mirror something shuffled around. Like we'd woken something up. You don't keep prodding a sleeping bear, do you? So I stopped at four times. Tay and Abi said her name a fifth time though. They didn't see. They didn't stop.'

'You only said it four times?'

Bridget nodded. 'It was enough though. Enough to let her in. She's waiting on the line for number five.' The girl started to rock gently back and forth. Her foot started tapping. 'Always waiting for me to say her name.'

Bobbie couldn't sit still a moment longer. She joined Bridget on the bed and placed a hand on her knee to stop the tapping. 'Bridget, it's okay. That was years ago . . . she isn't coming for you.' It all made sense. Bobbie had been living with this for three days, whereas it had been hanging over Bridget for more than thirteen years. It was no wonder.

'I see her in my dreams. I see the graveyard. She hasn't forgotten me . . . she's waiting for me to slip up.'

'What happened after you summoned her?' Caine asked. 'Did you start seeing stuff?'

'We broke up for the Easter holidays the next day. We all went home. I was in Italy and I hadn't thought about it, until I got a text from Abi. At the time I didn't think anything of it . . . why would I? I was clueless . . . stupid little idiot in front of a mirror . . . *say her name five times.*'

'What did the text say?'

'It said, "Hey, hon, how are you? Anything weird going on?" I ignored it and then they both vanished. That's when I looked in a mirror . . . and saw her waiting.'

Bobbie chewed her lip, deep in thought. There was nothing

in her story they didn't already know, and nothing that would help. 'Bridget. When you see Mary in your dreams . . . does she show you things?'

'Only the graveyard.'

'Which graveyard?'

'The one at St Paul's. She's laughing at me. I can hear her laughing in the graveyard.'

Bobbie shuddered like there was ice in her bones. 'I think . . . I think she's trying to tell me something. So that we can stop this. So we can help her.'

'No!' Bridget gripped Bobbie's wrist. 'Why? Why would you help her?'

'I think . . .'

'Don't *help* her. Keep her in the cage. Dog on a chain. She's a dog on a chain, tied to the school.'

Bobbie looked to Caine for support, but he only shrugged. 'I think M— I think *she* needs help . . . I think she's lost . . . unhappy.'

Bridget laughed bitterly. 'Misery loves company. She's dragging us down into her grave.'

Is that what this was? Mary was so sad, she wanted them all to feel it too? Bobbie was sure there was more to it than that. In a weird way she wished she could just get the spectre face-to-face. 'I'm not giving up,' Bobbie said quietly. She prized Bridget's fingers off her wrist.

'Neither am I,' Caine added.

'We still have two days left. We can stop this.'

The giggling continued. She spoke in a girlish, sing-song voice. 'You don't get it, do you? *She* won't give up. She hasn't

139

given up on meeeeeeeee . . .'

Bobbie frowned. 'What do you mean?'

'Look out of the window.' But Bridget herself turned inwards, resting her head against the plaster wall. Bobbie felt her skin crawl once more, the hairs pricking on the nape of her neck. She rose from the bed and slowly crossed to the window. Outside she could hear freckles of rain dotting the glass. They hit the windowsill in thick, heavy drops.

Bobbie opened the curtains, not sure what to expect. She made an involuntary gasp at what she saw. 'What is it?' Caine asked, squinting as grey daylight flooded the sterile cell.

Rainwater trickled down the window, but two handprints were clearly distinguishable where palms had been pressed against the pane. 'Handprints.' Bobbie ran a finger over the glass.

'So what?' Caine said.

Bobbie turned to face him. 'They're on the *outside* and we're three storeys up.'

Chapter 14

Stigma

Caine pelted out of the dingy room without another word. Bobbie threw an apologetic look to Bridget and followed. 'I'm sorry.'

'You will be.' Bridget turned back to her wall.

'Caine, wait!' Bobbie called after him. By the time she was out of the side room, he was already halfway down the corridor, the patients in the breakout space turning to see what all the commotion was about.

'Sorry . . . I had to get the hell out of that room. I couldn't breathe. It was doing my head in.' He leaned against the wall, resting his head on the fire-procedures poster.

Bobbie gave his arm a rub, but the gesture was awkward. 'I know. But I don't believe what Bridget said . . . Mary is showing me the past for a reason. Why would she do that if she just wanted us dead? She's trying to lead us somewhere, I know it.'

Caine looked weary, when she needed him to be strong. Bobbie remembered how it felt to be Mary: how ashamed she'd been in the lesson and how scared and lonely she'd been hiding in the toilet. She wasn't *evil*.

Dr Kahn bustled down the corridor, glaring at them. 'What's going on?'

'Nothing,' Bobbie muttered.

Dr Kahn looked into Bridget's room and then frowned back at them. 'I knew this visit was a bad idea.' She regarded them coolly. 'How do you even know Bridget? You're clearly a lot younger than she is.'

It was time to leave. 'We're friends of the family. We're going now. We're sorry if we upset her. We didn't mean to.'

'TWO DAYS LEFT.' Bridget's drunken voice echoed throughout the shared space. Caine tugged his arm away from Bobbie and stomped down the corridor. With another vexed glance from the doctor, Bobbie followed Caine towards the exit, pulling him back by the sleeve.

'Caine.' Bobbie lowered her voice and leaned in, aware that this wasn't a conversation you wanted the staff of a mental facility to overhear. 'Please. If ghosts are spirits trapped on earth, maybe she needs to be released. Perhaps if we can figure out whatever unfinished business she has, we can stop this from happening over and over again. Just . . . trust me.'

Caine softened and looked at her. Their faces were only centimetres apart – this was the closest she'd ever been to a boy's lips. They were dangerously inviting. 'I do.'

Bobbie couldn't stand it. Being that close to him was intoxicating and she needed a clear head. She pulled away. 'Okay. Bridget dreamed about the graveyard – perhaps we could go and check it out. I wonder if she's buried there.'

Bobbie wondered if her headstone might hold a clue – the name of a relative or something, someone, who could give them an insight into what Mary's unfinished business might be.

'It's worth a look.' Caine seemed to resign himself to the quest. 'It just seems that whatever we do . . . How can we stop something that can float up at windows? Something that lives inside mirrors?'

Although the mention of the impossible handprints was enough to send a wave of goosebumps up her arms, Bobbie wouldn't admit defeat. 'I don't know.' She lowered her voice again. 'But sitting in a dark room and rocking isn't going to help, is it?'

Caine laughed for the first time in ages. 'You have a point. Let's get the bus into Oxsley. And I reckon it's about time for some sugar too, I'm Hank Marvin.'

The mere thought of food made her empty stomach rumble. 'Okay. I wouldn't say no to chocolate either. I need to use the bathroom first.'

They left the ward and it was immediately lighter and fresher, as if the ward existed in its own sorry dimension. David, the nurse, showed them to the nearest toilets. Bobbie had to admit she was starting to feel Bridget's aversion to rooms with mirrors in, especially after what Caine had shown her last night. 'Wait here for me, yeah?'

He understood her unease. 'Sure.'

Bobbie entered the toilet, disappointed to find both cubicles empty. A single strip light hummed overhead, filling the room with bleached, stark light. There was a mirror above the sink, but she pointedly looked away from it – knowing that if she looked hard enough, she wouldn't be alone in the room. She did her business as quickly as possible, but, as much as she wanted to get out of the room, she *had* to wash her hands or she'd feel grimy for the rest of the morning.

Eyes avoiding her reflection, Bobbie rinsed her hands under the tap. That was when she first noticed. Where she'd pulled the sleeves of the Barbour jacket up to avoid wetting them, she saw a sore red scratch. How had she done that? It wasn't bleeding; it was more like a scar that was healing.

Shaking the water from her hands, she pulled the sleeve back further. Her mouth fell open. There were cuts all over her forearm. 'What the . . . ?' Vicious grazes criss-crossed her skin – some a centimetre or two, most of them tiny nicks, but some thick gashes. In desperation, Bobbie rolled up her right sleeve and found much the same. Her arms were covered in cuts that had never happened.

Chapter 15

Grave Matters

In a futile attempt, she brushed at her skin, trying to get them off. She closed her eyes and counted to five, praying this was all in her head – another dream moment – but when she opened her eyes, the angry scarlet marks were still present. An exasperated sob rolled off her tongue. 'Caine! Caine!' she yelled, unable to conjure words beyond that.

He burst into the bathroom, ready for a fight judging from the flared nostrils and clenched fists. Bobbie threw herself at him, only just keeping her voice on this side of hysterical. 'Look! Look at my arms!'

He grimaced as his fingers traced her skin. 'What happened?'

'Nothing! I don't know! They were just there!' It was all too much. She'd reached a tipping point and she couldn't hold it in a second longer. All the hard work she'd done at remaining positive and upbeat was gone in a heartbeat. Mary had *scarred* her.

'Oh God.' Caine held his arms out and she crumbled into

his embrace, her eyes wide and unblinking. She was worried if she blinked she'd push tears out, and she *wasn't* going to cry. His sweater smelled of 'meadow' fabric conditioner – clean and safe – he smelled like home.

It wasn't fair. She wanted to help Mary, she really did, but now this. What next? 'Why is she doing this? What does she want from us?'

Caine didn't answer but held her tight.

Half an hour later, Bobbie finished her Kinder Bueno and washed it down with some Fanta Lemon while they waited for the bus. 'That better?' Caine asked.

'Marginally.' Bobbie blushed. The terror had subsided, although the cuts had not. They were all she could think about. One more thing to add to the list of impossible things that had happened in the last three days. This was the worst though – this one affected her body. She felt violated, vulnerable and it made Mary feel *realer* somehow. She wasn't some gaseous spook, she could *get* them.

Caine had soothed her, accepting his shift as the rational one. He'd pointed out that although the cuts were real, she wasn't in any major pain, so it could be a lot worse. Bobbie kept her fresh fears to herself – they didn't need verbalising, they were clear from the marks on her arms. 'Sorry for my meltdown.' She attempted a quip but her voice wavered. 'Can we blame it on dangerously low blood sugar?'

Caine smiled. Dimples. 'I'm down with that. Nah, all things considered I think we're all doing pretty well.'

'Right.' Bobbie swallowed down the scream brewing in her

throat. *Crying is counterproductive* – how many times had she said that to Naya when some random guy had failed to reply to a text. 'Maybe if we had two weeks we'd have more time to stand around sobbing on each other and wailing.'

'Still.' Caine downed his second Red Bull. 'If you wanna cry, cry. I gave my pillow a pretty good punch this morning.'

'Is that a euphemism?' Bobbie couldn't resist, but wished at once she hadn't said it. Oh God, now he might think she was 'sassy'. There was nothing worse than 'sassy'.

Caine snorted Red Bull down his nose. 'Nice. I see what you did there.'

'Sorry. That's super-inappropriate.'

'No, it's not.' Caine opened a bag of Doritos. 'Let's talk about *anything* other than ghosts. That's literally all we've ever talked about.'

It was true. She didn't actually know anything about her partner in crime beyond the fact he went to Radley, rode a little BMX bike and sort of dated Grace. That was it. Oh, and the turbulent family history. 'You have a point. Go on then, tell me something else.'

'Like what?'

'Like about you.' Maybe if she focused on him she wouldn't think about the marks on her arms. Just thinking about them made her skin crawl. *Just think about Caine*.

It started to rain again – drops tapping on the roof of the bus shelter, which was half covered with slick, wet, orange leaves. 'Er, I dunno,' he said. 'I'm pretty basic.'

'Hardly.'

'I'm studying Sport, Art and Photography. If . . . you know

147

. . . if there is a next year, I'm *meant* to be off to uni to do Graphic Design.'

Bobbie's eyes lit up. She ignored the bit about Mary. *Just think about Caine.* 'Oh cool. I didn't have you down as a "creative".'

'Ha! That's what my hippy Art teacher calls himself. What makes you say that?'

Bobbie shrugged, embarrassed. 'Just a misconception, I guess. I saw the hoodie and the BMX and had you down as a . . . I dunno, a roguish rebel type or something.'

Caine grinned. 'Is it cos I is brown?' He winked and they both laughed. 'That's Radley High. It's a pretty hard-core school – you do what you gotta do to get by. You only show people what you want them to see, you know? Either that or you get your head kicked in. It was the same in Croydon.'

'Yeah. Piper's Hall is just as bad. Everyone in their boxes: like you have the hockey girls, and the choir girls, and the pretty girls; even the alternative girls are identikit. You can pick any box you like except the one marked *you*.'

He nodded. 'It's a killer. Like trying really hard to look like you're not trying. I try to mix it all up. My sketches, my skating, street-art influences. Look.' He lifted his jumper up to reveal a grey T-shirt with an anatomical diagram of a dissected frog printed on it. 'I made this.'

'Oh wow – that's actually really cool.' As he lifted it up, Bobbie caught a glimpse of the top of his boxers. He wore the baggy cotton kind and they bunched up over the waist of his jeans, the elastic tight over the muscular ridges running over his hips. Something warm and rosy stirred inside her. *Just think about Caine* was really working. He was just the tonic

148

she needed.

'Thanks. I wanna do more of them – maybe sell them online. Again, that's if . . .'

'I hear ya.'

'What about you? Is it all crochet and stuff up at the hall?'

'Ha! Not quite! God, I dread to think what you've heard.'

'Everyone's rich?'

'Nope.'

'Lesbian orgies?'

'Only the last Wednesday of the month,' Bobbie said wryly.

'Disappointing. Sex, drugs, rock and roll?'

'No, no and only the goth girls.'

'Fail. Is everyone well posh?'

'It's all relative. We have a minor royal in Lower Three, so compared to her I'm pretty much a pleb. There's an entrance exam, so if you're dead clever you can get scholarships and stuff.'

'What about you?'

'Did I get a scholarship?' Bobbie tugged her sleeves down where they rode up – she didn't want reminding of the phantom injuries until she could get undressed properly and see the full extent of the damage. The cuts constantly niggled in the front of her temple like there was a fly trapped in her skull. 'No. Despite the glasses I'm not actually that brainy. My mum was a pretty big actress in the Eighties – she was Desdemona in some old film version of *Othello*. She's always working in weird places so she sent me to boarding school for "my own good".'

'That sucks.' Caine finished his crisps and put the packet in the bin. 'You are brainy though. The way you talk and stuff.'

'Would I get my head kicked in at Radley?'

'Oh without doubt! Without doubt!' he laughed.

'I like writing,' Bobbie admitted. 'I don't know if I'm any good at it – I can barely use full stops – but I'd like to be a writer. Like an author.'

Caine smirked. 'A "creative"?'

'Yeah.' Bobbie smiled back. Through the murk, the bus hissed down the street, brushing and clacking against the overhanging trees as it did so, ruining the moment. Damn. She didn't want her chat with Caine to end.

They boarded the bus with a flash of their passes and Bobbie was hit by an almost tangible wall of BO. The steamed-up, damp vehicle was rank – it smelled like sacks of wet compost left in the sun. 'Dude, it reeks,' Caine muttered and Bobbie was about to reply when she saw something that froze her mid-thought. 'What is it?' he said.

'Just keep walking,' Bobbie told him, leading him to the very back seats. In the third row sat a day boarder called Elodie Minchin. God knew why she was taking the bus into school at almost midday, and it didn't matter. They'd been seen.

Caine saw what she saw. 'Oh bum. You reckon she'll grass you up.'

'Again, it's not Price I'm worried about.'

'Grace?'

'Grace.'

Caine must have picked up on *something* – perhaps she was making the same face she made when she was forced to eat dreaded olives or capers – because unprompted he said: 'You know, there's nothing happening with me and Grace.'

150

Bobbie feigned disinterest, as if this was of no consequence to her, although there was a marching-band victory parade in her head. Another part of her brain tried to push black Mary clouds to the forefront, but she ignored it. Life is all about minor triumphs. For now, on the back row of the 38 bus, she permitted herself to revel in the satisfaction of knowing that Caine wasn't interested in Grace Brewer-Fay. 'Oh, really? Does she know that?'

'If she doesn't she should. I've been straight with her.'

Bobbie chose to pursue it further, attempting to sound as breezy as possible. 'Why not? Grace is super-hot.'

'You think?'

'You don't?'

Caine's mouth turned down at the edges. 'She's Team Hot, but she's not Team Fun, you know what I mean? She might wanna try smiling some day.'

Bobbie stifled a laugh. 'Burn.'

'Yeah. I shouldn't be shady about her. She's okay, but . . . just no.' When she didn't reply, he went on. 'It's hard to say, ain't it – why you fancy some people and not others? You just sort of do or you don't.'

Bobbie thought of pithy comebacks, but was propelled to play it straight. 'I know what you mean. You can't help it.'

Caine nodded and rubbed a porthole for himself in the steamed-up window. 'Some people just shine a bit brighter than others and it's got nothing to do with what they look like.'

Bobbie suddenly couldn't speak for the lump in her throat.

***

151

By the time they reached St Paul's the rain had eased to a shroud of fine drizzle. The churchyard was empty aside from a lady with a pram leaving fresh flowers on a grave and pulling up the weeds that encroached on her monument. Bobbie briefly wondered who she'd come to see – a husband, perhaps her mother or father. Either way, the pair passed her in respectful silence.

They followed the path around the church to the seemingly endless rows of graves that waited around the back. 'Where do we start?' Caine asked.

'I have no idea. I guess we look for a headstone with Worthington on it . . .'

They split up to save time – yes, it was Horror Film 101, but there really were an awful lot of graves to inspect. There was no obvious order to the cemetery; even the pathways through the graveyard were winding and nonsensical. Looming oak trees were dotted amidst the graves, blocking out the light. Every few hundred metres there was a bench, but these were the only things that acted as landmarks.

As she walked through the tombstones, Bobbie could feel a sense of peace, of restfulness. Was it morbid to think that everyone dies and that's okay? It was the people left behind that *felt* the death. That was why Bobbie couldn't go just yet. Who'd look after her mum?

The heartfelt inscriptions on the headstones – just names to her – made Bobbie wonder if, once everything ends, you live on as a memory. Some of the graves had fresh tributes, but many had fallen to ruin, chipped and moss-eaten, with no one left to put a face to the name of the body that decayed below. Bobbie wondered if that's how long you truly live for – until the last person who remembers you, until the final bouquet on your grave.

An angel wept over a family plot, holding a worn stone hand to her face. Bobbie read the names of those interred within. Whole generations in one grave. But not a single mention of Worthington. This was starting to feel like a needle in a haystack job.

A faint noise turned Bobbie's head. A girl laughing. It carried on the wind, but the airy sound was faint, as if from a long way away or a long time *ago*. It was so delicate, so lacy, that Bobbie wondered if *this time* she really was imagining it.

She saw Caine make his way down the adjacent footpath. She met him at the junction, under a clump of grand, gnarled oaks. 'Did you just hear that?'

'What?'

'Nothing. Well . . . I thought I heard a girl laughing.'

'Laughing? Doesn't sound a lot like Mary.'

Bobbie nodded. 'That's what I thought.'

A frown drew Caine's brows together. It was kinda cute. 'This all feels a bit creepy though.'

'What? A graveyard? Seriously?'

He grinned. 'No, like major déjà vu.'

Any other week, Bobbie would have rolled her eyes, but in this case she believed him without question. 'You think you've been here before?'

'I *have* been here before – but this is different.' He shrugged. 'But I can't say how.'

Frustrating. 'That's okay . . . any sign of a Worthington?'

'Nope.'

'Me neither.' The heavens opened again, thick splatters of

rain quickly turning into rods. 'Ah! Let's find shelter!' Bobbie held her hands over her head. They sprinted for the nearest clump of trees, leaving the safety of the footpath.

There was a giddy strobe of lightning followed almost immediately by a rumble of thunder that sounded like the sky cracking. Bobbie remembered that if thunder instantly follows lightning, that meant the eye of the storm was close at hand. They dashed further into the woods, heading for denser cover. Under the browning autumn leaves, they were protected from the worst of it. Bobbie looked around the little forest and realised they weren't exactly alone. They were still surrounded by graves.

Almost completely obscured by trees was an ivy-strangled mausoleum set some way off the main path. Rusty leaf litter was built up around the squat stone structure. Bobbie had never noticed it before, tucked away in the shadows, but once it would have been quite beautiful: low steps led to pillars that framed an ornate metal entrance, with finely moulded bars twisting and curling around a guardian angel deep in prayer. Sadly, now neglected, it was covered in graffiti – not fabulous street art, but nasty, squiggly 'tags' and lewd representations of the male anatomy. Coke bottles and faded crisp packets climbed the walls with the leaves.

It had been a long time since anyone had brought flowers to this monument, Bobbie thought. Its neighbours – flat memorial slabs in the ground – were covered with wild grasses, weeds and yet more litter. This whole corner of the graveyard had been forgotten.

'It doesn't make sense,' Bobbie said, exasperated. Rain continued to tip-tap in the canopy. 'Why is Bridget dreaming of this place?'

'Why not? We all come here. Maybe girls used to come here in Mary's day too?'

Bobbie scrunched her nose. 'It's not fair. We're trying our hardest, we're following all the clues, but we're getting nowhere. We've learned nothing today that can help us at all.'

'Hey.' Caine moved closer and took her hand. His skin was hot to the touch, warming her cold, damp fingers. 'We're getting there. We're doing everything we can. Maybe . . . maybe we need to rest on it.'

'We haven't got time.'

'We still have two days. It's gonna be fine.' He gave her hand a squeeze and she almost believed him. Their bodies were close now, too close, closer than you ever would be to a friend. She tilted her head up a fraction, until her eyes met his. There were gems of rain on her lenses, but she could still see the way he looked at her. He wanted to kiss *her*. She wanted to kiss him. She wanted him to want to kiss her. She'd always wondered what her first kiss would be like, but she'd never dreamed it would be in a rain-soaked graveyard.

Their lips were only centimetres apart, but even that was too much distance. He leaned in, seizing the moment. The second his lips touched hers, an alien, balmy breeze blew in, a summer wave. Dry, humid July air with a hint of mown grass, wild garlic and lavender. And perfume . . . she could definitely smell perfume. Brown, amber, yellow leaves whipped up around them in a graceful tornado: twirling, dipping and diving like a waltz. The strange dance was accompanied, undeniably this time, by a coy, girlish laugh.

155

Chapter 16

Friendly Advice

Bobbie pulled back at once, their lips having scarcely touched. 'You can hear that, right?'

'Er, yeah.' The colour fell out of Caine's cheeks. 'Who is that?'

The spell broken, the spiralling leaves settled to the ground, rustling like scrunched paper. 'I'll give you precisely one guess.'

Caine released her hand. Bobbie sensed that *they* were causing this; they were stirring up the past. Or was there something in the air that had made Caine act like *that*? She really, really hoped that wasn't the case. Caine scanned the clearing. 'I think we should get out of here. Like now.'

What Bobbie wanted to say was, *No, kiss me again, right now,* but instead she nodded. She started down the path towards the church, not daring to look back. First survive, *then* kiss.

Somehow, the issue of getting *back* into school hadn't really crossed her mind. The only saving grace was, as she'd been signed off sick, no one would question why she wasn't in uniform. That, however, wouldn't save her skin if she was caught off the premises. Bobbie thought back to their sighting of Elodie on the bus. 'Grassing' was a mortal sin at Piper's Hall, but that only applied to teachers. All Elodie had to do was tell one person, and that person would pass it on, and then on, *ad infinitum*.

Bobbie arrived back at school during period five having already said goodbye to Caine in Oxsley. As they'd needed to get different buses there hadn't been a repeat of the kiss. They hadn't spoken of it either, so her doubt about what had happened in the graveyard was added to her mental pile of worries.

Sadie's original tale played on loop in Bobbie's mind. Mary had supposedly been hooking up with a local boy. A local boy just like Caine. This giddy feeling she felt every time she saw him – was it real or was it some sort of enchantment? Were they just playing out the past? Bobbie had never felt this way for a boy before so there was no way of telling. The way it felt like his name was written on her heart now, it might as well be supernatural. It was certainly alien.

Waiting until a group of gym-kitted girls trudged from the changing rooms to the hockey pitch, Bobbie slipped in through the back entrance without attracting attention to herself. Essentially, now that she was on-site, there was only so much trouble she could be in. Still, avoiding as many people as she could, Bobbie tiptoed through the secret passage back to her room.

Brontë House was deserted, naturally, while everyone was in lessons. As soon as Bobbie's rear hit her mattress, she knew she was exhausted. The day had kicked the crap out of her and it wasn't even three in the afternoon. She'd been scared witless, cut and kissed in the space of a morning. A major adrenaline crash felt imminent. She let herself lie down. A power nap in comforting broad daylight was infinitely more inviting than sleeping at night, and her eyes were drowsy the second her head hit her faux-fur cushion. Guilt nagged in her head, but she really did feel like they'd run out of avenues to explore. The only lead they'd got from Bridget was the graveyard, and except for the kiss-that-never-was, the trip was redundant.

Caine had decided to blow off the rest of the day, but had gone home to make sure the school office hadn't left a message on his mum's answering machine. There was no way she was going to smuggle him into Piper's anyway – she'd flirted with all kinds of trouble already today.

Kicking her shoes off, Bobbie closed her weary eyes. In her head, she played the almost-kiss on repeat. Imagination-wise, the moment had taken on cinematic proportions: sweeping violins; her dissolving into Caine's arms; her back gracefully arching like a dancer with him pouring over her. It would have been *so perfect* if it hadn't been for the ghostly interruption. No. She wouldn't let Mary ruin her movie moment. Her first kiss (kind of). Her heart felt full of blossom and her head soon caught up with the sentiment. She drifted away.

The serenity continued into her dream. She was downstairs in what was now the Lowers' Common Room but seemed to be a library then. Bobbie sat in the bay window seat, mostly obscured from the rest of the world by the thick, green velvet curtain. Warm spring sunshine doused the room and she bathed in it, feeling the rays on her face. There was a book on her lap, but she ignored it. Instead, she looked out of the window at the other girls in the playground. They laughed, shrieked and joked, tagging each other in some sort of chasing game.

Bobbie had never felt so removed from anything in her life. This must be what goldfish feel like.

Everything about them was different to her. The way they wore their hair rolled up at the neck and the way hers hung in its plait, the perfectly tweezed, stencilled brows. Suddenly she became aware that a girl with gorgeous ginger ringlets on the other side of the window was staring and pointing at her – she'd been seen. Somehow she knew it was Susan Fletcher. 'Did you see her? She looked right at me.' The cruel words were audible even through the glass.

'Just staring at us! How queer!' another girl laughed along.

Bobbie closed the book, ready to find another hiding place. She swung her legs off the reading seat and gasped, the book falling to the floor and bouncing. She wasn't alone. A handsome man, a teacher she guessed, stood watching her, his arms full of books. 'Oh I'm sorry,' he said. 'I didn't mean to scare you. I thought you knew I was here.'

If Mary replied all those years ago, Bobbie didn't now. She'd never known shyness like it, heavier than chainmail. She couldn't even look him in the eye. The teacher wore a simple grey suit with a tie the colour of red wine, although the cut of both seemed unfashionable to Bobbie's eye. His auburn hair was slicked back neatly, parted like a feather at the side of his head. He had a kind smile, dimpled chin and strong jaw. He was far more attractive than any of the current crop, even Mr Granger.

'It's Mary, isn't it? The new girl?'

159

Bobbie nodded.

'What are you doing inside all by yourself? It's such a beautiful day out.'

Bobbie was tongue-tied, but the conversation moved on without her.

'Ah, I see. Let me guess. Some of the Ladies have been less than welcoming?'

Time moved on. She was only seeing his half of events, like Mary couldn't take her eyes off him. 'What are you reading? Oh, *Moby-Dick* is one of my absolute favourites . . . "Call me Ishmael"– such a wonderful first line, don't you think? Yes . . . and Ahab's obsession . . . yes, I agree . . . very much so . . .'

By the time they had finished discussing the white whale, Bobbie – no, Mary – was in love.

The lightness in her heart was still there when she awoke, and she was initially disappointed that it had been a dream – only to remember Caine, and feel somewhat like she'd betrayed him with the gorgeous teacher. The dream was the most potent yet, like having a crush on a film star but with ten times more kick. Sadie's ghost story had omitted one vital detail: it wasn't a local *boy*, it was a local *man*.

Naya shook her awake. 'Gerroff,' she murmured, still dozing.

'Time to wake up, sleeping beauty.'

'What time is it?'

'Almost supper. How did it go at the asylum?'

Bobbie sat up straight and rubbed her eyes. 'It was a total waste of time. Bridget didn't tell us anything we didn't already know and I ended up covered in cuts. Look.' Bobbie pushed up her sleeves and Naya inhaled in shock, examining the scars.

'Oh my God. How did you get these?'

'No idea. They just appeared.' Bobbie unbuttoned her blouse to get a better look. The grazes went all the way up to her shoulders.

'Do they hurt?' Naya traced her skin, her lips curled back.

'No. Well, they're sore. Like everything this week, it doesn't make any sense, does it?'

'Sure you're okay?' Naya grimaced and Bobbie nodded, passing up another opportunity to freak out. 'Now . . . you missed a whole ton of stuff while you were "sick".' She made little bunny ears with her fingers. 'Do you want the good news or the bad news?'

Bobbie fastened her shirt up. 'Oh God, what now? The good news, I suppose.'

Naya folded her legs underneath her body. 'Well. Because Sadie's been gone for almost forty-eight hours, it's about to become an official missing persons inquiry, or at least that's what Jennie Pham said and her dad's a cop. Anyway, at lunch, Dr Price came into the canteen and was like, "We're extending Exeat to Thursday." Everyone's leaving Wednesday evening.'

'Oh wow. I wonder why.'

'We think it's probably so they can do like forensics and stuff.'

'Or because they think we're not safe.' Bobbie ran a hand through her hair, trying to get her thoughts in order. 'What about us?' Exeat was the first weekend of every month – Friday and Monday's lessons were suspended and *most* girls went home, leaving a skeleton staff behind to look after the international students, like Naya, and those who couldn't go home, like her.

'We're staying.'

'But that's when . . .'

'Time runs out. I know.'

The glow of her afternoon with Caine now seemed like a dim and distant memory. After lessons tomorrow, they'd be left in a near-deserted school with a ghost edging ever closer. 'Oh God. How is that good news? What are we going to do?'

'At least there'll be police all over the joint.'

Bobbie snorted. 'I'd like to see what they're going to do against a dead girl in a mirror.'

'On the bright side, if we don't die, it's a day off lessons.'

Bobbie raised a smile for her friend. 'And what's the bad news? Will I need a sedative before I hear this?'

'Dr Price wants to see you in her office.'

The mattress suddenly felt like a waterbed. Or maybe it was just her head swimming. 'Brilliant.'

Perched on the sofa between the Infirmary and Isolation Room, Bobbie wrapped her arms around herself like a straightjacket, waiting to be called into Price's office. For whatever reason, the old wing was always ten times colder than the rest of the school. In the distance Bobbie could hear the chatter of girls filing into the dining hall for supper. There was a Christmas-like hum about the place now that they'd been given the gift of a day outside of school. Those, like her, who weren't going anywhere said nothing at all, not wanting to rain on anyone else's parade.

'Roberta, would you like to come in now?' The door opened and Dr Price beckoned her in. 'Sorry I kept you waiting, I was on an important phone call.'

'That's okay.' Head down, Bobbie entered the office. She'd only been in the room a handful of times over the years. With prospectus claims that Piper's Hall favoured reward over punishment, only girls in serious trouble usually saw the inside of these walls.

Dr Price sat behind her grand desk, the wood gleaming like a freshly polished conker, and motioned for Bobbie to sit opposite. She found her feet rooted to the leaf pattern on the rug, however. She'd forgotten all about the mirror.

The defining feature of the Head's office was the ostentatious mirror that filled the wall behind the desk. It was clearly an antique, although Bobbie wouldn't care to say from *when* in the past it came. It had an intricate, almost vulgar, gold frame – like something straight out of the Palace of Versailles. If memory served her correctly, the mirror had been a gift to the school on its grand opening. Of course, what troubled Bobbie wasn't the flashiness of the ornament, but the reflection. The entire room was held within it, and Bobbie knew, if she looked hard enough, *she'd* be waiting too. 'Are you all right, dear?'

Bobbie dragged herself into the present, eyes avoiding the mirror. 'Erm, yeah, still a bit off.' She sank into the plush padded seat.

'Yes, I heard you were sick. That's why I wanted to talk to you. I've noticed you've not been quite yourself these last few days.'

The fact that Price even knew what she was like on a normal day was cause for surprise. Their paths had hardly crossed in five years. 'I think I was coming down with something.' She couldn't meet her gaze.

Price rested her chin on her fingers. Her nails were painted the exact shade to match the rose-colour scarf around her neck. 'Roberta, do you know what *in loco parentis* means?'

Bobbie sat on her hands. 'Yeah, doesn't it mean parental responsibility or something?'

'That's right. Literally *in place of parents*. I know we haven't talked all that often, but I pride myself on getting to know all my young ladies. You know, I never had my own children. I never felt like I needed to when I had all you girls.'

Her head teacher speaking so personally was unsettling to say the least. Bobbie had always subscribed to the idea that teachers went to sleep in Tupperware boxes in their store cupboards. The notion they had sex lives was plain weird. 'So I can tell when something is troubling one of you,' she concluded.

Bobbie felt too hot all of a sudden, flustered. 'I'm fine. Seriously. Just ill.'

Dr Price considered her, green eyes as clever as a fox. 'Bobbie, if this is connected to Sadie, and I think it is, I absolutely *have* to know. You might think you're protecting someone . . . maybe you think you're protecting Sadie, but every minute that she's missing, things become more serious. More serious for you too if you know something.'

Bobbie had to purse her lips to contain a bitter laugh/sob. As if she didn't know all this. Time was gurgling down the drain and there wasn't a thing she could do to stop it. Less than two days left. She was exhausted. Perhaps it was just time to come clean. 'You won't believe –'

'What? What won't I believe?'

Bobbie froze, the sentence unfinished. *She* was in the room.

In the mirror, in the furthest corner where the row of cupboards ended but before the window began. Mary was pressed into the shadows, only the palest white of her cheekbones and chin catching the light from Price's lamp.

'Bobbie . . . what won't I . . . ?'

Bobbie instinctively twisted in her chair to see if Mary was *really* in the corner. Predictably, she wasn't, but as she turned, the cupboard nearest to where Mary had stood popped open. A ring binder and some files fell from the top shelf, apparently pushing the door open and sending leaves of paper spilling over the office floor.

'Oh bother.' Price stood and emerged from behind her desk to tidy the mess. 'That's what you get for piling things in willy-nilly.'

Bobbie crossed the office and crouched to help her. Wow, teachers really did have to do a lot of paperwork, Bobbie thought as she scooped up the records. God knew what they were – copies of school reports from the look of it.

'That's okay, Bobbie – leave it to me, please. These things will need to be refiled in the correct . . .' Her voice trailed off and it took Bobbie a second to understand why. Absentmindedly, she'd rolled up her sleeves to lend a hand, revealing the scars. Oh crap. 'Bobbie, what have you done to your arms?'

'Nothing!' Bobbie squeaked, knowing exactly what it must look like.

'Have you been hurting yourself?'

'No! God no! I swear it's not that. I promise.'

'Then what exactly is it?'

Bobbie scrambled for a decent-sounding excuse. The wheel

165

of lies landed on only terrible ones that she'd have to try to make sound convincing. 'A kitten.' In that instant she knew she couldn't tell her the truth. She'd be made to see a doctor or something and they had precious little time to begin with – she wasn't going to waste her potential last day on earth having a psychological assessment.

'A kitten?' Dr Price straightened herself up and closed the cupboard.

'Yeah. There's this boy. He's called Caine. He lives in Oxsley. I've been seeing him at the weekends and he just got this new kitten. She's really cute, but she scratches without mercy!' Bobbie tried for a jocular smile. *Gosh, I'm so QUIRKY!*

Dr Price looked at her as if she were *insane*. The ghost version might have elicited a better response. 'Roberta. Self-harm is very serious. I take well-being –'

'I know. I promise it's not that. I wouldn't.'

Not even remotely satisfied-looking, Price returned to her desk. 'Bobbie, I'm going to be watching you like a hawk. Is that understood?'

'Yes, Miss.'

Another shrewd, piercing glare. 'And you're quite sure there's nothing you'd like to share?'

'No, Miss.'

'Good. You'd better get to supper while they're still serving.'

'Yes, Miss.' As Bobbie scurried out of the office, she chanced a look back. Mary was nowhere to be seen in the mirror.

Pinning the cuffs of her jumper under her fingers, Bobbie made her way towards the dining hall, her stomach clenched to the size of a pea. There was no way she'd be able to eat, even though it was rhubarb crumble and custard night, her favourite. Having Price breathing down her neck was going to make the next two days even harder. If only she knew what tomorrow had in store.

Most girls were finishing up now and drifting back to the houses in clumps of two or three. Bobbie didn't see Grace until it was too late. 'Oh hi, Bobbie, can I have a word?' The blonde was seemingly covered head to toe in men's names – Jack Wills, Tommy Hilfiger and Abercrombie & Fitch.

Bobbie was instantly on edge. This was the first time in memory Grace had called her by name and not Blobbie. 'Yeah, sure.' Bobbie poked her glasses up her nose and subtly looked around to ensure they had witnesses. They didn't. The corridor outside the dining hall was empty – with only clanging trays and plates echoing through the hall.

Grace fixed her in a flawless liquid-liner gaze and said in a low, solemn voice, 'Look. I know you were off grounds today. Elodie Minchin said she saw you on the bus with Caine.'

'Grace, I can explain –'

'You really don't have to,' Grace replied, voice dripping with golden syrup. 'I know it's my responsibility as Head Girl to report these things to Dr Price, but my God, we're friends. What kind of monster do you think I am?'

It took every ounce of self-control Bobbie had not to laugh, gape or give an honest answer. Since when had they ever, *ever* been friends? 'It's not what it looks like.'

Grace smiled, but perhaps her face was physically incapable of warmth. The edges of her lips turned up, but her eyes remained inert. 'I wanted to talk to you because I was concerned,

167

that's all.'

'Concerned?'

'Yeah. You should know that Caine Truman is a total player.'
Ah. *Here we go.* This was fascinating. The fact that Grace wasn't
merely threatening physical or emotional damage meant that,
for the first time, she wasn't only acknowledging her existence,
but also identifying her as competition. This was *enemies closer*
territory, but wholly unnecessary given how much further up
the food chain Grace was – like a tiger having a quiet word
with a tabby.

'Really?' Bobbie decided to play along. 'He seems okay?'

'Oh, Bobbie, they all seem okay to begin with. That's how
they get what they want.'

'Right.'

Grace nodded earnestly. Too earnestly. 'I just don't want to
see you humiliate yourself.'

'Humiliate myself?'

'Boys like Caine . . . He was probably doing it as some sort
of bet or something. They see us Piper's Ladies as trophies
to brag about at Radley. Just don't give him the satisfaction,
okay?' It was hardly a question, more a command.

Bobbie was near speechless. It was the verbal equivalent of
an acid attack. 'Er . . . thanks, I guess.'

'You're welcome. Us girls have got to stick together, right?'
Grace flashed a shark's grin. 'Let's hug it out.' She seized her,
although Bobbie pointedly left her arms hanging at her sides.

'I have to get to dinner,' Bobbie muttered, pulling away. As
if she didn't have enough to worry about.

Price, Grace and the dead girl.

Chapter 17

Apport

The whistle of air through Naya's nostrils coming from the next bed was enough to eventually lure Bobbie into a thin sleep. This time, she was almost hoping for a dream, searching for another clue from Mary's past. But tonight, there came only fragments, parts of a patchwork quilt come undone.

In the first, she was in a cold hall – the little theatre. She recognised it by its fusty odour and same folded velvet curtains hanging in front of the stage. It was empty and all the lights were out. Bobbie sat at a worn upright piano like the one they still used for choir practice – they only ever wheeled out the grand when there were parents in the audience. Her fingers hovered over the keys, unsure. She became aware that she wasn't alone. His scent hit her before she saw him – clean and soapy with just a suggestion of oak cologne. It was both masculine and intoxicating – exactly as she remembered from their first meeting in the library. The handsome teacher. He leaned on the end of the piano, watching her play. 'You play beautifully,' he told her. 'But let me show you.'

Bobbie started to rise from the piano stool. 'No, stay where you are. Watch my hands.' He nudged her along the stool so that they could share it. His thigh pressed against hers, his shoulder to her shoulder. He was so warm, she was sure she must feel like a block of ice next to him. He played the chords expertly, his fingers moving like water over the keys. 'Now you try.'

She tried to copy him, but her fingers felt as knotted and hefty as a string of sausages. The notes she made sounded pained next to his. 'Like this.' He took hold of her hand and manipulated her fingers, positioning them in the correct formation. 'See?'

She did see. This time, the keys worked together in harmony. As his hand left hers, it rested on her knee. She did nothing to shake it off. The contact was exquisite and she didn't want to lose it for a second. She felt her cheeks burn and a matching prickly heat in her breast, like there was a volcano erupting at her core.

Some other things happened, although they were too ephemeral for Bobbie to capture – snippets of colours and sounds. The next thing she clearly saw was a frozen playground. Icicles hung from the shelter surrounding the courtyard and tracks had been shovelled through orange grit-stained snow. Pathetic talcum-powder flakes swirled, somehow defying gravity, as girls darted to and fro, throwing snowballs or rolling boulders. Bobbie barely noticed them.

On the other side of the playground, nursing a steaming mug of tea in his gloved fingers, was her teacher. As he blew on his drink, his eyes never left her. She sat alone, as always, on the bench, swaddled in her winter coat. In the eye of a storm, they saw only each other.

Their little secret.

She had never felt so special.

Bobbie felt the fragments of images blow away like smoke. She awoke with a start, aware of a body next to hers. Her mattress springs moved and creaked as Naya sidled into bed alongside her, apparently spooked from her own dreams. 'Naya, are you okay?' Bobbie croaked, clearing her throat.

There was a murmur from the bed opposite. Even in the grey murk of the room, Bobbie saw Naya roll to face away from her.

So who's in my bed?

Bobbie shrank back, her knees jolting to her chest. She pinned her body into the corner where the wall met her bedstead. Her eyes wide open and wide awake, she dared to sit up and take a look. There was someone under the duvet – a slight, human form, its head making a tent of the quilt. 'Naya!' Bobbie cried, but the word caught at the back of her throat. She clutched her knees to her chest, not wanting the exposed skin of her legs to touch the intruder. 'Naya!' she repeated, but her friend only muttered, not stirring.

The figure was now still, squatting under the duvet halfway down the bed. Bobbie's mouth hung open uselessly, her eyes sore. A tear rolled down her face but she couldn't move; the fear gripped her like a vice. She was paralysed.

For some reason, God only knew why, she was reminded of a time when she'd been living near Sydney while her mum was in a soap opera out there. Late one night she'd heard a rustling noise in her bedroom. Initially, she'd been excited at the thought of a cute mouse or possum, but she'd opened her eyes to see a mammoth, hairy spider scurrying across her pillow. This was the same fear. Even when each synapse in her brain was telling her to run, every last muscle turned to stone.

The hunched figure, whom Bobbie could only assume was Mary, was equally still. They mirrored each other at opposite ends of the bed, heads at the same level. Even through the duvet, Bobbie was certain Mary was watching her. 'Naya . . .' Bobbie tried one last time, but knew she wouldn't wake her room-mate.

Mary still didn't budge. From under the duvet, Bobbie heard a hoarse, sickly rasping. 'M-Mary?' Bobbie breathed. 'Is that you?' It was a dim question, but it was the best she could do. As she reached for the bedside lamp, the shape lurched forward – only an inch but enough for Bobbie to squeal and grind her spine even harder into the bed frame. 'Why are you doing this?' Another tear ran down her cheek. 'I'm . . . I'm trying to help you . . .'

The figure was statue-still, although the duvet rose and fell with the dead girl's breaths. Just like with the spider, Bobbie tried to rationalise that this thing in her bed couldn't hurt her, but one look at the scars on her arms said otherwise. Regardless, she had to face her, get a proper look at the girl who was haunting her. 'Tell me, Mary. Tell me what I'm supposed to do . . .' Her head felt hollow and dizzy, and her hand trembled, but she reached for the quilt. It was time. Tears flowed to her lips and she tasted their saltiness.

It was some kind of reflex, but as she took the edge of the duvet, she emitted a scream, like all the adrenaline took physical form in her throat. In one swift matador flick, she whipped the cover off. Like a hoary stage magician's act, the solid form under the sheet evaporated into thin air. There was nothing, and no one, under the blanket.

No, that wasn't right. Even in the darkness, and even without her glasses, Bobbie saw a shape at the bottom of the tangled bed sheets. Naya *now* awoke, snuffling to life. Bobbie wondered if Mary had somehow kept her unconscious. Twisting in bed, Bobbie clicked the lamp on and reached for her glasses. 'What's up?' Naya groaned.

'She was here.'

'What?'

'In my bed.'

Naya sat bolt upright. 'You're kidding.'

'Do I look like I'm kidding?' Bobbie wiped the tears from her face and gingerly took the corner of the item at the foot of her bed. In the light, she could see it was a book of some sort, with a plain London-bus-red cover.

'What's that?'

'I . . . I think she left it for me.' Bobbie pulled it out of the sheets by its corner. It was an exercise book, totally different from the ones they used though. It looked old, antique almost; the pages had that tea-stained effect, only in this case no tea was required. Bobbie assumed it was Mary's book and flicked it open. The handwriting was an immaculate cursive script, somehow girlier than Bobbie was expecting. It looked to be some sort of jotter or notebook – filled with doodles and 'love calculator' equations. Nearly all of them were testing boys' compatibility with Mary Worthington. Bobbie turned the page to see a particularly cruel (not to mention *crude*, given the nature of the illustration) drawing of a girl who could only be Mary – why would she draw mean self-portraits? It was only then Bobbie thought to check the name on the front.

It belonged to one Judy Frier. Judy? That was familiar. It took Bobbie a second to think where she'd heard the name before – the dream in the girls' toilet. Judy Frier was one of Mary's tormentors.

DAY FOUR

Chapter 18

Judy

Bobbie set her alarm extra-early the next morning, not that she really slept after her night-time encounter. Her eyelids felt gluey when the alarm went off at six, but she forced herself up, ignoring the seasick feeling in her tummy.

The first thing she did was access the Piper's Hall alumni pages on her phone, a painstaking task given the meagre phone reception so near the cliffs. By half hanging out of the window, she attracted sufficient signal to load the website and search for Judy Frier. This answered two questions. One: Judy had been a pupil from 1949 to 1955. That at least narrowed down Mary's time at the school. Two: Judy had never left Oxsley. Her page proudly announced she was 'born and bred' and, until she retired, had been the Head of a local primary school.

For whatever reason, Mary was pointing the way to this woman. It wasn't a lot, but it was something. With a day left, Bobbie wasn't going to look any gift clue in the mouth.

The second thing she did was Google 'phantom objects'. By

this point, Naya was awake and doing sit-ups on the dorm floor, noisily puffing and panting. 'You're insane,' Bobbie reminded her.

'I have put on like three pounds!' Naya complained. 'I want my washboard abs back!'

Bobbie tutted. After scrolling past a load of paranormal forum trash, she clicked on a wiki labelled 'Apport'. Turned out, this was a 'thing' – at least to parapsychologists. According to the page, an apport was the 'paranormal transference of an object from one place to another or from an unknown source'. The phenomenon was related to poltergeist activity. No kidding. There were also a few YouTube videos of infrared cameras recording such ghostly activity: cups sliding across counters; drawers sliding open of their own accord; toys mysteriously stacking themselves into neat piles.

Shaking off a fresh wave of heebie-jeebies, she turned to Naya. 'Nay, have you been having weird dreams?'

'No, Ma'am.'

'You're sure?'

'Sure I'm sure. I'm off for a jog. Coming?'

'Are you kidding?'

'If a terrifying mirror ghost comes for me, I wanna be able to outrun her!' She grabbed a water bottle and swished out of the dorm.

The final thing Bobbie did was text Caine. Whether Dr Price was watching her like a hawk or not, she'd rather be expelled than dead. They'd have to use the same trick as yesterday and hope for the best. To Bobbie's surprise (and also delight), Caine texted back almost right away, something Naya had led her to believe (a) almost never happened and (b) meant that a guy kind of liked you.

'Sure. I got car today. More weird dreams?' he replied.

'Worse. Had a visit. Got a new clue.' She debated putting an X but noted he hadn't so she left it professional. The strict business of ghost hunting.

'Cool. Same time n place,' came his response. Still no kiss. Which was fine. JUST FINE. Bobbie threw her phone onto the bed and went to shower before the early-morning rush began.

With Exeat starting early, the school would be manic today: most girls leaving as soon as lessons finished and some getting collected even earlier. Not surprisingly, once news of Sadie's disappearance had become common knowledge, a number of parents couldn't get their kids out fast enough: a few girls had gone home last night. In all the chaos, Bobbie hoped sneaking out and in again might be easier today.

She locked herself in the shower room and peeled off her robe. Not even caring if Mary was in the mirror (although she *couldn't* see her), Bobbie examined the phantom scratches. She grimaced. They had spread. The wounds now covered her collar bone, ribs and thighs. She was covered in sore little lines. It made no sense. All she could think was that Mary *had* cut herself – it wasn't too uncommon amongst the current pupils, with some hardly bothering to hide the scars at all. Bobbie didn't understand, but certainly didn't judge. But in those cases, the girls seemed to cut their arms or legs and there was usually some order to it, even neatness. These marks seemed utterly random – all different sizes and locations. There was a madness to it, an insanity.

One thing seemed pretty clear to Bobbie. This was why Bloody Mary was bloody.

After she'd showered (and discovered that no amount of soap removes ghostly wounds), Bobbie changed into jeans and a flea-market woolly jumper, and slipped out of Piper's Hall with ease, blending in with a small group of girls being collected early for Exeat. With other girls out of uniform it was about a million times easier than it had been yesterday.

The process was aided by the freezing-cold mist that invaded from the sea. It rolled across the front lawns and driveway as thick as dry ice, straight out of Jack the Ripperville. Bobbie could barely see a metre in front of her and had a sudden fear of the cliff edge creeping up on her unawares.

Caine was parked in the same spot as yesterday, next to the leaning signpost pointing to the school on one arrow, Oxsley in the opposite direction and the coastal path in the other. This time the car was a true Barbie-mobile – a pearl-colour soft-top VW Beetle. This *had* to be Caine's mum's car. Sure enough, as she stumbled into the passenger seat, she noticed a load of cuddly toys lined up in front of the rear windscreen and cushions on the back seat. 'Nice ride,' she smirked.

'Do you like my Beanie Babies?' Caine grinned back. Bobbie laughed and he immediately looked wounded. 'I'm not kidding. They really are mine. I collect 'em.'

'Oh. I'm sorry, I –'

'I'm totally kidding, you muppet.'

Bobbie breathed a sigh of relief. 'Just drive, foolish young man.'

They drove deep into grey, murky countryside, taking the bends with excruciating precision as the fog refused to lift. The headlights failed to cut through it, and the trees lining the twisting roads were becoming more and more bony as they gave up the last dead leaves they clung to.

Squirming in her seat as she did so, Bobbie relayed the events of last night to Caine, who, to his credit, accepted everything she said without question. 'Man, that's messed up. In your bed?'

'Yep. I may never sleep again. The closer we get, the worse it's becoming.'

Caine took his eyes off the road for a second to look at her and they were full of concern. 'You're getting it worse than the rest of us.'

That hadn't really occurred to her until that moment. 'Yeah, I guess so. Haven't you seen anything else?'

Caine shifted uncomfortably. 'There is one thing . . .'

'Go on.'

'Take a look at my phone.' It rested on the dashboard, so Bobbie picked it up and swiped the touchscreen open. 'Look at the pics.'

Bobbie raised an eyebrow. 'Do I want to be doing this?' God only knew what sort of gallery a seventeen-year-old boy's phone contained.

'It's safe. Kinda.' Bobbie did as instructed. The photo gallery started, as ever, at the most recent images.

They were all of Caine. Of Caine sleeping peacefully, face down in his pillow.

'Who took these?'

A pause. 'Who do you think?'

'Oh God.' Bobbie gulped. 'It's like . . . it's like she *wants* you or something.' Bobbie recalled how much Mary had wanted the teacher, how all-consuming it had been, and couldn't help but wonder what that meant for Caine. It was like the dead girl was fixated on them, never letting either of them out of her sights. Spirit stalker, much? With each passing day, Mary's power seemed to increase – becoming more intrusive, more *impossible*, as they counted down to the fifth day. By tomorrow, who knew how powerful she'd be. What she'd do to them.

Caine went on. 'And I'm still dreaming. It's like they're getting louder in my head, you know what I mean?'

Bobbie nodded. 'Yeah. What happens in yours?'

More shifting. Definitely uncomfortable. 'They're pretty X-rated, man. I can't tell you . . .'

'Because I'm a girl? I'm not a nun, Caine.'

He blushed. 'It's not that, they're just pretty hot and heavy. It's not . . . it's not what I'm like. My mum taught me how to treat women right.'

Bobbie didn't know what to say. She hadn't believed a word of Grace's mark-my-territory warning, but she sort of *had* assumed that Caine was a 'lad's lad' – a polite word for 'slut' that girls don't get the benefit of. It was an absolute given that he'd have more *experience* than her. 'Caine. I need to know what you've seen. It might help. Somehow.'

'Okay,' he sighed. 'Well, I'm not me, that's for sure – for one thing I'm white. I'm with a girl, although I can't see her face. It's like I'm in the dark and I get these flashes of images. I can see trees, and the moon sort of coming through them. Pale skin – like a girl's back or her tummy or neck. It's cold, but I'm hot and sweaty, like it's running down my back. I'm . . . um . . . definitely naked and so is she and we're . . . you know. The weirdest thing is, we're on a stone thing. I think it's the graveyard.'

'Our graveyard?' She wasn't sure when it had become *theirs*, but the words left her mouth before she could halt them.

'Yeah, I think so.'

'Graveyard sex. Dignified and not-at-all creepy.'

Caine grinned. 'Ha! You just said sex!'

'Child!' She playfully punched his bicep. 'My dreams are edging out of PG territory too.'

'For real?'

'No, er . . . sweatiness, but in the dream, I'm Mary. I'm . . . she's in love with a member of staff. A teacher, I guess.'

'Ew, skanky.'

Bobbie allowed herself a small smile. 'I know. At first I thought it was pretty hot, but now I'm not so sure. I mean, he was so much older than her. It freaked me out a little – he was totally taking advantage of her.'

'What a perv.'

She sighed. 'It's not like he's a dirty old man. From Mary's point of view, it didn't feel *wrong*. Right or wrong aside, it was what Mary wanted. She was into it in a major way.'

'Wow. Pretty kinky.' He smiled back and said no more. Bobbie became aware of a now familiar heat inside. Suddenly there seemed to be less air in the car; in fact the whole vehicle felt smaller and Bobbie was very aware of their proximity. She really wanted to touch Caine, put a hand on his thigh the way the teacher had touched her in the dream. She resisted the urge. Caine finally spoke, changing the subject and clearing the hot haze from the air. 'According to your directions, we should be there.'

Bobbie squinted through the fog. High hedgerows towered over them on both sides, closing in around them. The car shot past a narrow opening in the hedge through which Bobbie caught a glimpse of a cottage. 'Stop!' she urged. 'I think we just went past it.'

'Oh. Okay. I need to find somewhere to park.' The nearest layby was about two minutes down the lane. Caine parked up and they walked the rest of the way back towards the cottage. Judy, it seemed, lived in the middle of nowhere – a remote thatched cottage on the periphery of a clump of trees. Somewhere close by a fast-flowing stream sounded like applause. It was so peaceful out here.

Bobbie pushed through a creaking wooden gate and followed the uneven flagstone path to the front door. The picturesque cottage, cute as it was, was somehow foreboding, reminding Bobbie of the gingerbread house. With a last wary look at Caine, she tapped the lion's-head knocker. After a minute and no response, she tried again. 'Oh God, she *has* to be in,' Bobbie moaned, a new sense of hopelessness washing over her.

'Can I help you?' said a voice from behind them. Both she and Caine sprang back in cartoon surprise.

'You scared me,' Bobbie said, hand to her chest.

An elderly woman had come around the side of the cottage. Her white cotton-wool hair was swept up into a bird's nest atop her head and she wore a wax jacket, with pink fleece-lined slippers on her feet. In her hand she held a bucket of chicken

184

feed. 'Is this a penny-for-the-guy thing? There's a sign on the letter box that says I don't want nuisance calls. Or menus for that matter – I don't care for pizza *or* curry thank you very much.'

Bobbie pulled herself back together, remembering her finest Piper's Hall manners. 'I'm sorry to disturb you, but are you Judy Frier?'

Shrewd grey-blue eyes narrowed behind glasses even thicker than her own. 'I haven't been Frier for forty-five years. I'm Judy Ledger. Who's asking?'

'Hi. I'm Bobbie and this is Caine. I'm from Piper's Hall.'

The old woman smiled. 'Crikey, are they delivering the newsletter by hand now? I didn't realise it was required reading.'

Bobbie smiled – Judy took the 'Piper's Legacy' about as seriously as she did then. 'I . . . we need to talk to you about something that happened a long time ago. It's about Mary Worthington.'

At the mere mention of the name, the colour drained from Judy's cheeks. She looked to the path underneath her feet. 'Goodness me, it's a long time since I heard that name. You'd better come inside.'

Through the patio doors, Bobbie could see the gaggle of chickens picking grain from the cracks in the paving. They sat at a simple wooden table in the centre of a slate floor, with low-beamed ceilings creating a dark yet cosy cottage feel. There was fresh bread in the oven as Judy carried over the teapot.

'So are you related to Mary or something? Is she your grandmother?'

'God no,' Caine blurted out, helping himself to a third Hobnob.

'I thought not.' Judy joined them at the table. 'I admit, I never thought I'd hear that name again – such a long time ago. So long ago it doesn't quite feel real – like that entire period was a story someone once told me.'

Judy poured tea into Bobbie's cup. Bobbie said, 'I know this must sound really weird, but we need to know anything at all you can tell us about Mary.'

Pouring a cup for herself, Judy said: 'It's more than sixty years ago, my dear. Ooh, this tea's a bit anaemic.'

'I know . . . but anything might be helpful.'

The old woman regarded her over the top of the china cup. 'Something's wrong, isn't it?'

Bobbie's stomach flipped, but she knew she couldn't tell her the truth – they'd be out on their ears in seconds. 'What makes you think that?'

Judy pursed her thin, lined mouth and took a sip of tea as if readying herself for confession. 'When I was a teacher, there were always the good kids and the rogues. That's just children for you, isn't it? But every once in a blue moon, there was a little boy or girl who was that bit different. Something dark in their eyes – they'd look right through you and it'd chill you to the bone. They simply lacked *kindness*. Sometimes even their own mothers were wary of them. Mary was one such girl. There was something *not quite right* about her, you know? From the first time you saw her, it was quite apparent.'

'How do you mean?' Caine muttered.

'I wish I could say it was *this* or *that*, but it was more of a feeling. When she was around, it was . . . unsettling. Gosh, how to describe it? Rather like when you find you've swam out too far from the shore – that sudden sensation of being out of your depth.'

Caine shrugged. 'I don't get it.'

'And nor did we. But being around her was . . . again, unsettling.'

'Is that why you were so mean to her?' Bobbie didn't know why she said it so abruptly, knowing full well it was rude, but she supposed she wanted an honest reaction.

Judy smiled sadly. 'Nothing could excuse how cruel we were to her. Once you realise you've been something of a bully, you don't ever stop feeling guilty.'

'So why did you do it?'

She threw her hands up. 'It's school! I was a teacher for fifty years and the places never change. It's survival of the fittest and all that jazz. There will always be the Susan Fletchers and Mary Worthingtons.' Grace's Venus flytrap smile instantly flashed into Bobbie's head. 'It's curious though – do you know what happened to Susan Fletcher once we left Piper's Hall?'

Bobbie shook her head.

'Absolutely nothing. Nothing at all. At school she was a queen, and then . . . nothing. The rest of the world had plenty of pretty schoolgirls, thank you very much, and she was surplus to requirements. Once you leave that school, nothing really matters any more.'

Bobbie bit her tongue to stop herself from saying there wouldn't be a future beyond tomorrow for her and Caine unless they stopped Mary. 'But what happened to Mary?'

'You tell me, dear. She vanished.'

'Vanished? Brilliant.' Caine scowled.

'Oh I felt so guilty. I think even Susan did, deep down, although she never said anything.'

'What happened?' Bobbie held her breath.

Judy paused to mull her next sentence. 'What you have to understand about Mary Worthington is that she arrived under a black cloud. She appeared at Piper's Hall one day, without a word as to where she'd come from, so naturally there were questions. Rumours.'

'What sort of rumours?'

'Gosh, I do hope you're planning on becoming either a detective or a journalist, young lady.' Bobbie smiled but said nothing, willing Judy to continue. 'There were so many it was impossible to separate fact from fiction. Some people said she was an orphan, some people said her parents were in jail – goodness, some people said she'd fled Europe in the war. Some people went so far as to say . . .' Judy trailed off.

'Say what?'

'Oh nonsense. Mumbo jumbo about gypsies and curses and devils. All I know is that when that girl arrived, a shadow fell over our school. It had nothing to do with what she looked like – she was very beautiful in her own way – but it was that *feeling*. That awful, ominous feeling that accompanied her everywhere she went.'

'When did she vanish?'

'It was 1954, I remember it so clearly. I don't know if it was true, but Mary gained quite a reputation for herself. Susan took it upon herself to spread the rumour that she was sneaking into Oxsley and, well, *seeing* young men. Now that wasn't especially unusual. Contrary to what you may have heard, even back then we were all partial to a spot of . . . bother, shall we say, but Mary was often found loitering in the churchyard at St Paul's. It was queer.'

Bobbie remembered Sadie's original tale. Even though it had only been last Saturday night, it felt like a lifetime ago. 'You think she ran off with a guy?' It hadn't even occurred to Bobbie that Mary might have been seeing more than one person.

Judy dipped her head. 'That was the most popular explanation.'

'She didn't hang herself?' Caine sprayed crumbs as he spoke.

'Hang herself? Oh goodness me, no. At least not that we ever knew about.'

Bobbie and Caine shared a glance. That poured water on the official version of events. 'What do *you* think happened?'

'Mary had such a difficult time at Piper's Hall. I wasn't surprised when she ran away, but I will say this: as soon as she left, things got better – like a shroud had been lifted. No one missed her, look at it that way.'

Bobbie felt tears prick her eyes. 'She wasn't evil, Mrs Ledger. She was just lonely.'

'And how would you know?'

'Because I know.' Bobbie swallowed back a bitter mouthful of anger and pity. 'She just needed a friend.'

Judy shook her head. 'If you'd been there, you'd have done exactly the same as we did.'

'I doubt that.' Bobbie felt for her rucksack. It was time to go. 'I don't think Mary ran away. I think something happened to her and no one cared enough to find out what.'

Judy looked angry and then just sad. 'We'll never know.'

'We will,' Bobbie said defiantly. As she swung her bag onto her shoulder, she had one final thought. 'Oh. When you were at Piper's Hall, was there a teacher with short reddish hair? A man?'

Judy frowned. 'Well, yes. That was Mr Millar. Kenton Millar.'

Bobbie eyes widened. Oh, she'd been so stupid.

Chapter 19

Immortal

Bobbie and Caine stood together in the empty main hall, with only distant footsteps and giggles for company. They'd lingered in Oxsley until after lessons finished to make sneaking back in less of an issue. Most of the remaining girls were in the Accy Area, Bobbie guessed, either waiting to be collected or bedding in for the long, extended weekend. At her side, Caine had a hood pulled over his head. 'If anyone asks, you're a very butch Upper, got that?'

'Do I have a name?'

Bobbie smiled. 'Pretend to be Naya.'

'Sure thang,' he said in the worst American accent Bobbie had ever heard. 'What are we looking at?'

Bobbie pointed up at the oil painting. The hair had receded, and there was a neatly groomed ginger beard, but she was pointing at a portrait of Kenton Millar, former head teacher.

'That's the guy in the dream?'

'Yep. I'm such a freaking idiot. I have looked at, slash ignored, that picture every day for the last five years and I didn't even recognise him in my dream.'

'I guess he was younger.'

'Yeah, but still.' Bobbie blushed. He had literally been under, or rather above, her nose the whole time. 'We have a whole wing named after him.'

'And you really think he was getting it on with Mary?'

'I'm certain.' Of course, they'd asked Judy if it was possible, but she'd dismissed the suggestion. Of all the rumours circulating about Mary Worthington, the possibility of a sordid affair with a teacher wasn't one of them. Bobbie did question if her dreams were mere fantasies, but she *knew* they were more than that – she'd *smelled* Kenton Millar's cologne.

'When was he in charge?'

'According to this he was Head from 1974 to 1985.'

'How old did he look in your dream?'

'Young. He can't have been teaching for very long in 1954.'

'Man, why do girls always fancy the teachers – even if they're fug?'

Bobbie turned to him. 'I don't. The whole thing creeps me out.'

'Really?'

'Yes, really! But I guess it's a whole big power trip. Or daddy issues – which I don't have. Hardly surprising given that my dad was an anonymous Hungarian dude with a plastic beaker.'

Caine looked to her for permission to laugh, which she gave him with a smile. 'Sorry. I shouldn't find it amusing.'

'Are you kidding? If you think my dad's funny, wait till you meet my mum!'

That silenced them both. As Bobbie understood it, meeting the parents is a big deal. At least it would be if there was a future for either of them.

Bobbie dragged focus back onto Mary. 'Caine, it was *wrong*. He was her teacher . . . and she was so lonely. Vulnerable.' Bobbie glared up at the smug 'gaze into the future' face Millar wore. For them there was no future to gaze into. Sighing, she pulled herself onto the stage at the furthest end of the empty hall, letting her legs dangle over the side. 'This is useless. I don't know why Mary wanted us to see Judy so much . . . we're no closer.'

'We are.' Caine joined her on the stage, keeping his hood up. 'We know that she didn't kill herself.'

'No, we don't. We just know that she didn't kill herself *here* . . .'

'It's still something.'

'We . . . we're running out of time,' Bobbie said mournfully. As ridiculous as it seemed, she'd never really noticed how much she liked being alive until this week. It was the ultimate 'taken for granted'. 'I really, really don't wanna die.'

If she was being really honest, this week was the first time she had even felt truly alive. In her attempt to blend in and go unnoticed, she saw now that she'd lived a beige existence, only coming to life through her fiction. She was a fictional girl. This week, as awful and scary as it had been, she'd *felt* every minute and now she didn't want it to end. That was in no small part because of this strange new creature next to her.

'Me either,' Caine admitted, staring at his hands.

'Like, I don't know about you, but I totally took things for granted. It's not just this week. I've been counting down the days at this school. I've been waiting for five years for this purgatory to end so I could start living, but now there isn't going to be a life to live. I haven't done anything, Caine. I've literally achieved nothing except a few grades and some stories under my bed.'

'Man, that's bleak.'

'You should read the stories sometime.'

Caine smirked. 'If we get through tomorrow I'll read anything you've got, and I *never* read.'

'Thanks.'

'My mum is always talking this "live in the now" chat. I guess this is what she means. Don't put stuff off that you can do today.'

'Because you might be dead,' Bobbie finished. 'It's a bit late to start a bucket list I suppose.'

'What would you do?'

Bobbie knew what she *wanted* to do, but wouldn't even know how to go about getting it. 'I dunno. I never thought about what I actually wanted to do. I thought there'd be infinite time to work it all out.' It was true. The two things that Bobbie had taken for granted were that she had time and choices. As it happened, she had neither. It felt so stupid and so, so childish – she'd almost seen herself as immortal.

'It's a conundrum,' Caine said from out of nowhere.

'Steady there with the big words. What do you mean?'

'If we hadn't done the stupid dare, we'd have never met. But because of the stupid dare, we won't find out what happens next.'

'I'm not sure that's strictly a conundrum, but I see what you mean.' Bobbie took off her glasses and rubbed a speck from the lens. 'Anyway, what do you mean, "what happens next"?'

Caine looked at her out of the corner of his eye, too coy to face her. It was too cute to be legal. 'You know, if we're a thing or not.'

Bobbie's heart flung itself around her chest like a gleeful Labrador puppy. 'Would you want us to be "a thing"?'

This time he did look her right in the eye and it was more than she could stand. 'Yeah, I reckon I would.'

'I would too.' Bobbie couldn't even pretend to be cool; the words came out high and light like she was a scared little girl, and wasn't she just.

Caine leaned in closer and she could feel his warm breath on her cheek. 'I'd better live in the now then, hadn't I?' They met in the middle and she closed her eyes, hoping above all else that kissing was something you could be innately good at the first time you tried it. The graveyard didn't count – this was the real deal. No ghosts, no spells.

They kissed.

So this was what kissing was like. It was warm and intensely intimate. In her head it was at once both noisy and quiet – the kiss blocking out everything else.

It was all about his lips.

As they brushed against hers, as light and airy as feathers, she started to worry about the Frenchness of the kiss. She thought it best to follow his lead and when he parted his lips, she did the same.

This was the best feeling she'd ever experienced. It was

no small wonder all the other girls were so keen. Bobbie was briefly annoyed at herself for not giving it a go sooner before letting herself melt into Caine's embrace, lose herself to him. She finally let herself touch him, her hand sliding under the rim of his hoodie. The skin was smooth and hot and he shuddered under her touch. She took that as a good sign.

His lips curled into a smile. All things considered, for a first attempt, Bobbie was quite proud of her efforts. He tucked her hair behind her ear and, smiling, went in for round two. The kiss was a door into something completely new. She wasn't sure what waited on the other side and she didn't care. She felt a sense of graduation.

Before they could get back into their rhythm, a familiar sound brought her back with a bump onto this astral plane. Her phone sounded harsh and horribly indelicate next to the wonder of the kiss. 'That's me,' she said apologetically.

'That's okay. I'm not going anywhere,' he said. 'Not yet anyway.'

Bobbie took out her phone. A local landline number was displayed. 'Hello?' she answered.

'Oh hello, is that Bobbie? It's Judy Ledger here.'

Bobbie had left her number just in case. 'Oh hi. It's Judy,' she told Caine.

'I'm sorry I wasn't more helpful earlier, but something else occurred to me after you'd left. It was a silly thing. Just more gossip, I'm sure.'

Bobbie still felt flustered from the kiss, like it had turned her brain to love-mush or something. 'Oh, okay. Like what?'

'Well, a lot of the girls, when she vanished . . . you have to understand, Bobbie, having a baby out of wedlock back then was a very different affair to how it is now.'

Bobbie caught up to the same page. 'Oh . . . you mean that Mary was . . .'

'Yes. People were saying that Mary was pregnant.'

Chapter 20

Ever Closer

'Quick – the coast's clear.' Bobbie hauled Caine out of the secret passage staircase and into Brontë House. Bobbie thought about how most of the Piper's Hall Ladies were now at home, eating Mum-cooked food and sitting in front of proper fires and widescreen TVs.

They didn't stop until they were safely inside the dorm. Naya was waiting anxiously by the door. The second they crossed the threshold, she slammed the door shut behind them.

'I can't breathe.' Caine was bent double, hand on his heart.

They were greeted by a mightily unimpressed side-eye. 'Having a sleepover with a guy,' Naya pouted, responding to a text Bobbie had sent her earlier. 'Gotta say, this expulsion plan of yours is right on track.'

Bobbie brushed her off. 'We need to stick together. I don't know why. We just do.'

'Mum's on a night shift tonight.' Caine told Naya the same thing he'd told her. Yes, having him sleep over was an insane risk, but it seemed a whole lot less deadly than letting him sleep in an empty house.

Naya relented. 'Whatever. I lifted as much food as I could from the cafeteria. The dinner lady must think I'm a hoarder or compulsive eater or something.' She pointed to the array of wrapped sandwiches, crisps and yoghurts on the writing desk under the window. Quite the midnight feast.

Kicking her trainers off, Bobbie flopped onto her bed, crossing her legs, Buddha style. 'This is finally starting to make some sort of sense.'

'It is?' Naya uncurled a hoop earring while Caine propped himself against her bed on the floor.

'Yeah! If Mary was pregnant that explains the baby crying in Mark's video for one thing, but it also gives her a reason for running away.'

Caine nodded. 'Did they have workhouses in 1954? I bet she went to one.'

Bobbie stroked his head, her smitten hands reluctant to be anywhere other than on Caine. 'Wrong century, but nice try.'

'Would she have been able to have an abortion back then?' Naya asked, mirroring her stance on her own bed.

'I don't know,' confessed Bobbie. 'I'm guessing even if it was legal, it probably wasn't something you chatted about over brunch with your sassy gal pals.'

Naya suddenly shot about a foot in the air. 'You know *Dirty Dancing*?'

'Yes . . .' Bobbie looked to Caine, unsure of where this was going. His head rested against her calf and for now that was enough, but she estimated she'd jettisoned approximately twelve per cent of her brain functioning to lingering memories of the kiss.

If Naya was noticing the ever-increasing closeness between them, their need to be within a millimetre of each other, she didn't acknowledge it. Bobbie suspected she'd get the interrogation once they were alone. Whether their future held gossip sessions remained to be seen. 'Well, in *Dirty Dancing*, the dancer, Penny, gets a backstreet abortion from some quack and almost dies.'

Bobbie processed the theory and it tested well. 'That's not a bad idea. If she was young and scared and desperate, perhaps she would have done anything to get rid of the baby.'

'But that's not what you saw in the dream,' Caine reminded her. 'You said that Mary was happy when she was with Millar.'

'Yeah.' Bobbie frowned before quickly filling her room-mate in on the identity of Mary's potential secret lover. She now understood the bliss that Mary had shared with her teacher, because she'd had her first taster during the kiss in the hall, like a child sneaking a sip of champagne at a wedding. Mary's dreams were like an Instagram picture of the same high-def multi-colour explosion she'd just experienced first-hand. There was nothing in the dreams to make her think Mary was anything other than enamoured with Millar. But she *was* lonely, and perhaps if she was tired of being alone . . . 'Maybe she had the baby . . .'

'Maybe she had the baby and DIED IN CHILDBIRTH!' said Naya with an inappropriate level of morbid glee. 'That was huge back then.'

'My God, you are full of gruesome factettes tonight!'

Bobbie pulled a distasteful face. 'But it's also a good idea. It's all connected. Mary, Millar, her baby. We're getting close now, really, really super-close.'

Caine huffed. He clambered to his feet and poked about in the food Naya had snaffled for them. 'Good thing too, cos we've got less than a day left.'

That dampened the mood to say the least. Bobbie turned to Naya. 'Naya, are you sure you haven't seen anything in your dreams?'

Her friend shrugged, flipping metres of black hair over her head. 'I told you, I haven't dreamed this whole week. Nothing. Nada.'

Caine looked at her doubtfully. 'What? You haven't had a dream all week? As if.'

'Well . . . I don't know. It's like I am dreaming – you know how you know you've had a dream? But there's nothing happening.'

'Eh?' Caine picked the salad out of a ham salad sandwich, grimacing at the abundance of mustard.

'In the dream there's nothing – just a big black blob. It's cold though.'

Bobbie sat up straighter. 'That *is* a dream. You're dreaming you're in a cold, dark place somewhere.'

'Maybe. I'm not moving though. Like I'm stuck.'

Ice crept up the vertebrae of her spine. 'Stuck? Or buried?'

Naya shuddered. 'I . . . I don't know. I guess. I hadn't thought of it that way . . . but yeah.'

Caine swallowed a mouthful of his sandwich before discarding the rest. 'Okay, that's messed up.'

'Oh God, I don't wanna think about it.' Naya hugged herself.

Now Bobbie couldn't think of anything else (except for that twelve per cent). *What happened, Mary*, she thought to herself. *Is this it? Is this all you're giving us?* They'd been given five days – five days might not be enough.

'What do we do now?' Caine asked.

'I don't know. We can't risk wandering around the school. The fact that no one's seen you is a miracle.' With most of the girls now away until Monday, the school was quieter than normal so Mrs Craddock would be all the more focused on the few who remained. 'I think we should get rid of the mirror somehow.' Bobbie motioned at the wardrobe. The thought of the cupboard door creaking open in the middle of the night . . .

'You're right,' Naya agreed. 'How do you want to do it?'

It turned out the thing was screwed inside the door. It only took a couple of minutes to unscrew the bolts holding it in place. If Mary was in the mirror, Bobbie couldn't see her this time, but she avoided looking right at the reflection. She and Naya took hold of the glass and carried it like a stretcher to the Accy Area while Caine hid back in their room. They were spotted by a chubby Lower, who was dismissed with an unnecessarily strong word from Naya. 'Come on,' Naya said, leaning the mirror up against the wall. 'We shouldn't leave you-know-who alone up there.'

'Wait.' Bobbie hung back. 'There's something I need to do.' Checking no one was in earshot, Bobbie doubled back to the Lodge, not even turning the light on. Naya returned to their room so Caine wasn't tempted to come looking for them.

Bobbie took a deep breath and dialled her mother's number.

Her mum answered on the fourth ring. 'Hello, darling, how are you?'

'I'm okay. Are you busy?'

'No, no, it's fine. We're on a break. Between you and me, darling, Jared's being an absolute pain. He won't do a thing unless the director fools him into thinking it's his idea.' Bobbie smiled. Elsewhere, life went on exactly as normal. If she should die, in time, her mother would still be her mother. 'What's new with you?'

'Nothing. I just wanted to say sorry for being so weird when I last spoke to you.'

'Don't be silly. It's what I'm here for! I was worried, sweetie. You so rarely ask me for things, I seriously thought about booking myself onto the red-eye.'

Bobbie closed her eyes. She would *not* cry. Her last conversation with her mum would not be a tearful one. 'Don't do that. I'm fine.'

'Are you sure? Isn't it late for you, darling? Shouldn't you be in bed?' In the background, she heard someone shout 'Five minutes!' and the wail of an NYC ambulance. It sounded noisy, like her mum was on the street, probably with a bucket-sized latte and a cigarette.

Bobbie hadn't prepared a speech and sort of wished she had. Last words are supposed to be epic, moving and memorable. She had nothing. 'Mum, I'm fine. I don't want you to worry about me, like ever, because I'm fine. So you just have a good time and don't even think about me.'

'Are you a bit drunk, sweetie?'

She laughed. 'No, I'm not. I just thought I'd have a go at saying what I really think for once.'

'You should. I taught you to always express yourself.'

'You did. So basically, I love you.' That was so not a British thing to do and it felt ridiculous coming out of her mouth. 'I really do.'

This time her mother laughed. 'Well, I don't know what's come over you, Bobbie Rowe, but I like it. I love you too. More than anything in the whole wide world.'

Oh, it could be worse, Bobbie thought. Who said a life had to be *long* in order for it to be considered a success. She was probably going to die tomorrow, but she did feel *loved*. She always had. That was an achievement. 'Okay, Mum, I have to go.' More or less the truth of the situation. She wouldn't cheat her with a *catch you later* or *speak soon*. 'Goodbye, Mum.' Turns out, knowing it's your last goodbye doesn't make it any easier.

When she'd dried her eyes (her resolve had crumbled the second she hung up) and returned to the dorm, Caine had his back to the wall on her bed, legs up with his elbows balancing on his knees. He was chatting to Naya but broke off to ask a question. 'You think we should have smashed it?'

'I think we've chanced enough bad luck with mirrors, don't you?' Bobbie half smiled, hoping it didn't show that she'd just lost half her body weight in tears. 'I don't need another seven years on top of this week.'

Caine returned her smile, gazing out from under dark brows. 'There's no way I'm sleeping. What if she comes in the night?'

'Totally,' Naya agreed. 'We could sleep in shifts?'

He shook his head. 'No way. I don't wanna die in my sleep

like some old granddad. If she comes . . . if she comes, I'm putting up a fight.'

A silence followed in which it went unsaid that Bobbie and Naya wouldn't take it lying down either. This was it. *One more sleep.* The thought of what the morning might bring was too much for her weary brain to process. On the other side of tonight *something* awaited. When the quiet became too much to bear, Bobbie said, a glint in her eye, 'Does anyone know any ghost stories?'

DAY FIVE

Chapter 21

Unexpected

Eventually, Bobbie could no longer resist the heaviness in her eyelids and she drifted off. One moment she was listening to Naya recount her near-death experience in a Brooklyn drive-by and the next she was in the graveyard.

It was a sweltering, humid night, the damp air kissing her skin. A welcome, much-needed breeze rustled the summer leaves as she ran through the woods, her gingham summer dress brushing her thighs. She was giggling. He was chasing her – hide and seek. Bobbie knew this wasn't the first time they'd been here; this was their special place – a place they could meet away from the prying eyes of Piper's Hall.

Bobbie ducked behind a tree, her hand over her mouth to muffle her laughter. *He won't find me now*. Of course, she very much wanted to be found. When she could no longer hear his footsteps, she chanced a peek around the thick trunk only to find him ready for her on the other side. With a lion-like roar, he pounced, and she fell into his arms.

He spun her around and around, pirouetting between the gravestones. This part of the churchyard was hidden from the eyes of the school *and* the church by the trees and hedgerows. *Their place.*

With a warm hand, he cupped Bobbie's face. Tonight his flannel sleeves were rolled to his elbow and she wore only the Piper's summer dress and open-toed sandals. Her hair was down, free. No longer shy with him, she kissed his lips first, hungrily seeking his tongue. With one strong arm he lifted her effortlessly onto a long, flat sarcophagus. Bobbie lay back, grateful of the cool stone on her hot, sticky legs. Kenton climbed atop her. As he nuzzled her neck, landing kiss after kiss on her skin, she opened her eyes long enough to see over his shoulder and wonder at the smattering of stars in the night sky. She'd never seen so many, and it felt like they were all out for them.

An exquisite shiver rippled through her body, and she let herself go.

Bobbie awoke with a start, and tugged hair out of her face like cobwebs. She mistook her duvet for Millar, frantically pushing it off. It took her a second to realise where she was. So much for not falling asleep. Half fearing Mary to be in her bed again, she whipped her knees up to her chest, sitting upright.

The dream had frightened her – as much as any ghostly scars or visions in the mirror. She felt unclean, as if Millar's hands really had been on her skin. It was getting uncomfortably real. Mary may have enjoyed it, but she most certainly did not. *How could Mary have been so stupid?*

The room was still, however. Pearly dawn light seeped under the curtains and two bodies slept peacefully with her: Caine was stretched out on the floor in a sleeping bag, his hands tucked behind his head. Bobbie had the strongest urge to nestle her shoulder under his armpit and use his shoulder as a pillow, to seek comfort in his arms. The sunny feeling inside she got when she was with Caine was the exact opposite of how she'd felt with Millar – that felt as dark and suffocating as tar.

In a weird way she was grateful; Mary had brought her and Caine together. If this was her last week on earth, she could at least say she'd felt *it*. It was like spring had finally arrived after a lifetime of winter. Looking at Caine now, his eyes closed and full lips ever so slightly parted, she finally *got it*.

His eyes opened and Bobbie looked away, hoping he hadn't caught her staring. On the periodic table of creepy, watching people sleep was surely number one. He blinked and frowned, like he was momentarily confused by the alien surroundings before coming to. 'Hey,' he croaked. 'You okay?'

'We're still alive.' Bobbie tucked her hair behind her ear. 'Or Hell is a girls' boarding school.'

'Both could be true,' Naya said, head still facing her pillow. Bobbie knew how she felt. The urge to stay in bed and somehow sleep through to day six was sorely tempting.

'No,' Caine went on, 'I meant your face.' Even with puffy eyes and creased clothes, he was still gorgeous. Bobbie shuddered to think how hideous she must look a minute after waking up. Last night she'd discovered (with some shame) that she didn't own anything even resembling cool or sexy pyjamas. Her baby-blue-with-fluffy-white-cloud flannel pyjamas, unbelievably, were her *least* embarrassing pair.

The concern in his eyes, however, soon outweighed her

embarrassment. 'What? What about my face?'

'You have new cuts on your face.'

Bobbie's hands flew to her cheeks. Aware there wasn't a mirror in the room, she traced her skin. Sure enough there were four or five new scars on her forehead and over her cheekbones. 'Oh God,' she said, and saw panic fill Caine's eyes. 'No. No, it's okay. They don't hurt, I promise.' They did hurt, just a little.

Naya's head twisted towards her. 'You sure, hon?'

Bobbie nodded, although was desperate to see herself. She'd resist the temptation.

'This is it then.' Caine sat up and smoothed his T-shirt down. 'Day five.'

'It feels like any other day,' Bobbie noted. The birds were as chatty as ever in the trees outside their window, gossiping away without a care.

'I sort of didn't expect it to get light,' Caine admitted. 'I stayed awake until the sun came up, just in case.' Maybe he'd watched her sleeping. Oddly, she didn't mind. It made her feel safe.

'Sorry for nodding off.' Bobbie put her glasses on. 'I couldn't help it.'

'No worries.' Caine looked a lot like he wanted to join her on her bed. 'So what do we do now?'

Bobbie climbed off her bed and pulled open the curtains to a swear word from Naya. It was another foggy, drizzle-soaked day. Just a Thursday. No one else had got the memo about how important this Thursday was. God knew what the birds had to be so chirpy about. 'I don't know, to be honest. I didn't have a plan for if we got this far. There's no lessons today. I

212

guess most of the girls will go into Oxsley or just hang about watching TV.'

Caine didn't look impressed with those options. 'Maybe we have until the end of the day – like a full five days. That still gives us like sixteen hours to work out how to stop this mental witch.'

Bobbie nodded. 'You're right. I just can't think of what else we can do. I mean, we have exhausted every weird half-clue we've been given. It's almost like Mary doesn't want us to work it out.'

'If she's buried she could be anywhere,' Naya muttered from under her duvet. 'Literally anywhere. What are we meant to do? Start digging?'

Bobbie chuckled. 'It's not a terrible idea.'

Naya pushed the duvet back. 'Are you serious?'

'I didn't mean the digging part, I meant the bit about finding her body.' Bobbie sat at the desk chair and put her glasses on. 'We know Mary was a real-life person because Judy went to school with her, but there aren't any records of her being at the school and she isn't on the alumni pages.'

'Perhaps we could talk to Dr Price?' Naya suggested.

'Hmm. She's suspicious already and she didn't start here until a few years before we did so I don't see how she could help, really. Caine and I looked at the graveyard yesterday and she isn't buried there.'

'That don't mean anything,' Caine said. 'She ran away. She could be buried anywhere. Like anywhere in the world.'

Bobbie narrowed her eyes. 'I think it's something worth considering though. Isn't that like a thing? If you don't lay a body to rest on hallowed ground and all that?'

Caine shrugged. 'I dunno. The graveyard might be worth another look – both me and Bridget dreamed about it.'

Bobbie sighed. 'Me too. Caine, I think our dreams finally matched up last night.'

His eyes widened. 'Yeah?' He blushed. 'Oh right.'

'I see why you didn't want to talk about them . . .'

He glanced up at her and couldn't keep the suggestion of a smile off his lips.

'Oh get a room,' Naya chided. 'Preferably someone else's.' She kicked off her duvet, resigning herself to being awake.

Bobbie's mouth fell open. *No way*. She blinked, but it didn't change a thing. She was really, truly seeing this.

Naya climbed off the bed and Caine backed away, wriggling across the floor in his sleeping bag like he was scared to go anywhere near her.

Naya balked at their reaction. 'What the hell is wrong with –' And then she stopped because, stood up, she could see it too. Her hands shot to cover her mouth. Her breath shook and she whined like a lost, fragile infant.

Naya was heavily, *heavily* pregnant.

Chapter 22

Phantom Pregnancy

Naya pulled up her now-stretched pyjama top and Bobbie's jaw fell further. *It was real.* Naya's olive skin was swollen across her abdomen, her belly button protruding. Under the taut skin, something moved, as if something inside her friend was writhing around, kicking to get free. Something *alive.* 'Oh God!' Naya cried, hands fluttering. 'Oh God!'

Bobbie dragged herself off the mental ledge. Now, more than ever, Naya needed her to keep it together – even if she had to pretend. She shot off the desk chair and took hold of her friend's wrists. 'Naya. Look at me. Try to stay calm.'

'Bobbie . . . Bobbie . . . I'm . . .'

'You're not!' Bobbie shouted louder. 'You're *not!*' Bobbie remembered Naya banging on about her little tummy and weight gain. Oh God – she'd been feeling sick all week too – morning sickness! All this time, Bobbie thought that Naya had got off lightly, but that clearly wasn't the case. What if she *was* . . . ? No, there was *no way*.

'Are you sure you're not . . . ?' Caine asked somewhat sheepishly. Both girls turned to him with disdain. The very mundane question brought them both down a few notches.

'I *can't* be pregnant!' Naya wailed. 'I definitely can't be *this* pregnant!'

'I know, I know.' Bobbie tried to soothe her. Forcing herself to take another look at the freakish bump, Bobbie swore it was smaller than it had been a second ago. The thing inside her kicked again and Bobbie flinched. 'Naya, this is Mary's . . . doing.'

Naya didn't seemed comforted by this news. 'Your cuts are real!'

No. No way. There was *no way* there was a real-life baby inside Naya, but that thought read all over Naya's face. Bobbie tried to steady her, but she pulled away, unwilling to be comforted. 'This isn't the same.'

'Get it out of me!'

'Oh God.' Caine's face was now horribly ashen. Bobbie sighed, she couldn't deal with a full-tilt panicking Naya and a squeamish Caine.

'Caine – don't you freak out on me now!'

'Sorry . . . but this,' he pointed at Naya's belly, 'this is next level.'

'Bobbie, please . . .' Tears rolled down Naya's face.

Bobbie took a deep breath. Her head was pounding, like blood was gushing into her brain too fast. It really did feel like her head might pop. How much more could they take? Mary was *torturing* them. 'Naya, sit down. Someone in your condition shouldn't be standing up.'

'Bobbie. This isn't funny.' The joke actually went some way

to calm her down; instead of hysterical, Naya now looked annoyed.

'I know, but we all need to decompress. This,' she gestured around the room like their panic was a tangible entity, 'isn't helping. This isn't real.'

'It feels real.'

'The dreams felt real. When I thought Mary was in my bed, that seemed real . . . but there was *nothing* under the covers. This is just the same. Literally a phantom pregnancy. There is no way there's a real baby inside you.' Naya wiped her cheeks, this time listening. The swelling seemed to go down further. 'See? She just wants us to know. She's telling us her story.'

'Man, this is so twisted,' Caine said, blinking like a normal human once more.

'I think I've figured it out.' Bobbie knelt at Naya's feet, still holding her hands. 'Why she takes five days. She isn't waiting . . . she's building her strength.'

Naya sniffed. 'What do you mean?'

'On day one, we just had the nosebleeds. Since then, she's become worse and worse, like she's gaining power . . . getting a better grip on us. Look at me. I'm covered in cuts. She can make you seem pregnant.'

'I guess I've got off pretty lightly.' Caine sounded apologetic.

'I'll say.' Bobbie shrugged. She recalled the way Mary had watched Caine sleep and wondered if he was re-enacting the role of Millar – someone for Mary to adore. Or maybe she had more tricks up her sleeve before the day was through. 'But let's not speak too soon. We still have a whole day left.'

Caine didn't look too thrilled at that prospect. 'This means

Judy was right, though. Mary must have been up the duff.'

'Charming.' Naya examined her bump again. It was rising and falling with her breathing, expanding and decreasing like a balloon inside her.

'Is that it, Mary?' Bobbie now spoke to her directly, raising her voice to the ceiling. 'We worked it out! You were pregnant with Kenton Millar's baby! So what now?' Predictably, there came no response. Bobbie wondered if the other Piper's Ladies, the ones from before, had got this far. If they'd even tried. Would Mary give them points for trying? A new thought crossed Bobbie's mind. What if Mary had given birth to a son or daughter? Was that who they were supposed to track down? If so, sixteen hours just wasn't going to cut the mustard.

Naya sprang off the bad and ran her hands over the diminishing bump. 'I think it's going.'

'See? I told you . . . she wanted us to know, to be sure, about the baby, I think.' At this stage, after everything she'd put them through, Bobbie wasn't sure she could vouch any longer for the dead girl's benign nature.

'Okay.' Caine breathed a sigh of relief. 'This doesn't really change anything – we still have to find where Mary's body is. Before it's too late.'

Bobbie nodded.

'I need a shower.' Naya shuddered. 'I feel majorly dirty and weird.'

'No,' Bobbie insisted. 'You can't go to the shower room. There's a mirror in there.'

Naya considered this for a moment. 'The prefects' bathroom has a bath and no mirror.'

'But you're not a prefect.'

Naya wiped her damp cheeks, her spirit returning. 'A – they're not here, are they? B – I'm carrying a ghost baby, I think they'll understand my need for a little pamper time.'

Bobbie hugged her friend. If she could make a joke out of it, she was on the road to being cool. 'Okay. You go first and then I'll freshen up before we head back to St Paul's.'

'Cool.' Naya grabbed her wash-bag and secured a robe around her waist, although the huge third-trimester bump had now faded to almost nothing more than a food baby. She ran her hand over it, but said nothing. *It wasn't real*, Bobbie reminded herself.

'Stay away from any mirrors . . . including the one we abandoned in the Accy Area. I'll be up in a sec – we should stick together.'

'Yes, Ma'am. Thanks, Bob, for, y'know . . .' Bobbie guessed she meant for the support. 'You're amazing. Love ya, girl.' Naya embraced her and Bobbie felt her cheeks flush. She didn't feel amazing, she felt like a pretender – someone playing the role of a girl who could cope. As long as Caine and Naya believed she was keeping it together, that was all that mattered. Naya gave her a peck on the forehead and left, letting the door slam behind her.

Bobbie was alone again with Caine for the first time since their kiss in the hall. She glanced up at him and looked away, suddenly shy. Another great mystery solved – why did so many Piper's Hall Ladies trot into Oxsley every weekend to lurk outside shops with boys? Answer: because it's addictive. All she wanted to do was kiss him again, partly to see if it was as good as she remembered, but also because it put her in a state unlike any other she'd ever felt before.

She wanted to recapture what she'd felt in the hall: the gallop in her chest.

Bobbie mentally shook it off. Spending her last day on earth kissing the beautiful boy was either the best or worst idea she'd ever had. 'Well, I wasn't expecting that.' She flopped onto her bed, already wiped out despite only having been awake ten minutes.

'I know, right? That was messed up.' The room suddenly seemed bigger, like they were too far apart. As if he sensed this, Caine kicked off the sleeping bag and joined her. 'Is this okay?'

'Yeah.' Somehow Bobbie knew that he wouldn't make a move. For whatever reason, she just really, really wanted to touch his skin. She stroked his neck, feeling the fuzzy hairline where he'd shaved his head. This time, she kissed him. It was every bit as good as she'd remembered – better.

Caine pulled back. 'Morning breath!'

'Me?' Bobbie was horrified.

'No! No! I meant me!'

'You're fine,' Bobbie smiled back before giving him a less risky, fleeting kiss on his lips. He pulled her into an embrace, holding her tight. She felt safer than she had in years; locked up securely in strong arms. When had someone last held her? Oh, Grace had, but that was totally different. And Naya was as touchy-feely as they come, but her mum hadn't hugged her since she'd been tiny – years had passed. She realised how much she'd missed the contact and why people did this – why they dedicate all those hours to finding boyfriends and girlfriends.

It's for someone to *hold*. She rested her head on his broad shoulder. A tear found its way out and soaked into the thin cotton of his T-shirt.

'Are you crying on me?' His voice sounded like he was smiling, teasing her.

Pulling away from him, she wiped her eye. 'No. It's just my eye leaking. Sorry. Not massively constructive, I know. I just don't want *this* to go away.'

Caine stroked her back, strumming her with his thumb like a harp. 'Yeah. I know.'

Bobbie took his hands. She didn't know why, but she voiced one of her greatest fears. 'You don't think I'm weird, do you?'

This time he did look at her. 'Only in a good way.'

Another tear threatened to make an appearance. She held it back. This was a good thing. If she was taken by restless spirits she could at least say she'd died having met someone who *got* her. That was pretty cool. 'Do you want some breakfast?' she asked. 'I could smuggle us some up.'

'Yeah. That'd be good. Can you pass some water?'

'Sure.' Their glasses from last night were arranged on the desk. 'Which one was yours?'

'The taller one.' She handed him the glass, still half full with water from the evening before.

'Thanks.'

Bobbie looked around the room for some clothes she could throw on to fetch breakfast. The shyness was back – she both did and didn't want to strip in front of Caine.

'Whoa!' Caine's cry came about a second before the glass shattered on the threadbare carpet.

'Wh—'

'She was in the cup.' Caine pulled his legs off the floor.

'What?'

'I could see her in the water. Look!'

Bobbie looked at the puddle spreading across the floor. The carpet was so thin it was hardly absorbent and the water advanced in a black circle. For a moment, Bobbie saw only herself in the puddle, but another face appeared from behind her, as if she was *right behind her*. Bobbie screamed and threw herself back, colliding with the wardrobe.

Then something else happened.

The tip of a dead, blue-white finger emerged from the puddle: from reflection to reality. Bobbie screamed again. This was it, she was coming for them.

Unable to take her eyes off the corpse fingers, she didn't see Caine grab hold of her duvet, but a second later it landed on the wet patch, the fabric soaking up the water in an instant. Bobbie sprang to action, dabbing at the damp. She pulled back the bedding. The puddle, and the ghostly fingers, were gone.

She looked up at Caine. No words necessary. It was game over. She was on her way. 'She doesn't even need a mirror any more. She's strong enough to come through *any* reflection.'

Caine's head fell into his hands, only for him to spring upright at once. 'What about Naya?'

Bobbie frowned and then something that felt like an anvil crashed to the pit of her stomach. 'Oh God! The bath!'

They both sprinted into Brontë House, Bobbie not caring who saw them any more. It didn't even cross her mind how much trouble she could be in if Caine was caught. Nothing else mattered but this.

'Where's this bathroom?' Caine shouted, a couple of steps ahead of her. The doors of Brontë were a blur as they careered past.

'Next floor up! End of Dickinson.'

'Where?'

'Follow me!' Bobbie took the lead and headed for the main staircase. By now they'd made enough of a commotion that some left-behind girls poked their heads out of a door in Austen House.

Bobbie was moving too fast to see who they were, but she definitely heard one of them say, 'Oh my God! A BOY!' A few days ago, that would have been her amongst the scandalised masses.

She took the stairs two at a time, with Caine right on her heels. *Not Naya . . . please not Naya.* Her throat was so dry and tight it was painful. They reached the landing between Christie and Dickinson. 'Naya!' Bobbie screamed. She tugged on the double doors into Dickinson, her socks skidding across the cool, tiled floors.

The prefects' bathroom was next to the main Dickinson bathroom, and was the only actual bathtub pupils got to use. The perk was pretty much the only reason to become a prefect. Bobbie fell into the door and tugged on the handle. It was locked. 'Naya!' Bobbie hammered on the wood.

'Bob? What's up? I'm okay, the bump went down.' Naya's voice came from within. Bobbie heard the sound of water sloshing as Naya sat up in the tub.

'Naya, get out of the bath!'

'What? Why? Are you desperate for a pee or –' The sentence was cut short.

Bobbie pressed her ear to the door. 'Naya?'

Caine banged on the door. 'Naya, get out! It's not a joke.'

'Naya!' Bobbie tugged and shook the door handle. Not being a prefect she'd only peeked inside the room once or twice and couldn't remember what type of lock it was. She threw all her weight behind it, but the thing wouldn't budge. 'No!' she wailed. She couldn't lose her best friend; life without her didn't stand thinking about. Naya's unconditional friendship was one more thing she'd taken for granted. 'Caine,' she pleaded. 'Do something!' *No no no no no no no.*

He rammed the door with his shoulder, prompting more doors to open in Dickinson House. The door dented, but didn't burst open.

There was a mighty splash and a gasp from within, as if Naya had breached the surface, struggling for air. 'Bobbie!' came her gurgled plea. Someone was pulling her under.

Bobbie fell to her knees, struggling to breathe through her tears. There was a minute gap between the handle and the door frame. A sliver of light shone through. With one eye shut, Bobbie peered through the crack.

Steam filled the room. A tatty opaque curtain hung out of the chipped enamel tub. The room was still and silent, with no suggestion of the struggle she'd just heard. 'Naya?' she whispered. Her friend was gone.

Silence. Only a steady *drip, drip, drip*.

From within the bath, fingers curled over the rim of the tub.

Clammy, grey, dead fingers. Fingernails like slate. Blood-tinged pink water dribbled down the enamel all the way to the floor. A soaked head of black hair emerged.

Mary hauled herself out of the bath.

Chapter 23

Isolation

Bobbie sprang away from the door, crashing into Caine. She tumbled backwards onto her bottom, taking him down with her. 'She's coming!' The words tore from her throat.

'What?'

She scrabbled around to face him. 'Mary! She's in there! She took Naya!'

The double doors at the end of the corridor smashed open, a gust of wind wafting into the hallway. 'Just what on earth is going on here?' Mrs Craddock clomped down the hall, carrying a slice of half-eaten toast. 'Roberta Rowe! Exactly what do you think you're doing?'

Bobbie stumbled to her feet and spun to meet her, getting a mouthful of hair in the process. 'Mrs Craddock, you have to help us. She's got Naya.'

Confusion creased the old woman's face. 'What? What *are* you on about?'

Tugging at her sleeve, Bobbie dragged her away from the

226

bathroom door. 'Mary. Mary Worthington. She took Sadie and now she's after us too.'

Mrs Craddock's expression changed from one of annoyance to one of worry. 'Bobbie, dear, you need to calm down. Are you okay? And who is this young man?'

Caine stepped into the breach. Beads of sweat glistened on his forehead. 'She's telling the truth. There's a ghost in there.' He pointed at the door with a shaking finger.

And the annoyance was back. 'Oh for crying out loud! Stop this nonsense at once! Where's Naya?'

'Stop asking questions!' Bobbie snapped. 'There isn't time!'

'That is NOT how we speak to members of staff.' The thin, angular silhouette of Dr Price stood in the door frame. Arms folded, lips pursed. 'Roberta, you have precisely one minute to explain why there is a boy in Piper's Hall and why you are screaming up and down the corridors at eight in the morning.' Her voice was as flatline as ever.

Bobbie couldn't hold it back any longer. Losing Naya had punched a hole in the dam and now the torrent of emotion she'd been holding back gushed through. 'Dr Price. Please, please help us. You have to. You have to help us.' Her nose was running. She didn't care.

'Bobbie, stop this now. Pull yourself together.'

'But she took Naya. She took Sadie.'

'Who on earth are you talking about?'

'Mary Worthington.' Bobbie had to stop herself from screaming the name, and then, 'Bloody Mary!'

The Head rolled her eyes, a brittle smile on her lips. 'Oh for God's sake, Roberta, I haven't got time for silly stories.'

'You have to believe us,' Caine barked.

Price hit him with a blast of arctic frostiness, regarding him with thinly disguised disgust. 'You are trespassing. I don't want a word out of you.'

Bobbie clung wildly to her headmistress, all self-control gone. 'It's true! Five days ago we said her name in front of a mirror. On the fifth day she comes for you. She's in there now! She took Naya!' The awful truth sunk in. If there had been anything in her she would have thrown up; as it was her stomach just heaved painfully. 'She took Naya.'

Price pinched the bridge of her nose and sighed. 'Just when you think you've heard every excuse in the book. I mean this really takes the cake, Bobbie.' Her heels tapped across the tiles as she approached the prefects' bathroom.

'No! Don't open the door! Mary's in there!'

'It's locked from the inside,' Caine reminded her.

Dr Price rapped on the wood. 'Naya Sanchez? Are you in there? This is Dr Price, let me in immediately.' There was no reply. Price reached for the handle.

'No!' Bobbie screamed.

Dr Price turned the knob and, without any resistance, the door popped open, steam rolling into the corridor. 'It isn't even locked.'

'What? No way.' Caine frowned. 'I swear it was . . .'

'I thought I said I didn't want a word?' Price stepped into the room. Bobbie forced herself to look. Mary, of course, was gone. She wondered if Mary physically *couldn't* manifest to those who hadn't invoked her. That would go some way to explaining why Kellie and Lottie hadn't been disturbed the night Sadie vanished. She wiped her wet face. For now, they were safe. The bathwater still swayed up and down the tub, settling. 'Roberta, what is going on?'

'I already told you,' she said, feeling stronger.

'Where's Naya?'

It was too late. They were too late. Naya was gone. It didn't seem possible. How could anything as important as Naya vanish with so little ceremony? Sadness flooded her. She wasn't sure what Naya's future would have held, but *anything* she did would have been *spectacular*. Bobbie's vision blurred. 'Mary took her,' she whispered. 'She's going to take us too.'

A small congregation of left-behind girls had gathered to see what the commotion was. They twittered like bitchy sparrows, whispering in each other's ears. Bobbie was too wound up to care that Grace and Caitlin were amongst the onlookers.

'That's enough!' Price raised her voice for the first time. 'This is serious. Roberta Rowe, where is Naya?'

'I told you! Mary took her!' Bobbie's voice grew shriller and louder.

Dr Price arched an eyebrow. 'Okay, that's your final warning. I will not be spoken to like that. Where. Is. Naya?'

Bobbie felt like a rubber band, being stretched to her very limit. And then she snapped. 'What's the point? You won't believe us! I am telling the truth – Mary killed Naya and now we're – me and Caine – we're going to die too and if you don't listen to us, it'll be all your fault!' She turned to their small audience. 'Grace! Grace, you were there with us! Tell her what we did – tell her about the dare!'

Grace paused before holding her empty hands up. An almost

undetectable smirk flickered on her lips. 'Dr Price, I have no idea what she's talking about.'

'You bitch!' Bobbie shrieked.

'She's lying!' Caine added.

Dr Price put herself between Bobbie and Grace. 'Enough! We'll talk again when you can behave like a Piper's Hall Lady.' She looked for assistance. 'Mrs Craddock, Grace, would you help me escort Miss Rowe to the Isolation Room?'

'Of course.' Grace could not have been more eager to help.

'You can't put me in there!' Bobbie backed away, further inside Dickinson House, but Grace and Craddock came to her side. 'I won't be able to get away if she . . .'

'Don't touch her.' Caine stepped into Grace's path, but she didn't seem fazed by his height in the slightest and batted him away like a fly.

Price took Caine by the arm and guided him towards the door. He yanked his arm away. 'If you're not off my school premises in the next two minutes I'm calling the police. Is that clear?'

'You can't!'

'Try me.' Dr Price led the way onto the main stairwell. 'Roberta, you will calm down in the Isolation Room until you can speak to me maturely. Is that understood?'

Grace and Craddock started to drag her towards the stairs. 'Please . . . no! Please don't put me in there!'

'I'm not giving you a choice in the matter.'

The Isolation Room was little more than a store cupboard next to the Infirmary on the ground floor. Caine had been hustled out of the main entrance and the door slammed in his face. Bobbie could still hear him pounding on the wood as she was led towards the cell. 'Please!' she begged. 'Don't leave me alone!'

'You need to calm yourself,' Dr Price repeated, leading the way.

'If you leave me alone she'll get me!'

'Perhaps we should call Dr Robinson?' Mrs Craddock suggested.

'Let's see. If she doesn't stop ranting and raving we might have to see about getting her sedated.'

Bobbie stopped struggling at once. If she was sedated there was no way she'd be able to fight when Mary came for her. 'Please. Just . . . can someone watch me?'

Dr Price regarded her with something like pity. 'I assure you we'll be watching.' She entered the Isolation Room and held the door wide. 'Now in you come. Take off your glasses please. Clearly you've been hurting yourself.'

In the chaos, she'd forgotten her face was covered in scars. Resigned, Bobbie handed her glasses over and was immediately disoriented. Grace took unnecessary relish in pushing her into the boxy room. It was a narrow cuboid with only two high, thin slit windows at the top of the far wall. Underneath them there was a single hospital cot bed, no blankets. 'In.' Dr Price said.

Bobbie shuffled further into the room. On a bright day, it would be dank. On a dank day it was oppressively dark.

'I'll be back to check on you in an hour.' She turned to Mrs Craddock. 'We need to look for Naya. If she's missing we need the police here ASAP.'

The door closed, sealing her in the concrete box. Bobbie wasn't great with small spaces – even lifts made her feel claustrophobic and, as the lock crunched in the door, this felt worse. *The police*, she thought, *good luck with that*. They wouldn't find Naya. No one would. She was gone.

At the thought of Naya, an acute ache flared up in Bobbie's sternum. She bit her tongue to hold back a scream.

She crumpled onto the bed, the springs resisting with a cranky screech. Closing her eyes, Bobbie focused on long, deep breaths – exactly what her mum would tell her to do if she were here. It brought scant comfort. Caine was out there, all alone, in a world full of mirrors. Not just mirrors any more, anything that held a reflection. He was as good as dead. Scanning the room, the only positive thing about her cell was that there was nothing reflective at all.

That meant she was the only one left: Sadie, Naya, Caine any second now, and she was in captivity. They were beaten. Bobbie had never felt so useless. All she could do was wait.

The one thing she had in the dungeon was thinking time. As much as she tried to keep Naya memories out of her head, she couldn't: the party they went to in costume as Bellatrix and Dobby; Naya groping the bare bottoms of statues at the British Museum before being escorted off the premises by a security guard; the 'anonymous' Valentine Naya sent her every year without fail. Bobbie was going to miss her *so* much. She stifled a resigned chuckle; there was some comfort in knowing she'd only feel this hollow in her heart for a maximum of twelve hours. Who knew, perhaps they'd all be reunited.

She thought about Caine too. Caine had done a real fairy-tale number on her: he'd woken her up with a kiss. She'd lived more in five days than she had in sixteen years. Now he was gone and she wanted him like she'd never wanted anything else (including the vintage typewriter she'd begged for when she'd been twelve).

In the Isolation Room she had no way of knowing how much time had passed. She was still in her pyjamas with no watch and no phone. Outside she heard the waves crashing into the cliffs and the steady patter of rain on the quad. A gutter or something must have been leaking too, because a continuous drip splattered to the pathway outside of her window.

No . . . wait. *Of course*, she thought. *Mary* . . . dripping onto the tiles in the hall; the shower room; the prefects' bathroom. She'd been hearing that drip all week . . . just out of earshot. It had now reached fever pitch.

Bobbie remained on the bed, until her legs and buttocks became so numb she resorted to pacing to keep the circulation flowing – not that there was much room to pace in. The room became darker and darker, and seemingly smaller and smaller, as the storm outside grew worse. Thunder started to rumble like the sky was hungry and lightning flickered in jittery intervals.

Every once in a while a blurry face appeared at the frosted Perspex panel in the door. Bobbie guessed it was Price checking up on her, but couldn't be certain. As the minutes turned to hours (probably) Bobbie could feel her grip loosening. Caine and Naya, Naya and Caine. Panic turned to anger, her hands twitching with nervous energy.

Finally, she boiled over and threw herself at the door. She couldn't wait a second longer. Forcing her voice to stay even and sane, she called through the glass: 'Hello! Is there someone there? I'm calm now! I'm ready to talk.' There was no reply. She pressed her face to the window, but couldn't see or hear anything in the corridor. 'Can someone please tell me what's going on?'

Nothing. She was cold. She rubbed her arms to warm them and sloped back to the camp bed. She pressed her back against the cool plaster and fixed her eyes on the door. She *was* calm now, but she wouldn't lie. If necessary, she'd start at the beginning and tell the whole story: the dare, Sadie, Bridget, Judy. As crazy as everything sounded, no one could deny that something impossible, dictionary-definition paranormal was happening. God, if she had to, Bobbie would force Price to ring Judy or the hospital. All the clues were there if you looked hard enough – anyone would see a weird pattern.

Bobbie closed her eyes and rested her head against the wall.

Outside the window, the trickle of water slowed to a precise *drip, drip, drip*.

Drip, drip, drip.

Her eyes opened. Out of the corner of her eye, in the outer edges of her peripheral vision, something moved.

Bobbie yelped and rolled off the bed onto the floor.

Where the wall was once smooth and flat, there was now an imprint of a face looking in – a girl's face. The wall stretched and flexed like it was made of latex, fingers pressed either side of the face, like she was trying to force her way *through* the wall.

Not daring to look away, Bobbie backed along the floor on her bottom. The face sunk back into the plaster and it was just a wall once more. 'Oh God . . .'

The wall to her left, the one nearest to her, rippled and a hand once again tried to push its way through, like it was feeling for her blind. Bobbie cried out and jumped to her feet, pressing her back against the opposite wall. Two thin arms reached through, clawing for her. The ghostly hands couldn't quite reach. They withdrew.

A second later, Mary's imprint face emerged right next to hers. Bobbie spun back to the door. 'Let me out!' she screamed, banging on the wood. 'She's trying to get in! Please!' She was aware this wouldn't help her sanity plea, but better crazy than dead. 'Please! Can anyone hear me?'

Mary's face, her mouth gaping open, swam across the wall, the whole surface elongating, stretching as she tried to push her way through. Bobbie whirled to face the dead girl. 'There are no mirrors in here, Mary! It isn't going to work.'

The outline of the face stopped and turned quizzically towards her. 'What is it you want?' Bobbie muttered, terrified. 'I've done everything you wanted . . . I tried and tried to help you . . . why won't you just leave me alone?' Why her? Why, out of all the girls in all of the world who'd said her name? Why had Mary latched onto her like a parasite?

The face retreated, slowly, almost trance-like. Bobbie clung to the door frame like it was a life raft. Mary's power was stronger than ever, but apparently she still needed a reflective surface to cross properly into reality.

'Let me out.' Bobbie leaned her head against the door, knowing that no one was listening. 'Please,' she added feebly.

The dingy room was still. The walls were just walls. The only sound was her own ragged breathing. Bobbie, her back pressed to the door, scanned the cell. Mary wouldn't give up so easily, not when she had a captive audience. 'Mary?' Bobbie whispered. 'Where are you?'

Drip.

The noise was louder than ever. Closer.

Drip, drip.

Bobbie saw it. High above her head, heating pipes ran across the ceiling – vanishing into the wall at both sides. There was a rusted joint in the centre of the antiquated pipe and Bobbie saw a thick, fat droplet leak from the corroded part. It trickled down the joint, pooled like a teardrop, hung for a second before plummeting to the floor with a moist splat.

Bobbie's mouth fell open. This was Mary. She was making it happen.

Drip, drip, drip.

The drops started to pool in the centre of the linoleum. Mary was creating a way in. The drops turned to a dribble, the leak worsening.

Bobbie turned back to the door and pounded on it with both fists. 'Oh my God, get me out of here!'

A hand as white as chalk reached through the puddle.

Chapter 24

Losing You

Bobbie heard a key twist in the lock. The opening door smacked into her and threw her forward, almost into Mary's waiting fingers. She felt hands grab her shoulders and pull her backwards out of the room. Bobbie slammed the door shut, hopefully trapping the dead girl within.

She whirled around to find herself face-to-face with Caine. Falling into his arms, he moved her into the safety of the corridor. Buried in his chest, she could only dimly hear the continuous droning clang of the fire alarm. 'You're okay,' he whispered into her hair. 'You're okay.'

Looking up, she kissed him hard on the lips. This was for several reasons. One, she'd never been so pleased to see *anyone* in her life – she would have considered kissing Mrs Craddock. Two, it was Caine. Three, she'd really thought she was never ever going to see him again, and if it were the case that there were no more kisses, she wanted a really good finale. She pulled away, but he didn't let her out of his arms, like he couldn't bear to let go either. 'You're alive,' she said breathlessly.

'I am.'

'How . . . ? How did you get back in?'

'I set off the fire alarm . . . couldn't you hear it?'

'Not in there . . . but I wasn't alone.'

'What?' Caine whipped his head round to look into the room. 'Are you okay?'

'I am now. We need to get away from here – I don't know if doors can stop her.' Clinging to one another they started down the corridor. 'What time is it?'

'Nearly three.'

'I've been in there *all day*?'

'Pretty much. This place has been crawling with police. I had to wait for them to head off before I risked coming back inside.' He handed Bobbie her glasses. 'Here, these were on the shelf outside.'

It was so thoughtful she almost kissed him again, but it would have to wait. 'I guess they're looking for Naya.' Bobbie tried to get her head back in the game. 'They'll have to check she hasn't run away or whatever before they announce anything.'

Caine took her hand and pulled her towards the dining room. 'Come on. We haven't got long. They'll work out it's a false alarm in no time and someone's bound to remember you were shut in there.'

Bobbie followed him towards the exit by the kitchens. She knew that, during fire drills, staff and students had to report to the hockey pitches. That gave them a few minutes at least, but not enough time for her to change or even grab some shoes. She tugged on his hand to slow him down. 'Thank you for coming back for me.'

He looked puzzled. 'Are you kidding?' He appeared to search for the right words. 'I got your back.'

She smiled, knowing that was as much as he could reasonably say so early into their relationship, if indeed that was what it was. 'Thank you.' And just so that they were both sure of their relationship status, she kissed him again. She was going to exploit every last remaining minute.

He blushed. 'Come on. Getting me excited isn't going to help me run away . . .'

Bobbie realised what he meant and was about to comment but he was already pulling her towards the exit. The fire alarm continued to ring as they ran into the quad connecting the old building to the Millar Wing. The sky was a violent bruise, as dark as the middle of the night. Rain teemed from the sky, bouncing off the concrete flagstones. Vast puddles formed like lakes across the courtyard

Bobbie let go of him and held her hands over her head. 'Wait. Where are we going?'

Caine stopped and stood in the centre of the courtyard, rain running down his face. 'I dunno. Just away from here before I get arrested for kidnapping you or something.'

'We'll head to the graveyard. Maybe we can find –' She saw what was going to happen way too late. The first thing she thought when she saw that Caine was standing slap bang in the middle of a giant puddle was, *He'll get wet feet*. The second thing was . . . 'Caine!'

A marble-white hand reached out of the water and clamped itself around his ankle. As he realised what was happening,

Caine's eyes widened and his mouth fell open in a shocked, silent scream.

His foot disappeared into the puddle as if a trapdoor had opened up below him, the hand pulling him in. By the time Bobbie reached him, he was swallowed up to his waist. 'Caine!' She grabbed his right hand with both of hers and tugged as hard as she could. He weighed so much more than her and whatever held him was *beyond* strong.

'Bob—' Caine gritted his teeth, his left hand looking for something to grab hold of. His fingernails scraped along the wet paving stones trying to gain a hold. He was submerged to his chest.

Bobbie pulled back with all her might, throwing herself backwards, using her feet to anchor herself. It wasn't enough. Her knees buckled and she fell onto her bottom, being pulled along with him. 'Don't let go!'

He sank to the neck. Caine tipped his head back to stop his face going under. Bobbie wrenched on his arm, feeling his shoulder pop. It was no good. 'Bobbie,' he said. 'I –'

Caine closed his eyes as he went under, only his arm sticking out of the water. 'I won't let go of you!' Bobbie hissed through her teeth. Her wet socks scraped along the slabs and she struggled to find a grip. His hands were wet and her fingers slid over his skin as if he were covered in grease. *Don't let go.* With a cry, Bobbie felt Caine being torn away from her. *I will not let go of him.*

Toppling forward, Bobbie fell head first into the puddle.

darkness

total darkness black and blind

Caine . . . don't let go . . . Caine . . . please . . . Caine . . . CAINE

falling

fading

formless

nothingness

endless and infinite

Where am I?

Bobbie Rowe

Caine?

void

vacancy

vacuum

Bobbie Rowe

Where are you? *Where was his voice coming from?*

My arms . . . I can't feel my hands

dissolving

evaporating

weightlessness

howling, screaming wind. A storm. A gale.

Bobbie Rowe

Caine, Caine, I'm falling. I can't stop.

Crumbling . . . decay . . . hollow . . .
smoke . . . shell
Bobbie Rowe

emptiness hopelessness sorrow ache suffering grief misery torment

a light
a window

I see it . . . I see it

Bobbie Rowe

Chapter 25

The Truth

Hands outstretched, Bobbie tumbled through the mirror and landed in the centre of a well-trodden rug. Rolling onto her back, she gasped for air, like she'd been drowning in the darkness. It felt as if the emptiness filled her lungs. Scanning herself, Bobbie checked to make sure she was back in one piece. *Two arms, two legs* . . . she was okay. What *was* that place? It felt like . . . like *oblivion*. She'd felt so, so lost and alone. In that wilderness, she'd had no form, no physical sensation, only a feeble consciousness being tossed on stormy waves.

'Caine?' she croaked. 'Caine?' There was no reply. It was his voice. His voice had guided her to the mirror, so where was he? Was he still in that . . . nightmare?

Bobbie forced herself to breathe steadily and took in her surroundings. She was in a dingy, smoke-filled room. She'd landed in front of a low coffee table around which four plump, old-fashioned armchairs were arranged – bottle-green leather with metal studs bolting the material around the frame. An overflowing ashtray sat at the centre of the table.

Under the dark window, a single green banker's lamp shone over a desk piled high with exercise books, ready for marking. Feeling stronger, Bobbie pulled herself off the rug, her legs still jelly (but at least she could feel them). *Wait a second . . .* she *knew* this room. It was Dr Price's office. The mirror she'd fallen in through was the grand gilt mirror. Dr Price's power-desk wasn't there, but the gaudy gold mirror was still hanging where it always did.

Bobbie looked down at herself and saw she was back in the scratchy, vintage version of the Piper's uniform. She was Mary again.

The door opened and Bobbie flinched behind one of the armchairs, half expecting Mary to burst in. Instead, a familiar masculine figure filled the doorway. Kenton Millar. He clocked her and his mouth fell open in horror. 'Mary, what on earth are you doing in the staffroom?' Ah, so in 1954, the Head's office was a staffroom. 'What are you thinking? We were supposed to meet in the graveyard at eleven, like always.'

'I'm sorry,' Bobbie said, unable to hold the words in. Mary had control of her. The words weren't her own even if the voice was. Mary was *strong* now. With Mary manipulating her like an invisible puppeteer, she rose to her feet. This was no dream; she was living Mary's memory and she was powerless to halt its progress.

Her teacher smiled and looked over his shoulder to check the coast was clear. 'Not to worry. You're here now, and it is getting a little nippy for the graveyard, isn't it? I don't suppose there's anyone much around to hear us anyway.' He pulled her into an embrace and kissed her hard on the lips. He tasted of cigarettes and strong coffee. With the dreamy gloss stripped back, he was repellent. She pulled back. 'What's wrong, my flower?'

Bobbie felt a fat tear roll down her cheek. Not her tears, but Mary's. Bobbie could guess the next sentence before Mary moved her mouth to say it. 'Sir, I think I might be pregnant.'

He flinched as if she'd hit him. 'What?' He exhaled long and slow. 'You *think*?'

'I . . . I am, Sir. I must be. Please don't be cross with me.' Bobbie couldn't stop the words. History was playing out through her body and her hand now rested on her abdomen.

Kenton Millar clung to the back of the nearest armchair, threatening to tip it over. 'Is this some sort of joke?'

'No . . . no, Sir.'

He turned to her, his eyes cold and cruel. 'And . . . and how do I know this child is mine?'

More tears fell. Bobbie's head was filled with Mary's confusion. Why was he being like this? 'You . . . you are the only man I've ever . . .'

He sneered. 'What am I meant to think? I've heard all the stories . . . all the boys at Radley. I mean, you certainly seemed to know what you were doing.'

Bobbie keenly felt Mary's bewilderment, her disbelief. This gentle, tender man: it was like when a dog turns on its owner – quick, vicious and violent. 'I swear there's no one else. This baby is yours, I promise.' She could hardly breathe for tears. She held her arms open to him. 'Please hold me. I've been so scared to tell you.'

Kenton Millar strode to the window, smoothing his slick hair with his hands. He turned back and reluctantly held her to his chest, stroking her hair half-heartedly. 'There, there. It's not the end of the world; it's fine. You were right to come to me. It's going to be fine. I have plenty of money and I'll . . . I'll pay for it to go away.'

Bobbie sobbed, feeling every ounce of Mary's sorrow. *He loves me, so why is he saying these terrible things?* She pulled away from him, looking up in horror. 'But . . . but that's not even legal!'

'For pity's sake stop wailing, girl!' he bellowed, clearly forgetting he could wake the entire school. 'Don't you understand? I already have a baby on the way!'

'What?'

'Mary, you were aware of the situation.' How it had escaped her attention until now was a mystery, but there was a simple gold band on his ring finger. Maybe she hadn't *wanted* to notice. 'Look. I have a real chance of becoming the new Deputy Head Teacher here – I'm hardly going to let some silly mistake get in the way of all that, am I?'

'Please!' Bobbie begged. 'You said you loved me!'

'Oh, Mary. One day you'll understand what this was. Just a bit of fun. It's okay to have a bit of fun, everybody does it, but that's all this can be,' he murmured, trying to appease her. 'You had fun, didn't you? Do you understand?'

'No! No, I don't! This is our baby.' Bobbie felt a surge of love – the pure, overwhelming love Mary felt for her unborn child.

His eyes darkened again. 'Oh was that your plan? Get

yourself pregnant so I'd leave my wife? Well, it's not going to work, Mary, do you hear me? What? Did you think we could play at happy families? That we'd elope somewhere? It's just not possible, Mary. You are my *pupil* – just a *girl*.'

Bobbie wiped her cheek with the back of a sleeve. He had *betrayed* her. The only good thing in her life was dead to her now. No reason to carry on, no reason to try. All the love inside her heart turned black, venom in her veins. She was going to cause him *pain*. 'You can't do this to me! I . . . I'll tell people what you did.'

He almost laughed in her face. 'You'll do no such thing.'

'I will!'

'Oh and who'll believe a common tramp like you? A *gypsy*. Like mother like daughter.' He came closer and she felt his hot breath on her face.

Bobbie stood her ground – she wanted to hurt him as much as he'd hurt her. 'I will. I'll have this baby and tell anyone who'll listen. I'll say you took advantage!'

As she reached for the door, he seized her by the arms and dragged her away. 'Listen to me, you bitch.' Bobbie struggled against him, wriggling out of his grasp. She ran for the door, but he grabbed a handful of her hair to drag her back. Bobbie howled in pain. 'There is no way you are having that . . . that *bastard*, you hear me? I don't care if I have to take a knitting needle to it myself.'

Bobbie screamed as loudly as she could, the cry shaking the walls. Millar tried to clamp a hand over her mouth, but she squirmed away. 'Keep still!'

'Help me!' she cried. Adrenaline coursed through her body

and she made a final, mighty bid for freedom, but Millar yanked on her arm, swinging her like an Olympian hammer thrower. Twice her size, he sent her reeling across the room. Unable to stop herself, with no time to even cover her face, Bobbie careered into the gilded mirror. As her nose made contact with the glass, she both felt and heard a painful crack. She wasn't sure which broke first – bone or mirror.

Dazed and woozy, Bobbie crumpled to the floor, trying to use the giant frame to keep herself upright. Her head was spinning, black stars dancing in her blurred vision. There was a loud snap – like a violin string pinging free. The floor beneath her felt like it was leaning in.

'Mary!' Kenton Millar cried.

It wasn't the floor tipping *up*, it was the wall tipping *in*. No, not the wall, the mirror. It had come clean off the wall. There was nothing that could be done.

The mirror crashed down on top of her, and the last thing that Bobbie saw was Mary Worthington's bloody, terrified face.

Chapter 26

Ellen Price

Bobbie was falling. Arms folded over her face, Bobbie crashed onto Dr Price's desk, scattering pens, papers and empty coffee mugs. She felt the impact on her hips, elbows and knees, the edge of the desk hitting her right in the gut and winding her completely. Bobbie slid to the floor, her eyes adjusting to the gloom in the empty office.

Outside, the sky was almost pitch-black – how long had she been in Mary's realm? It had felt like minutes, but the dark skies said otherwise.

The echoing drip was louder than ever. Pushing Price's desk chair out of the way, Bobbie clambered to her feet, aching all over from the impact of the fall. 'Ow,' she groaned, brushing down her crumpled pyjamas. So that was what had happened to Mary Worthington. The final piece of the puzzle fell into place. She'd died in this very spot sixty years ago. An accident, but an accident that was Kenton Millar's fault.

Something flickered in her peripheral vision, and Bobbie

knew just what it was. What a rookie mistake to make . . .

She had her back to the mirror. *It isn't over.*

Oh-so-slowly, Bobbie turned. No . . . sudden . . . moves. There *she* was in the reflection, inching across the room towards Bobbie's mirror image. Bobbie finally saw Mary properly. Judy was correct, Mary was beautiful in a way – full, defined lips, high cheekbones and icy blue eyes. She had a strong, Roman nose though, which, instead of pretty, made her almost handsome.

To get to that conclusion, however, Bobbie had to see past the blood. The falling mirror and shattering glass had left dozens of cuts all over Mary's face and body, and, unlike Bobbie's phantom cuts, Mary's bled. Vivid scarlet blood ran all down her face in thick, worm-like rivulets. Her uniform was saturated in crimson and her lank black hair was matted to her head.

Mary's eyes, burning through the blood, never left her. With each step, she edged closer to Bobbie, her hands reaching for her. Bobbie knew her time had come. Acting on instinct, Bobbie did the only thing she could think of. Grabbing the smaller chair at the side of the grand desk, Bobbie swung it at the glass at the very same moment Mary's red fingers reached through the mirror's surface.

With a shriek, Bobbie struck the mirror. There was an ear-splitting crack and Bobbie felt her arms strain as the chair bounced back. It was enough though. Jagged triangles spilled out of the ornate frame, jangling and shattering to the floor. Not leaving anything to chance, Bobbie took another swing, attacking what was left at the edges. Soon glass was piled up around her feet and she took a cautious step backwards. 'Good luck getting through that.'

Hands shaking, she let the chair fall to the floor. If the room would just stop spinning she might be able to figure out what to do next. Bobbie clung to the desk for support. All she could feel was sadness and despair circling around her, but she couldn't let them win when she still needed to work things out. Caine *and* Naya. She'd lost them. She'd failed them. That *emptiness* she'd felt in the darkness behind the mirror – was that what death was, just *nothingness*? Eternal nothingness, but a nothingness that you're aware of – it was too awful to comprehend. The thought of Naya and Caine falling through that vacuum forever . . .

Can they feel it? Are they awake? For their sakes she hoped not; she preferred to think that they were sleeping – dreaming of something nice.

There was a shrill creak behind her and she whirled round, half expecting Mary to burst out of a mirror on the far side of the room. Bobbie clutched her chest. It was just a wardrobe door swinging on a hinge that needed a drop of oil. For a horrible moment, Bobbie wondered if it had a mirror on the inner door like the ones in the dorms, but she remembered it didn't from when she'd helped Dr Price tidy up.

Wait a second. Bobbie no longer believed in coincidence.

'That cupboard *again*,' she said to herself, switching on the table lamp for a better look. Bobbie gave the heap of shattered glass one last check before stepping out from behind the desk. She recalled Mary lingering by that cupboard the last time she'd been in here *and* that it had tumbled open then too. Now that she thought about it, the very first time she'd followed Mary (when she'd taken her glasses), she'd been led to this room.

For whatever reason, Mary wanted Bobbie to see inside.

Bobbie decided that if she did somehow get through the next few hours, she was so expelled that a little cupboard break-in couldn't hurt. Tucking her hair behind her ears, she got to work. The cupboard contained files and files, most marked as some sort of policy: Food Policy, Religion Policy, Policies Policy. The top two shelves were made up of pupil records – the very top shelf held files called 'Former Pupils'. Bobbie knew exactly what she was looking for: 1954. There was a folder for every five years or so (Bobbie guessed about the time it took a girl to go through the school). Not caring how much mess she made, she tossed irrelevant files to the floor in her search for the right one. She was soon standing in a crisp, white sea of paper.

It was no good – they were all too recent, only dating back to the 1990s. On the very top floor of the school was a records room, where Bobbie guessed most of the older files were kept. But if that were true, Mary wouldn't have directed her here. 'Where is it?' Bobbie hissed through gritted teeth. She stopped and squashed all the remaining files to one end of the shelf. *Behind* the other files was a simple manila folder bound with a leather strap.

Bobbie pulled it out. The file was marked 'Confidential Pupil Records – For Head Teacher Only'. What the hell – Bobbie tore the band off and sat on the floor in the midst of her file destruction.

It was a folder full of girls' portraits. Taylor Keane and Abigail Hanson were on top, along with police and newspaper reports of their disappearances. There were more girls – all Piper's Hall Ladies, all missing. All *Mary's*. Now Sadie and Naya could be added to the gruesome roll call. Instinctively, Bobbie turned the pack upside down to find the first girl who'd gone missing – Mary herself.

Sure enough there was everything she hadn't found online. A school portrait, a year-group photo (with Mary stood slightly apart, no other girl wanting to be shoulder to shoulder with her it seemed) and her report cards. A life story too; Bobbie lingered on her registration forms.

Mary Eloise Worthington, born 1938. Father: unknown. Mother: Eliza Worthington (no fixed abode). There was a letter on Radley Comprehensive headed paper too – the school that would one day become Radley High, no doubt: 'Mary has struggled to settle at Radley, but due to her excellent attainment in all fields we firmly feel she could flourish at Piper's Hall. We have no doubt she would excel in such an establishment. Mary is a shy, withdrawn young lady who would benefit from the more nurturing environment boarding could provide.' Bobbie scoffed at that; there was nothing like sending your kids away to school to put an end to any nurturing one might have had. Bobbie didn't *hate* boarding school, but while she had felt safe, secure, even encouraged, she had never felt nurtured.

There was a separate sheet – a different handwritten letter to the then Head, Mr Fisk. 'Dear Mr Fisk,' it read, 'I am writing to you to insist that my daughter, Phyllis, is moved from her current dormitory in Brontë House. Her letters home are increasingly agitated since she was placed in a room with a young woman called Mary. Phyllis is quite simply terrified of her and has been struggling to sleep since she arrived at your school . . .' It went on in much the same tone.

The final sheet was a typed letter to Eliza Worthington from Mr Fisk. 'Further to our conversations, we wished to write to express our sorrow that we were unable to provide a safe environment for your daughter. All evidence suggests that on the evening of the 17th September, Mary absconded from Brontë House. You must understand that we operate a school, not a jail, and try as we might, if a Piper's Hall Lady chooses to leave the premises there is little we can do to stop her. We have fully cooperated with the police and I understand the search continues . . .'

A tear splattered onto the page, blotting even the old ink. Bobbie wiped her cheek. Poor Mary. It all made sense – a horrid sort of sense. Kenton Millar, on purpose or not, had killed Mary Worthington *and* her unborn child. God knows how, but a part of her had got stuck in that, and every, mirror.

Another tear rolled down her cheek. Mary was lost in that awful blackness, listening for her name. They'd called her, some sort of lighthouse, guiding her back from the other side of the ocean. The same way Caine had somehow brought her back.

Millar must have done something with her body. Bobbie rifled through the remaining sheets on her lap, but knew he'd never be stupid enough to leave evidence behind. There was nothing about a body in the pages, cementing Bobbie's certainty that the key to the haunting was finding Mary's resting place. *Think, brain, think!* She struggled to put herself in the guilty teacher's shoes – if it were her, what would she do with a body?

Bobbie didn't even notice the door opening. 'There'd better be a really, really good explanation for this . . .' Dr Price's eyes cut through the gloom like lasers.

Bobbie dropped the folder, shocked.

'And let's start by talking about how you got out of the Isolation Room.'

She was so over this. 'Or we could talk about how you left me in there even when you thought the school was on fire.'

'Touché. We knew it wasn't a fire. We decided to focus on locating whoever had set the alarm off. I imagine it was your *friend* from Oxsley.'

Bobbie glowered at her, no longer intimidated by the ginger witch.

'Now, given that your entire future at Piper's Hall depends on this, I suggest you explain yourself. Just what do you think you're doing?'

'You lied.' Bobbie stood, fighting to maintain her composure. Screaming and shouting wasn't going to get her taken seriously. 'You knew full well that girls go missing from Piper's Hall, and you've done nothing to stop it, and now Naya and Sadie are gone and I'll be next.'

'You don't know what you're talking about.'

'Yes I do and so do you. This is about Mary Worthington.'

'There was no such girl.'

'I have proof!' Bobbie raised her voice and pointed at the array of paperwork at her feet. 'There's actual evidence – although I see the school did a pretty good job of covering it up.'

Dr Price put her hands on her hips and smiled. 'Roberta, I have to hand it to you, you don't give up. Creativity, enterprise, perseverance. A perfect Piper's Lady.'

Bobbie bit down on her jaw, resolute. 'Mary Worthington died right where you are standing.'

In the dim lamp light, Dr Price's gaze looked to her office wall. 'Oh my God, what have you done to my mirror?'

'Listen to me!' Bobbie yelled. 'Kenton Millar got her pregnant and then killed her right here! Well,' she conceded, 'it was an accident, but it was his fault.'

The temperature in the room dropped to way below zero. Dr Price advanced and Bobbie had no choice but to back into the corner. 'What did you just say?'

Bobbie withered under the intensity of her stare. 'I . . . I said that the old Head, Mr Millar, he was having an affair with Mary – not while he was Head, but before that, in 1954.' She backed into a potted palm next to the wall. There was nowhere left to go, but Price continued to advance on her, cornering her.

'How *dare* you?' Price breathed. 'Kenton Millar was one of the most brilliant and generous Heads this school has ever had.'

'I swear on my life it's true. When Mary told him she was pregnant they had a fight and she died. He . . . he must have hidden the body.'

Price pinned her to the wall, both hands clamped on her shoulders. Bobbie was scared, far more scared than she'd ever been of Mary; there was nothing ghostly about the vice-like grip. The older woman's nostrils flared. 'I think I'd know if my father had killed someone, don't you?'

The 'sudden plummet' sensation in Bobbie's stomach was getting far too familiar. 'Wh-what?'

'My maiden name was Ellen Millar. Are you really trying to tell me my father murdered someone? I want you to think very, *very* carefully before you answer . . .'

Bobbie's lips opened and closed like a fish out of water.

Price was trembling with rage – her knuckles white and veins swollen in her forehead. Kenton Millar had killed to keep his secret buried and Bobbie couldn't help but wonder if his daughter would kill to keep it that way.

Chapter 27

Bobbie's Run

'How? How can you be Millar's daughter?' Bobbie was finding it so difficult to make sense of what was unfolding.

Price frowned. 'It's no big secret. I don't advertise the fact; I want to build my own legacy here, not just trail after my father's. However, he was a great man and a fantastic teacher and what you just said is *slander*!' Her lips curled, the anger firing up again in her eyes.

But Bobbie had come too far and seen too much to crumble now. 'I'm sorry, Dr Price, but it's true. Why would I make it up?' Her voice wobbled, but didn't break. 'You've seen how many girls have vanished. Don't you think it's weird? There's no way it's coincidence. It's all because of what your dad did to Mary. I know it sounds crazy, but it's like she can't rest because no one ever found the body.'

Dr Price's gaze fell to the floor, her eyes twitching like she was trying to solve an equation in advanced algebra.

'Please let go of me,' Bobbie said softly. 'You're hurting me.'

Price let go, her arms flopping to her side as if they were made from spaghetti. Shoulders hunched, she fell into the spinning office chair, which she pulled away from the shattered glass and gaping gold frame. 'Oh God. Is that what . . . ? All that time . . .' She seemed to be talking to herself. Her head fell into her hands.

Bobbie backed away to a safe distance. 'What?'

'I don't believe it.'

'Dr Price, *please*. She's coming for me . . .'

Price deflated like a balloon. 'Just before my father died, he was very, very sick. On his deathbed he was talking absolute gibberish, but he kept saying this one thing over and over.' She stopped, shaking her head.

'And?' Bobbie urged.

'He kept asking to confess. He kept asking for a priest, saying that he needed to confess his sins before he died.' Price muffled a laugh. 'We weren't even Catholic! I thought he was delirious . . . but now . . .'

'Mary *was* pregnant. He *was* responsible for her death,' Bobbie finished.

Price looked her dead in the eye. 'Oh God. He also said he was sorry. Over and over again. We never knew what for . . .' A tear fell off her cheekbone and splashed onto her skirt.

Bobbie shook her head. This whole situation was awful, but she wouldn't feel sorry for the man who'd preyed on a vulnerable schoolgirl. 'It was a little late for sorry.'

Price didn't reply.

'Did he say *anything* that might lead us to her body?' Bobbie asked. 'She died in here – he wouldn't . . . couldn't have gone far.'

'I have no idea.'

'Please, Dr Price, there must be something that stood out –' Bobbie stopped as she became aware of a steady dripping noise. The lamp on Price's desk flickered before dying entirely. 'Oh no.'

Price frowned and tried to turn the lamp back on. 'Strange . . .'

Behind Price, near the wheels of her desk chair, there was one broken fragment of glass larger than the rest – a vicious-looking scalene triangle reflecting the ceiling as it lay flat on the floor.

A dripping hand burst through, closely followed by the top of a head. Bobbie shrieked and stumbled away from the desk. Price sprang off the chair. 'What? What are you looking at?'

'You can't see her?'

'What on earth are you talking about? There's nothing there!'

Mary squeezed a second arm through the narrow shard, dislocating her shoulder with a moist crack to fit through the narrow gap. Splinters of mirror jangled as Mary pulled her body through into the room. Dripping crimson dots all over the carpet, she moved unnaturally fast, her joints and bones clicking and clacking as if she hadn't used them in a very long time. She emerged fully from the mirror and drew herself upright.

Bobbie backed away, colliding with an office chair. 'She's here! She's right behind you! We have to get out of here!'

'Bobbie, there's nothing there.' Dr Price's voice was cold with impatience.

Mary started towards them, heavy spots of blood splattering as she went. It ran from her fingers. The dead girl moved slowly, on uncertain legs, as if she wasn't accustomed to solid ground beneath her feet. Bobbie remembered the infinite darkness behind the mirror and shuddered.

'Please!' Bobbie cried. 'She's coming for me.'

Price seized her arm. 'You need to pull yourself together. We have to talk about my father. I will not have you going all over telling people what he did. You have no proof.' The teacher dragged her away from the exit and towards the silent, oncoming Mary.

'No!' Bobbie snapped. Snatching her arm back, she did something she wouldn't have thought herself capable of. She pushed Dr Price into the dead girl's path. The teacher was expecting it even less, her mouth falling open in shock. In true haunting style, Price fell *through* Mary as if she were made of smoke and straight into the nest of paperwork Bobbie had left all over the floor. One step onto the loose leaves and Price's court shoe slipped out from under her, sending her clattering into the open cupboard. With a shrill cry, her forehead clashed with the second shelf down and then the third as she fell.

Price lay in an untidy heap, half in and half out of the cupboard. She moaned slightly, hovering somewhere close to unconsciousness.

Bobbie backed away, not taking her eyes off Mary. There was only one problem: Mary now stood between her and the only exit. 'Mary, stop!' Bobbie pleaded, trying to stay cool. 'Where did he put you? Do you even know?' Bobbie's bottom collided with the desk, knocking an overturned coffee cup to the floor. Bobbie felt her way around the desk.

The pain in her sock-clad foot when she stepped on the

glass was excruciating. It shot up and down her spine and red flashed before her eyes. Howling, Bobbie stepped back further, only to tread on more shards. The pain was acute, intense, throbbing all the way up her legs. She leaned against the hole she'd made in the centre of the huge mirror, with Mary still edging towards her. Bobbie raised her left foot to examine the damage: a little-finger-sized glass sliver stuck out of her sole. Her white sock was quickly turning red. Gritting her teeth, she pulled it free – her own blood now dripping onto the carpet.

The wall beneath her shoulder felt strange – too flimsy to be a wall. It was wooden. Office walls aren't made of wood. That was when Bobbie noticed the outline. It wasn't a wall at all, it was a *door*: a small hatch concealed behind the mirror. Of course! Another secret passage, or a priest's hole – one of the legendary priests' holes.

Whatever it was it didn't matter. With all her might, Bobbie pushed on the hidden panel and it swung inward. The space behind the door was pitch-black, but Mary was only centimetres away. A blood-stained hand reached for Bobbie's face, and, with a gasp, she ducked to avoid it, clambering through the hole.

Ignoring the pain in her feet (which now seemed to *burn*), Bobbie reached up and slammed the hatch in Mary's face. It clicked shut but Bobbie had no idea if secret doors could stop ghosts. Leaning back against it, Bobbie strained to see in the darkness. Feeble grey light bled around the edges of the panel and it was just enough to recognise that she was at the top of a staircase, which had to lead *somewhere*. That meant it was more than just a hidey-hole; it could go anywhere in the school.

The penny dropped. This was exactly how Kenton Millar

must have moved Mary's body all those years ago. There's no way you could have a secret passage behind your mirror and not know about it. That made her mind up. Her only option was to follow the passage and pray it hadn't been bricked up over the decades. If she ran into a dead end, it was game over.

Bobbie hobbled forward, her feet stinging with every step. She left ketchup-red, sticky footprints as she went.

The stairs were steep, slick and icy cold. With each pained step, the air became staler, like she was descending into a cellar. Bobbie felt her way along the walls as the darkness crept closer. By the time her foot found flat slabs, she couldn't see at all; it was almost like being back inside the awful abyss of Mary's realm.

The echoing drops of water that fell from the ceiling – real this time – suggested she was in a confined space: a tunnel or cave – nothing like the functional servants' passages. She must be *underneath* the school from the sheer number of stairs she'd taken.

Something crawled over her toes. Bobbie cried out and kicked it off, the thing giving an angry squeak before tiny paws scurried away. The passage was infested with rats – Bobbie grimaced and set off into the shadows. Trying to run, but only managing a feeble limp while clinging to the walls, Bobbie hoped there was nothing in the darkness to cut her feet. *Oh . . . wait a sec . . .* Despite everything she laughed. Was that actually funny or was she hysterical? Either way the evil doll giggle she was making was more than a little creepy. *Stop. You have to keep it together. Keep going.*

Bobbie froze. She leaned against the wall, which, this far

down, was slimy with damp. Even over her unsteady, heaving breaths and chattering teeth she heard unsteady footsteps scraping down the stairs behind her.

That wasn't rats . . . Mary was on the stairs.

The hysterical laughter swung into a sob. Bobbie pushed off the wall and continued her excruciating run. At least the freezing stone tunnel went some way towards numbing her feet. She tried to stay on tiptoes to keep the pressure off the cuts in her soles and heels. Hobbling as fast as she could, Bobbie didn't even look back.

Mary was advancing in the darkness. She wouldn't see her until she felt those fingers.

The tunnel seemed endless. There were no bends, no corners, the blackness stretching on forever. Bobbie wondered if it was already over and this was Hell – one infinite, black tunnel.

She wheezed as she ran and her breathing switched to panting. Pausing for a moment, she heard feet shuffling behind her. *Way* too close. Bobbie ran on, hands outstretched. Within seconds she realised she could see brickwork up ahead. The fact she could see *anything* meant there was light entering the tunnel. With renewed vigour she charged forward, only for her spirit to wilt: there was a dead end up ahead. No, it wasn't a dead end, it was a wall. A wall with a ladder.

Bobbie threw herself at it and looked over her shoulder. If there was something moving back down the long corridor it wasn't close enough for her to see. Looking up she saw the light was filtering through a vent at the top of a narrow shaft. A way out. It felt like dawn breaking at the end of her longest night.

She grabbed the rung of the ladder at eye level. The wooden

rungs felt wet and greasy, covered in moss or mould. Bobbie feared the wood was rotten, still it felt sturdy enough. Gripping the ladder with the tips of her toes, she started to climb. Jolts of pain tore through her body every time she tried to put weight on her feet, so she tried as hard as she could to *pull* herself up the ladder, utilising all the strength she had in her arms. It hurt so, so much, but all she had to do was get to the vent and at least she'd be out of the tunnel and (hopefully) in fresh air.

There came footsteps from the bottom of the ladder and out of the corner of her eye Bobbie saw a shadow shift in the meagre light. She climbed faster.

The rusted mental vent overhead was within reaching distance, although God knew what was on the other side. Bobbie stretched for the final rung and heaved herself up.

There was a sickening crack and the rung broke off in her hand. She dropped it, scrabbling for something else to grab. The second the weight went onto her feet, she howled in pain and, in reflex, let go.

She fell. She fell fast, like a stone dropping down a well. All she could do was brace for landing. The end was mercifully swift. Bobbie hit the floor with a thud, her feet (her poor feet) taking most of the impact. At first she was too shocked to register any pain. She lay flat on her back, staring up at the shaft, blinking like an idiot. Then the pain *really* hit. If she thought lacerated feet had been bad, it was nothing to the agony that started to spread through her ankles like lava.

It hurt so much she couldn't breathe. Nor could she move.

Something warm dripped onto her cheek. Like a teardrop. There was another, then another.

Drip, drip, drip.

Bobbie was mobile enough to tilt her head back an inch on the cold stone slabs.

Mary stood over her, blood running from her fingers onto her face. 'No,' Bobbie muttered. After everything she'd done. After fighting so hard . . . it had done her no good.

Mary's cold, impassive face leaned towards Bobbie's own. Bobbie felt her shallow, raspy breaths on her skin, as if the other girl's lungs were filled with fluid. 'Please . . .' she begged.

A freezing, dewy hand touched her cheek. A bloody lock of her hair grazed Bobbie's lip. The stench of her breath was overwhelming – like the girl's insides were rotten. Bobbie whined and tried to wriggle away, but she was pinned down; Mary was right on top of her, leaning in. All Bobbie could do was close her eyes and wait for it to end.

Chapter 28

Tales from the Crypt

'Bobbie?'

She dared to open her eyes a fraction and came face-to-face with a leering skull at her side. She recoiled, only to remember that every inch of her body was battered and sore, like her bruises went all the way to her core. Her fingers brushed against something smooth and hard – bonelike. So bonelike, she realised it was, in fact, bone. More bones. She brushed it out of her hand, disgusted, as she became aware of someone leaning over her in the gloom.

Sitting up, she first saw Caine. He crouched by her side, helping her up. Her ankles throbbed – for now, she'd settle for sitting upright.

This had to be a mirage. If he weren't so grimy and dirty, Caine could be an angel. He cradled her head in a strong hand and kissed her hard on the lips. They didn't need words. There wasn't a word big enough for how it felt, and she knew that he felt exactly the same. Perhaps this was the big reunion in heaven, although Bobbie liked to imagine that, in heaven, she wouldn't ache quite so much. 'You're alive,' Bobbie whispered.

'Only just,' said another familiar voice. Naya! Tears, the good kind, suddenly flooded the cavity behind her nose. Naya was alive. They were *all* alive. It was too good, more than she could have dared hope. Dizzy, Bobbie's head spun, bits of silver glitter swirling in her peripheral vision.

Naya sat on some shallow stone steps that lead to an ornate metal door – a door Bobbie had seen before. Well, at least the other side of it. It was the forgotten mausoleum in the graveyard at St Paul's. In Naya's arms was Sadie, barely conscious. Oh how stupid they'd been. Two days ago they'd been metres from Sadie and left her there.

'Oh my God,' was all Bobbie could think to say. She tried to stand to get to her friend, but the pain in her ankles was too raw. 'Naya . . . I . . .'

Naya shook off the big, heartfelt reunion, there clearly wasn't time. 'She's going to die, Bob. She's been here for days.' Sadie looked in a bad way, her usually outdoorsy face sunken and her eyes hollow.

Bobbie examined her surroundings. They were in a dank, mossy chamber, infused with green-tinged light where vines and trees had smothered the tomb. Rainwater drummed on the roof. There was a grand stone sarcophagus in the centre of the room with smaller caskets lined up the walls in beautifully carved alcoves.

'When I got here and found Naya,' Caine said, 'I called for you . . .'

'I heard,' Bobbie brushed a cobweb out of his hair. 'I heard you say my name.'

Caine's brown eyes glistened. 'I thought you were lost in that . . . place.'

'And I thought you were . . .'

'Ahem!' Naya interrupted them. 'This is super-cute, you guys, but what do we do?'

'Do you have a phone?' Caine asked Bobbie.

'No, it's still by my bed from this morning. I didn't think to grab it.'

Caine nodded. 'Mine's up in your room too.'

Bobbie took a closer look at their tomb. The floor was strewn with bones. Human bones. Like some sort of hilarious mass grave, maybe half a dozen skulls grinned at each other, scattered around the floor like drunk students at a house party. Naya was wearing someone else's clothes. An old-style Piper's PE hoodie that hadn't been regulation uniform for about ten years.

And it all made sense. 'Help me up?' Bobbie asked Caine. He offered her a hand, and even though it made her ankles, back and hips *blaze* with pain, she allowed him to heave her upright.

'Are you okay?'

Bobbie ignored the pain and just said, 'I'm okay, but we have to find Mary.'

Caine frowned. 'What?'

Bobbie looked around the nightmarish space. It had the same awful, ghoulish feel as the catacombs in Paris where her mum had taken her on an ill-advised trip when she was about eight – the walls of skulls had given her nightmares for weeks. 'She's in here somewhere.' When Caine continued to look at her blankly, she said, 'Kenton Millar accidentally killed Mary and hid her body.'

'No way,' Naya chimed in.

'Way. There's a secret passage from Price's study that leads here. It must do . . . that's it!' Bobbie scanned the floor of the crypt. 'There!' Sure enough, underneath a weeping Virgin Mary statue in the corner, there was a partially hidden metal grate – the very same one she'd almost escaped through.

There were so many light bulbs going off above her head, it was like a paparazzi moment. 'Millar must have used the passage too – that's why he and Mary always met here. The tunnel leads under the field to the church. It *was* a priest's hole – or a priest's passage anyway. It let the priests who were hiding out get between the school and the church without anyone seeing them.'

'This is where we were dreaming about?' Caine said as Bobbie started to kick through the bones.

'Yeah. The forest was their place, I guess. He must have taken her body down the tunnel and hidden it here. Mary didn't want to kill us! I knew it! I knew she just wanted help. On the fifth day she brings you to where she was hidden. Here!' One touch from Mary and you were transported to her final resting place.

Naya scanned the human remains. 'But they all died, Bob.'

'I don't think she can help it – it's not like *she* sealed the tomb, is it? And the other girls didn't know what they were looking for. We do.'

Caine shook his head. 'So all that time . . . all the girls that went missing. They've just been in here the whole time?'

Bobbie sighed, weary from the tunnel – almost too tired to go on. Still she tried to understand. 'Yeah. Think about it.

Abigail and Taylor vanished from miles and miles away. Maybe the others did too. Why would the police think to search the graveyard? And you saw it. It's been derelict for years. Who ever comes here other than kids?' The more she thought about it the more it made sense. 'We know that Millar brought Mary here to make out . . . I guess he had access to a key – there'd have to be one for the priests, right? Does that make sense? And Naya . . . you dreamed that Mary was in a dark place. What's darker than a coffin?' Looking around, Bobbie wondered which skeleton was Taylor Keane's, which belonged to Abigail Hanson and whose clothes Naya had borrowed. 'Come on, Mary *has* to be in here somewhere.'

Caine threw his hands up. 'Bobbie, any one of these could be her! And we're locked in. Even if we do find her . . .'

'No!' Bobbie snapped, refusing to back down. 'This is all about laying her to rest.' She looked at the skeletons. 'There's no way he'd have left her lying around. He would have wanted to hide her in case anybody came looking. Check in the coffins. I bet anything one of them has two bodies in. Naya, help us.'

Naya rested Sadie's gaunt-looking head on the stairs. She'd been in here for three days with no food and only whatever rainwater trickled in. How long can you survive without food and drink? Bobbie guessed, from the look of her, not much longer. With little ceremony, Bobbie dragged the nearest coffin out of its alcove and it smashed to the stone floor. It was heavy, but the wood was rotten and old. Initial panic at seeing the coffin lid was nailed on turned to relief as she realised the nails would slide out of the sodden wood. Bobbie shook the lid off and let it fall. Only one grinning inhabitant lay within.

On the other side of the crypt, Caine and Naya pulled open their own coffins. 'Anything?'

'No!' Naya called, her hand over her mouth. 'God, this is sick!'

'Keep looking.'

'I can't get the lid off this one,' Caine moaned.

'Well, then neither could Millar,' Bobbie said, and then stopped. 'Wait. We'd be able to see if he'd tampered with one of the coffins, right?'

Caine and Naya stopped searching. 'Yeah.' Caine wiped dust on his thighs. 'I guess.'

'Well, that means . . .' All eyes fell on the grandiose sarcophagus in the centre of the room.

'No nails in that one,' Caine said, which was precisely what she was thinking.

'Help me.' Bobbie knew, just *knew* that this was it. She could see it now: sweating, panicking and desperate, Kenton Millar had carried Mary's body through the tunnel. He'd somehow got her up the ladder and into the mausoleum. Rather than risk taking her outside to bury her where he might be seen, he'd put her in the most secure of the graves – the most ancient.

Caine and Naya hurried to her side of the stone coffin. 'After three,' Caine suggested, reminding her of the last time they'd counted down as a group. It had been in front of a bathroom mirror five days ago. 'One, two . . .' They all pushed together. It was heavy, but not as heavy as Bobbie might have feared. There was a lip to the slab, so they had to lift and slide.

There was nothing on her body that didn't hurt. Bobbie had to let Caine and Naya do most of the lifting, but the slab

272

came loose. 'Push!' she cried and they slid the granite lid all the way off the tomb.

Bobbie's hand flew to her mouth. Naya screamed and jumped back.

Mary lay in the sarcophagus, perfectly preserved. Still flesh, still covered in blood. Eyes closed, she looked almost peaceful. She could so easily be sleeping. Alongside Mary, looking somewhat cramped, was the original occupant – mere bones.

Mary's eyes snapped open and now Bobbie yelped, clinging to Caine's arm just as he clung to hers. Mary raised a hand towards them. *No*, Bobbie thought, *it's over now!* A sigh passed Mary's lips and her eyes closed, her hand falling. A certain serenity fell over her. Relief and release.

Sixty years finally caught up with Mary and, like one of those time-lapse cameras on nature programmes, her face thinned, cheekbones jutting, the skin tightening around her bones, darkening like leather. Her lips peeled back into a perpetual smile and her eyes turned to hollows, skin rotting to nothing. The black hair fell and withered about her skull like a halo.

Mary Worthington was now at rest.

'Bobbie, your face.' Caine held her cheeks in both hands. 'The scars are all gone.'

Bobbie buried herself in Caine's chest. They'd done it. They'd actually done it. She was never, ever letting go of him, or Naya for that matter, ever again. She squeezed Naya's hand to let her know.

'Bobbie, look.' Caine prised her off.

'What?'

'Look inside the coffin.'

'Oh my God.'

Naya tentatively approached. 'What is it?'

Bobbie pointed inside the sarcophagus and things got just that little bit worse. There was literally writing on the wall. Near Mary's skeletal fingers was an engagement ring, presumably from her cellmate, which she'd used to carve letters into the side of the tomb.

'Jesus Christ.' Naya turned away, pale with sickness. 'That means . . .'

Bobbie finished the sentence, gripping Caine's forearm with white knuckles. 'She wasn't dead when he put her in there.'

'That's awful.' Caine's lips were a horrid grey. 'How long do you think she was in there . . . without food or water? How long would you survive?'

There was no way Mary would have been able to get the lid off alone, injured as she was. Bobbie closed her eyes to hold back the tears as the final piece of the puzzle slotted into place. 'I don't know, but at a guess . . . I'd say about five days.'

Five days. Five days to die. Five days to find her before it was too late.

Bobbie traced the letters she'd carved in her dying days. The last testament of Mary Worthington. She'd written in a frantic, jangled mess of letters:

no one BeLiEvED me i just wanted people to LIKE ME

Bobbie wished there was some way of letting her know that, even if she was ignored in life, after her death, people *did* believe in her. People all over the world said her name in front of a mirror, half expecting her to appear. Thousands and thousands of people *believed*.

As fanciful as they were, Bobbie recalled Judy's tales of 'gypsy curses', which she'd brushed off without a second thought, but maybe, just maybe, poor Mary *was* cursed. Maybe it was the freakish circumstances in which she died or maybe, like Judy said, she was simply born *different*. Whatever the reason, every time someone at Piper's Hall called her name she'd been a slave to their song, unable to prevent the awful side effect of the summoning. Saying her name was like winding a clock: once wound it would inevitably tick out to the conclusion.

And now the cycle was broken.

Once they'd managed to shift the statue – which wasn't easy – the grate under the Madonna lifted easily enough, revealing the ladder and tunnel. Bobbie could only think that Millar had concealed the passage in case Mary's body was one day found – the last thing he'd want was the police knowing there was a direct tunnel to his staffroom. It was lucky for her he hadn't bricked it up entirely.

The irony that Abigail, Taylor and the others had a hidden escape route metres from where they'd perished wasn't lost on Bobbie, but she put the sad thought out of her head. They had to rouse Sadie enough to get her to cling to Caine's back so he could piggyback her down the ladder. The top rung was already destroyed, but the crumbling ladder just managed to take their combined weight.

Naya went next, leaving Bobbie alone in the crypt. 'I'll be back soon,' Bobbie told Mary. 'Everyone's going to know the truth and we're going to get you a proper grave, I promise.' Bobbie lowered herself through the trapdoor.

Her head was about to vanish into the tunnel when brilliant white light flooded the room. The main doors creaked open and sunlight blinded her. Had they been gone so long that morning had arrived? Dr Price must have come to and organised a search party. Bobbie squinted into the aurora, daring to take one hand off the ladder to shield her eyes. There was no one racing in to save them, however – someone was leaving.

Mary stood in the threshold and she was beautiful. All the blood was gone and her uniform was smart and clean. A gentle breeze blew her loose black hair off her face, highlighting the incredible cheekbones and sky-blue eyes. She turned and looked at Bobbie, who was frozen to the ladder. What she was seeing *couldn't* be real.

In that moment it became clear that the window into Mary's world could be seen through on both sides. Mary had been watching, listening, learning, and they *knew* each other now. Looking as she did now, just a girl, Bobbie wondered whether, if they'd lived in the same time, they'd have been friends. Mary hadn't *haunted* her, she'd reached out to her. Two little Piper's Hall misfits separated by decades.

Mary didn't say anything, her lips didn't even part, but Bobbie knew in her heart that the other girl was thankful. Turning away, a faint smile on her lips, Mary walked out of the mausoleum and into the sun.

Chapter 29

On Reflection

Piper's Hall reopened the following Monday. How could it not? Dr Price was running the biggest PR campaign of her career. It had finally stopped raining and the pale blue face of winter emerged behind the clouds. Silver frost stiffened the front lawns as BMWs and Mercedes dropped pupils off, their breath hanging like speech bubbles as they said their goodbyes.

A collective whinge filled the halls. When the headlines hit everyone had been expecting the school to shut for at least a week or two, but Dr Price and the governors were adamant that it was very much business as usual, and that the grim discovery at St Paul's Church had *nothing* to do with them.

Bobbie who, of course, had never left, sat in the Accy Area with Naya. Thankfully her ankles were sprained, not broken. She was wrapped up like a mummy and the pain wasn't too bad, but she still had a crutch leaned against the arm of the sofa.

In the end, despite her promise to Mary, they'd changed their story. They'd had to. Initially Bobbie told the full truth, but however she'd said it, in a police station with a group of very tired and irritable police officers glaring at her, it had just sounded insane. It *was* insane.

In the end, it had gone something like this: Sadie had run away through the secret passage, got trapped in the mausoleum and then Caine and Naya had inadvertently got locked in while trying to rescue her until Bobbie had freed them. No one bought that story either, but at least that version didn't feature a dead girl who climbs out of Hell via a mirror.

The real investigation now focused on the other bodies. The current thinking was some serial killer had preyed on Piper's Hall Ladies for decades, using the crypt to hide his victims.

History would now say that Mary Worthington was the first victim of a serial killer. Not true, but at least her story now had a final chapter.

Likewise, Taylor Keane's mother had been on the national news. She'd seemed *happy*, happy that she finally had some answers about her daughter's disappearance. The Keanes had something to bury.

Dr Price was denying everything – even knowledge of the tunnel. Perhaps she wasn't lying. It was possible her dad had ensured the tunnel became a truly 'secret passage' during his time as Head. Price would lie through her teeth regardless. Bobbie watched her Cheshire-cat grin as she shook rich parents' hands, assuring them that there was nothing at all to worry about. But while Bobbie *had* told the police about Kenton Millar, her father's involvement wasn't public knowledge. Yet. As far as Bobbie knew he'd be a suspect for all the bodies. Bobbie quite liked having that trick up her sleeve for when she needed it most – like if there was ever any fallout regarding Caine or the struggle in her office. While journalists were circling the school like vultures, Bobbie felt she had some power over the Head.

'Hey hey hey.' Kellie Huang rushed over to where they sat, tossing her Birkin to one side as if it were worthless. 'How's Sadie? Everyone's saying it's you two that saved her.'

A few other girls gathered around to hear the latest. 'She's gonna be fine,' Naya said, loving the celebrity. 'Severe dehydration, but she's all hooked up with her very own drip and she'll be back probably by the end of the week.'

'Oh thank God!' Kellie clutched her chest. 'What was she even doing down there in the graveyard? She's lucky to be alive. If it weren't for you two being like detectives or something…'

Behind the little congregation, Grace and Caitlin sauntered past, rolling their eyes.

Bobbie had had three long days to prepare for the inevitable barrage of questions. She'd come up with about fifty possible cover stories, all of them vaguely plausible (she was a writer, after all). She thought about saying it really *was* a secret lesbian lover in the village; it was a hoax to freak them out after the dare; she was trying to score some pot. They'd all work, but it was urban legends that had got them into the mess in the first place, so Bobbie just said, 'I have no idea. You'll have to ask Sadie when she's better.'

A lofty voice cut in. 'You're so full of crap.' It was Grace, looking far from pleased at being on the outside. 'There was totally something weird going on. Nosebleeds, sneaking around, boys in your dorm. You should have seen Bobbie on Thursday

279

morning. She was totally having a bad trip outside the bathroom and we had to put her in the Isolation Room. She must have like drawn all over her face in red pen too. What a freak.'

'Oh shut up,' Naya scowled.

'Excuse me, I'm the Head Girl, you can't tell me to shut up. It's *so* obvious this is about drugs or something.'

Quite rationally, Bobbie took her crutch and rose from the sofa. She paused to smooth down the custom sweatshirt Caine had given her yesterday. No longer intimidated, she walked directly into Grace's personal space, took her arm and twisted her around. 'Ow! What are you doing?' the taller girl squealed.

They were now both facing the mirror she and Naya had taken out of their room on Wednesday night. The reflection held them both. A whisper ran through the crowd. The girls nearest edged away and Bobbie wondered just how accurate the gossip mill was on this occasion.

If she's called, she has to come.

Bobbie thought about it for a second. Perhaps Mary owed her one. Instead she said, 'Take a look at yourself, Grace. What do you see?' Her voice was steady and calm.

'What? Get off me, you freak of nature.'

'Do you know what I see? A needy little princess who knows her reign is coming to an end. Final year, Grace, and then what? Outside of Piper's Hall, you're *nothing*.' Bobbie emphasised the last word. 'Once you leave here, you're nothing but an averagely intelligent, pretty-ish blonde girl with nice legs but no sense of humour. Good luck. Let me know how that works out for you.'

Roughly speaking the crowd reacted with laughter, poorly

concealed glee or plain shock. *'Oh my God, did you just hear that? That's hilarious! She must have a death wish,'* etc.

Grace Brewer-Fay was speechless. Her cheeks burned scarlet and she yanked her arm out of Bobbie's grasp. But Bobbie wasn't done. 'In fact, I think I'll take that.' Bobbie reached for Grace's lapel and removed the Head Girl pin. 'I have a sneaking suspicion Dr Price will fully support my coup. No more *Elites*. Ever.'

'Amen to that!' Naya whooped and applauded. Kellie Huang took up the cheer and a few other girls joined in too.

Bobbie Rowe, the new Head Girl of Piper's Hall, attached the pin to her boyfriend's jumper and, with an arched brow, dared Grace to challenge her.

Later that night, Bobbie crept out to visit Caine. 'Crept out' possibly wasn't the right phrase to use given that she'd hobbled out of the main exit right under Dr Price's nose. She was hardly going to stop her, was she?

Caine lived in the most normal house in the world and Bobbie loved it. It was a semi-detached house on one of those new sandstone estates with identical dream-homes all in a row. There was an oval patch of green in the middle for the owners to take the dog out, scoop its poo and head straight back inside. Pretty much every home had a Mini Cooper or, like Caine, a VW on the drive. A lot of zippy convertibles too – hairdresser cars.

That night Caine's mum was back on the nightshift at the hospital, so it was just the two of them. Tomorrow morning her mum would arrive in London from New York – spending a whole week in Hampstead with Bobbie before flying back for opening night – so she wasn't sure when she'd see Caine again after tonight and therefore intended to soak up every drop. Caine had carried his duvet down into the lounge and they were about to attempt all of the *Avengers* films in the correct order, starting with *The Hulk*. Bobbie predicted they wouldn't get much past *Iron Man* before nodding off or making out.

The microwave pinged and Caine shook the popcorn into a bowl, cursing as he burned his fingers. There was a slight smoky smell drifting through from the kitchen – he'd obviously nuked it for too long. He carried it through sheepishly. 'Right, here's the popcorn. You okay for Diet Coke?'

'Yep.'

'Do you need anything else?'

'I don't think so.' Bobbie frowned.

Caine joined her and pulled the duvet over his lap and hers. 'So what's up? You seem quiet.'

There was something up. All day, she'd had the weirdest sensation. A feeling that she'd forgotten to do something, an overwhelming tip-of-the-tongue sensation that she couldn't shake. All she could think was that it was the lingering, niggling worry that Kenton Millar would somehow 'get away with it'. 'I'm probably just tired,' she eventually said.

He saw through that in a second. 'Or . . . ?'

Bobbie was worried putting her thoughts into words might make them true, but she was driving herself a little crazy. Last night she'd hardly slept a wink. 'Oh I don't know. I can't stop thinking about Bridget and Judy.'

Caine frowned. 'What about them? Did you speak to

Bridget?'

'No. The person I spoke to on the phone said she'd taken a turn for the worse . . .'

'Oh. Is that what's bothering you?'

Bobbie fiddled with the edge of the blanket. 'Can you remember what Bridget said about not letting Mary out of the cage?'

'Yeah . . .'

'And there was what Judy said about Mary being different . . . even before she died there was something strange about her, all those rumours. Then there was the letter . . .'

'What letter?'

Bobbie sat up straighter. 'In Price's office there was a letter from a parent about how, since Mary had started at Piper's, her room-mate couldn't sleep for having terrible nightmares.' Her throat tightened up. 'What if we didn't *set Mary free*, what if we *let her out*?' He looked at her sceptically so she went on. 'You said it yourself at the hospital – we only show people what we want them to see. We only saw what Mary wanted us to see.'

The words hung between them and, just for a second, she saw the panic in his eyes. He shook it off and leaned in for a kiss. His lips brushed hers. 'Bobbie, it's all over now. People aren't just "evil", that doesn't make any sense. It's all over,' he repeated.

Bobbie relaxed back into his embrace and tried to focus on the movie. He was right, of course he was. He had to be.

'I'm gonna get some more Coke.' He sprang off the sofa.

Bobbie cautiously swung her bandaged ankles onto the coffee table, knocking the local paper to the floor. It was open on a

283

page displaying an all-too-familiar image. The tomb. 'Are we in the paper?' she called.

'Yeah, well, the story is,' he replied from the kitchen. 'Sorry – I meant to bin it.'

'No. I wanna see.' Bobbie turned the paper over in her hand. The main image was one of the mausoleum decorated in police tape, forensics officers in white onesies ducking in and out. The inset image was a close-up of Mary's message, the one she'd carved into the sides of her coffin:

no one BeLiEvED me i just wanted people to LIKE ME

Bobbie raised an eyebrow. There was something about the frenzied, jumbled-up letters. It seemed odd somehow, even for the state that the poor girl had been in. In the crypt, Bobbie could only imagine Mary's *fear*, but, seeing the words again, it was the writing of someone who was really, really *angry*. And who had more reason to be angry than Mary Worthington?

That was when Bobbie froze. She stared at the photograph. She recalled the letter from Radley about Mary's exceptional attainment. Not the sort of girl to badly punctuate.

We only show people what they want to see.

She remembered the faint smile on Mary's lips.

Tears pricked Bobbie's eyes. Not tears of pity – scared tears. *What have I done?* Only certain letters were capitalised and they spelled out a new sentence.

BLEED LIKE ME

284

ONE WEEK LATER

The Southe

Friday, 13 November

Police Hunt Crash Surviv

Police have launched an urgent appeal to locate the passenger of the fatal car accident that killed a highly regarded head teacher.

Dr Ellen Price, principal of Piper's Hall School for Young Ladies near Oxsley, was killed when her BMW veered off the coast road last night. Eyewitnesses report seeing an injured teenage girl in the back seat of the car and, although no second body

was recovered at the scene, police are 'deeply concerned' for the girl's safety.

The passenger is described as 14–19 years old with long, straight, dark hair and was wearing the Piper's Hall uniform. One witness describes the girl as being 'covered in blood' before the accident, prompting speculation the pair may have been driving to the local hospital at the time of the crash.

Acknowledgements

Say Her Name marks a new chapter in my writing career, one for which I'm very grateful indeed. Thank you to Jo Williamson and everyone at Antony Harwood Ltd for managing me so well these last four years. Doesn't time fly!

Obviously a big, BIG thank you to Emma Matthewson and everyone at Hot Key Books for making me feel so welcome. Your enthusiasm for Mary is contagious and coming into Hot Key HQ is always a treat. Big thank you to Jet Purdie for the cover – if I hadn't written it, I'd buy it!

I also need to thank Simon Savidge for challenging me to write the scariest contemporary YA horror ever (what do you reckon, Simon? Did I do it?) and also Tanya Byrne and Kim Curran for their early feedback. Special thanks also to Aprilynne Pike for her kind words. More thanks to my critical readers Kerry Turner and especially Sam Powick who read *Say Her Name* despite her mortal fear of a) ghosts and b) horror stories – you had to read it because if it didn't scare you it was dead in the water!

UKYA Massiv – love you.

Finally a big thank you to YOU, the reader. Whether this is the first of my books you've read or my THIRD (where does time go?), thank you for choosing me. I hope you weren't TOO scared. Just FYI though…I still haven't dared to say her name five times. I always stop at four. Mary's out now. Just something to dwell on. Sweet dreams.

Find James Dawson on Twitter: @_jamesdawson
Or on Facebook: facebook.com/jamesdawsonbooks
And also tumblr: jamesdawsonbooks.tumblr.com
Or his homepage: jamesdawsonbooks.com

James Dawson

James Dawson is the award-nominated author of chillers HOLLOW PIKE and CRUEL SUMMER. A former teacher, he also wrote BEING A BOY, the ultimate guide to growing up for young men.

James lives in London and spends his time watching *Doctor Who* and horror films.

HOT
KEY
BOOKS

Thank you for choosing a Hot Key book.

If you want to know more about our authors
and what we publish, you can find us online.

You can start at our website

www.hotkeybooks.com

And you can also find us on:

We hope to see you soon!